CW00796948

www.goodbyemorecambe.co.uk

GOODBYE MORECAMBE

M N STEWART

ALBERTINA
– BOOKS –

For all our yesterdays

1982

SUMMER, SOMEWHERE ON THE FAIRGROUND

LEANING APATHETICALLY ON THE DOOR FRAME, STANTON LOOKED out across the sea of heads that filled the floor of the amusement arcade. They ebbed and flowed rhythmically like the tide in the bay, which he could just about see through windows caked with sand and grime.

"Fucking idiots," he said, under his breath.

Stanton needed this job because he needed the money and he wanted the girls who wanted his money. He was left with no choice but to suffer them; these miserable holidaymakers swarming around in front of him were part of the deal whether he liked them or not. Their stink, their stench, the stolid smell of weak humans lifted up into his nose. At that moment, he felt he could kill every one of them and not feel a thing.

Without warning, Tony, the arcade manager, appeared by his side.

"Did you sort that machine out at the back?"

"What?" Stanton answered distractedly.

"The one Brown told us about, the one-armed bandit. Needs some wood putting under it. He doesn't want it out of action, it's unstable and needs sorting."

1

Stanton looked at Tony, who had been doing this job for twenty years, his skin like leather.

"Yeah, I'll sort it."

"When?"

Stanton looked away. "Soon."

"I've asked you twice already to do it."

"Alright, *Jesus.* I said I'd do it."

"Well just get it sorted, Stanz. It's getting busy now and it's costing Brown money and you know how he hates the thought of that. Get some wood and get it stabilised now." The manager went back inside his office.

"Fucking dickhead," Stanton swore quietly, heading outside for a change of scenery. He stood in the shade with his hands in his pockets, before taking a cigarette from behind his ear and nonchalantly lighting it.

As he was enjoying the shade and peace away from tinny arcade noise, a pretty blonde girl wearing denim shorts and a bikini top caught his eye, heading into the arcade with her friend.

He might hate the people, but he loved his job. For a sixteen year old, where the stretched summer days felt like weeks and the weeks felt like months, it offered everything he needed in life – money, fags, beer and girls.

Stanton waited a few seconds before dropping his cigarette and smothering it beneath his heavy, laced boot, quickly checking his reflection in the window before following them inside.

He pretended to be distracted, strolling casually around the arcade, nervous with excitement, secretly searching with darting eyes for the pretty blonde. He soon spotted her playing an arcade game alongside her friend. Checking that his manager was busy, he went over and stood by them, arching his arm confidently over the machine.

"Watch out, they'll come out from behind those rocks."

"What?" said the girl.

"Told you, game over." Stanton laughed as the words came up on the screen

"That wasn't fair, you put me off," said the pretty blonde.

"You put yourself off. Where you from, then? Here on holiday?"

The girl leaned suggestively on the arcade machine. "Who's asking?"

Stanton smirked.

"Who's asking? Maybe the boy that's gonna give you a free game if you give him a kiss." He leaned closer in, holding her gaze.

The girl giggled. "You rate yourself a bit."

Stanton removed the chain of keys from around his neck. "Comes easy when you look like me."

"Come on Paula, let's go outside on one of the rides," her friend suggested. "It smells funny in here."

Stanton looked at the friend with disdain.

"You crack on, love. She'll catch you up. Now, let's sort out that free game, shall we?"

Bending down, Stanton was about to unlock the machine when, from somewhere in the arcade, there came a loud scream.

He ignored it. This place manufactured screams. It was part of the experience; screams were the currency of the fairground.

He turned the key in the lock.

Then another scream, but this one higher pitched, unmistakably packed with emotion and not the kind you get from winning a cheap prize. People looked away from the machines they were playing, some even began walking away from unfinished games.

But that lone scream now became a chorus.

Stanton rolled his eyes and stood up.

"Wait here," he said to the girl.

He put the key chain back around his neck and headed toward the commotion, aggressively pushing through the crowds as he went. Once he had made his way to the front, he looked down and froze. He was standing in a pool of crimson blood, important looking blood that could only have seeped out from somewhere deep. The kind of warm blood that should never see the cold light of day. The type of blood that should not be running, as it was now, across the dirty linoleum floor of an amusement arcade and staining the white trainers he had only just bought.

Amid the blood was a toy gun and next to the gun, a stool that had fallen on its side.

Stanton was rooted to the spot with shock.

The heavy one-armed bandit was on the floor and someone was underneath it.

By now the arcade manager had also pushed his way to the front where he stood, shocked and mesmerised by what he saw. He spoke under his breath.

"Shit. You better go and get Mr Brown. You've fucked it, Stanz."

But nobody moved.

The lights continued to flash and the pop songs echoed hauntingly around what was otherwise a deathly silent arcade.

1985

TUESDAY

ONE

"SON OF A BITCH."

Stanton jammed the gun into the armpit of his naked torso and silently slid the barrel out of the window. He took a final drag on his cigarette before placing it carefully on the windowsill and away from his line of fire.

He didn't want smoke drifting into his eyes.

He didn't want to miss. Stanton never missed.

Closing one eye, he put the target in the middle of the sight.

Across the road, on the asphalt roof of a garden shed, a seagull warming itself in the morning sun twitched its head nervously.

Stanton squeezed the trigger just as the seagull turned, and they unwittingly locked eyes. The weapon jolted painfully into his shoulder and Stanton looked up quickly. White feathers spun in the air, remnants of a bird that had quickly flown to safety. He had been too hasty, he had only managed to clip the bird. Next time he wouldn't be so careless.

Standing back up, he rested the gun on his shoulder, picked up his dying cigarette and breathed life back into it, knocking the ash thoughtlessly out of the window.

He had only just woken up and he was bored already.

Leaning against his bedroom wall, forehead on hand, he thought over his problems while appreciating the light breeze coming in through the window. It had been another warm night, and he hadn't slept well for days.

Stanton was in trouble. A lot of trouble.

As usual, he had no one but himself to blame. His inability to see the unintended consequences of yet more bad decisions meant he had taken to sleeping in his jeans and heavy boots. That way, if anyone came calling, he could be out the window and halfway down the drainpipe before anyone knew where he was.

Matters were coming to a head. In a few hours, he would have to visit Mickey and start explaining himself.

Mickey was a small-time criminal with big ideas who had been moving up in the world, or at least trying to. Stanton had been hell-bent on rising with him. He became the go-to for shoplifting and stealing car radios, before Mickey promoted him to selling the stolen goods around clubs and pubs.

But recently, things had got interesting. Mickey had met some people from the town across the river. They were looking for someone local to help shift their product – nothing heavy, just some hash, the easy stuff, as Mickey had called it. But if they played this right, it was going to move them into the big time, to the stuff the yuppies were shovelling up their noses. That was the future, said Mickey. That was where the real money was.

So Mickey had shaken hands with the Moroccans, promising them the world, before ringing Stanton and delegating the hard work. If Stanton could help sell a larger amount on his behalf, he'd give him a bigger share of the profits.

Stanton had jumped at the chance. Using his contacts from when he worked at the fairground, he had gone to the traveller camp at the back of the park and spoken with Big Tommy. A price was swiftly agreed, and Stanton had walked out of there with his pockets full of cash.

Today, exactly two weeks later, Big Tommy had sold all the drugs and Stanton had spent all the money. New boots, new clothes, new stereo, a brand-new air rifle, and fun, lots of it. Stanton couldn't deny he'd had the best two weeks of his short and chaotic life.

Staring with contempt out of his bedroom window, Stanton felt hemmed in by the suffocating, close-knit rooftops that filled his view. To him it was a miserable scene of slate-grey sea, stitched together row after row, aerial after aerial, chimney after chimney. Some of the fires were already lit, wispy smoke filtering out through the pots. In this town, even in summer, fireplaces were needed to warm the skeletal bones of the old.

Stanton despised what he saw. He hated this place and the people who lived here. Inhaling deeply from his cigarette as though that would be enough to suck up the decay and detritus of life that festered all around, he briefly closed his eyes, feeling the warmth of the sun as it rose across the bay. He was about to go and lie on the bed when something in the alleyway opposite caught his eye. Swearing under his breath, he swiftly reloaded his rifle and put the cigarette back on the windowsill.

This time he was looking at a young child, no more than three, playing in a yard across the street while his mother was busy pegging out some washing.

Stanton closed an eye. Gently placing his finger on the trigger, he slowly began to move the crosshairs from the mother to the child and back again. He did this a few times before deciding on the ample backside of the woman and was about to fire when, from directly beneath his feet, a loud thudding noise came through the floorboards. At first he ignored it, trying to concentrate on what was happening outside. But the thumping became louder and more frantic. Realising the moment had gone, Stanton reluctantly put the rifle down.

It was Margaret, his mum, although he had stopped calling her that many years ago. These days, she slept downstairs in what used to be the living room. Margaret was a cold, miserable, one-legged, bed-ridden woman and Stanton was resigned to being summoned each morning by her banging a broom handle against his bedroom floor.

He stomped his foot loudly. "Yes, okay. I'll shoot you next, silly cow."

For now at least, his fun was over. Pulling on a white t-shirt hanging over the back of a chair, he casually flicked the still-burning cigarette out of the window and went across the hallway into the small bathroom.

Standing at the bowl, he stared in the mirror, piercing eyes looking back at him. With his blonde hair shaved close to his scalp, he looked much older than nineteen. Spitting into the bowl and leaving it unflushed, he descended the narrow staircase, his heavy boots pounding the threadbare carpet, sounding like thunder rolling in across the bay.

Seething at his morning fun having been interrupted, he stormed straight into Margaret's bedroom without knocking.

"Cuppa, Margaret?"

That was as far as he got, the words catching in his throat as he winced. "Christ, it stinks in here."

The commode sat in the middle of the room like a throne, no doubt filled with her stinking piss, its smell mingling with the earthy aroma of an old woman who smoked and rarely brushed what was left of her teeth. Heavy velvet curtains hung across the window, shutting out the daylight and helping to keep in the acrid stench.

Margaret wheezed as she scrambled to sit higher in the bed.

"You daft sod, you should knock before entering a lady's room. Could've killed me with a heart attack."

"I'm not that lucky," Stanton mumbled, while throwing back the curtains and opening a window. "Do you want a brew or not, Margaret?"

"Aye, cup of tea," she rasped, making herself comfortable.

"Fucking stinks in here," Stanton repeated, closing the door behind him to stop the odour from permeating the rest of their tiny house.

He filled the kettle and placed it on the hob of a filthy, free-standing oven that was older than Margaret, scraped the only chair across the cheap linoleum floor and sat down. While waiting for the steam to whistle, he shuffled through some unopened brown envelopes on the table before tossing them dismissively away.

Leaning back, he stretched out his long legs and stared up at the stained and greasy ceiling.

∾

The meeting was not going well.

"Fuck off with your next week. You've had two weeks as it is. Do we have a problem here?" Mickey narrowed his eyes on Stanton's face and used a shovel-like hand to push back his thinning, greasy quiff.

It had been just after noon when Stanton had walked into the Smugglers. He'd loitered outside for a while, keeping an eye on Mickey's white van with faded red lettering and probably filled with stolen goods. Stanton was sure the van wouldn't be there when he came back out. The Smugglers was what Mickey liked to call his office, but it was just a dingy back-street pub set away from the promenade. The only rule here was, if it went quiet when you walked in, you weren't meant to be there.

Stanton sheepishly picked up his pint.

"No, Mickey, not at all. There's no problem. Everyone's just busy getting ready for the summer season. Left some messages, the word is out, it'll soon be sorted."

Mickey pursed his lips. "Well, sort it quicker. They're coming across Friday."

Stanton's throat went tight and he struggled to swallow the beer. He put down his glass, wiping his mouth with the back of his hand. "Friday? No way, Mickey, that's too soon."

Mickey feigned surprise. "Is it? Well, some might say two weeks ago was too soon and yet here we are."

"It's a lot of money and—"

Mickey cut him short.

"—I *know* it's a lot of money and do you know *why* I know it's a lot of money? Because I had to borrow it myself from people who *don't* happen to think Friday is too soon."

Mickey took a large mouthful of neat scotch before banging the glass back down. "So, Friday?"

Stanton was cornered.

"Yeah, Friday, no problem Mickey."

"Don't let me down, Stanz."

It was too late; Stanton already had. He looked at the shadows on the other side of the snug's frosted glass, watching as they laughed without a care in the world while his own life was unravelling before him.

He looked back at Mickey. "I'll get the gang together. Soon get it sorted."

It was Mickey's turn to almost choke on his drink.

"Those morons? May as well send your one-legged mother out, Stanz."

He leaned in closer so that their heads were almost touching. The meeting was coming to a close. "Get that money and get it to me quickly or we'll both be eating through a straw. Now, piss off."

Leaning back, he looked over Stanton's shoulder at his next meeting hovering nervously in the doorway.

Stanton picked up his glass and left the snug, purposely brushing past the man waiting to go in after him. He was no longer in the mood to finish his drink so put the glass on top of a fruit machine and walked outside, squinting as his eyes adjusted to the bright sunlight.

He looked across the car park. Mickey's van had indeed disappeared.

Stanton swallowed hard. If he didn't come up with that money soon, he might be next.

TWO

STANTON COULD FEEL HIS FINGERS GRIPPING TIGHTER AROUND THE phone the longer his call went unanswered. He hadn't expected to end up inside a stifling hot phone box on the promenade, looking out through its dirty and graffitied glass, hoping the only person he could trust in the world was home.

After leaving Mickey, Stanton had wandered around town trying to think how he was going to get hold of the money. The only solution he could think of was the obvious one. He was going to have to steal it back. But he knew he couldn't do that on his own.

He was about to put the phone down, when someone picked up.

It was a tired sounding voice that answered. "Hello."

Stanton watched the timer start to tick down. "Is he there?"

As the woman on the other end of the call recognised his voice, Stanton could feel the animosity crackle down the line.

He heard her put the phone down and shout, "Jason, it's for you."

There was a momentary pause while the phone was handed over.

"Yeah," Roper said, taking the phone.

Stanton mocked him in an effeminate voice. "Is that Jason speaking?"

"Funny as ever, Stanz. What's up?"

"What you doing?"

"Not much. You?"

"Same. But I've just been to see Mickey."

The line went quiet. Stanton bit a fingernail in the silence.

"What did he want?" Roper asked cautiously.

Perspiration was beading Stanton's brow, so he pushed the door open to let some cool air in.

No point wasting time. "The money."

Roper sounded tense as he spoke into the mouthpiece. "But we've spent the money. All of it."

"I know that, dickhead. But we've got no choice. We need to get it."

"Okay. When for?"

Stanton felt compelled to push the door a little further open.

"Friday." He knew Roper was smart enough to see it was already hopeless.

"This Friday?"

The pips started to signal there wasn't much time left on the call.

"Hold on." Stanton fed a coin into the machine.

"We could sell some of the stuff we bought?" said Roper as the line became clear again.

Stanton had already thought about that. "And who shall we sell it to, Mickey? We need to start thinking better than that."

"So what's the plan?"

"Haven't got one," Stanton replied truthfully. "Not yet, anyway. But I will soon. Let's me and you meet tomorrow and we'll work it out together. I'll bell you later."

Stanton put the phone down. He stepped back into the

fresh air, slumped on a nearby bench and took out his cigarettes.

He had no problem being a loner. If anything, he had more of a problem being around people than he did being on his own. But he made an exception with the gang, because each of them was as dysfunctional as he was. Jez and Bin Bag were there to make up the numbers and help with the fighting. Sally was there to give Stanton something to do on a Saturday night, and Kat was there as a shoulder for Sally to cry on when Sunday morning came.

But it was Roper that mattered. He held the others together and, if Stanton ever cared to admit it, he held him together too. Not as tall as Stanton, but he was wider, stronger, tougher, more handsome but not as pretty. All the girls fancied him, and all the boys wanted to be him. Stanton made sure to keep him close. They'd met on their first day of school with a recalcitrant nod of their heads and a few years later they were both expelled on the same day as well. One last attempt at selling Margaret's Valium at the Christmas disco had been the final straw.

Stanton jumped off the bench and walked over to the railings. Dark clouds gathered on the shoulders of the hills on the opposite side of the bay, dominated by one they called The Whale. The elongated, sloping shape gave it its name and its imposing form brooded over the bay and the people who lived there.

Stanton noticed his hands clutching the railing hard, his grip so tight his wrists began to hurt. Letting go of the cold metal he flicked his half-finished cigarette into the sea, watching it float for a moment on the water gently lapping at the sea wall.

Stanton had been reckless, got too confident, he had got in too deep.

He needed a way out, and he needed it fast.

THREE

HE NEEDED TO CLEAR HIS HEAD. HE TURNED AND WALKED DOWN the promenade, those already out for an afternoon stroll steering clear of him as he cut through the crowds like a knife, his menacing look intimidating them aside as his heavy boots ate up the sunbaked tarmac.

Stanton was annoyed with himself more than anything, not that he would ever show that to anyone. Weakness was for the weak. If there was one thing Stanton could look back on with pride, it was that he had never backed down from a fight even when the odds were stacked against him. But he was becoming bored of always seeming to be on the wrong side of whatever was in front of him – life, the law and some very poor decisions.

He reached for his cigarettes. But they weren't in his jacket pocket.

"Shit." He looked over his shoulder but he didn't fancy the walk back to the bench. He needed that cigarette because he needed to think and smoking helped the process. A young couple had stopped at the railings to look out across the bay.

Noticing that the man had a cigarette in his fingers, Stanton approached them.

"Cadge a fag off you, mate?"

"Sorry?"

"A fag, give us a fag."

"No, I don't think—"

"—I don't give a fuck what you think, just give me a fag."

Stanton moved closer, towering over the other man. He was in such a foul mood that if he had to hit him to get a cigarette, he would.

"Give him a cigarette, Terry," said the startled woman.

Stanton laughed. "Yeah, give me a cigarette, Terry."

The man, realising he had no choice, reached for his packet of cigarettes and held them open. Stanton took one before pausing and taking another to put behind his ear.

"For later. Cheers, Terry."

He winked, turned away from the couple and headed toward the town centre.

Now late afternoon, the day still stretched endlessly out ahead of him. It needed to be filled because in this town boredom was the enemy of youth. He thought about stealing something, anything, that he could sell later for fags and beer. But he needed to be in the right frame of mind and he clearly wasn't. He could meet up with the gang but they were the last people he wanted to see. Instead, he headed for the shopping arcade in the centre of the town. He only ever went there to go to the record shop, a small haven away from the troubles of his life.

The arcade was busy with mums dragging their reluctant kids around the shops as the elderly looked on, lost in thought about where their own time had gone.

Striding arrogantly past them all, Stanton went inside the

record shop, acknowledging as he did the man behind the counter. He thumbed through the laminated record sleeves, stopping occasionally to pull one out to look at in depth, front and back. Music was one of the few things that Stanton could get excited about, listening to anything played by the disenfranchised to an audience of the disaffected. But today there was nothing there, nothing new, nothing that made him want to stay. Looking up, Stanton hadn't noticed there were a couple of punks at the back of the shop, sharing a headphone each and no doubt listening to their god damn awful music.

"Fucking state of that hair," he muttered to himself. Turning to leave, he stopped and sneered at them. They did the same in return with hand gestures to match. Not here, not now thought Stanton, but at some point their paths would cross again. They always did.

Going back outside into the fresh air, Stanton felt hungry. He hadn't eaten anything today and until now he'd had no appetite. But he had cigarettes and he had a bit of money in his pocket and he certainly had time to kill.

Stepping onto the promenade once again, he headed toward his favourite café. It was at the end of the stone jetty that he could see up ahead, a jetty that stretched out into the bay that was now in full tide.

FOUR

Stanton liked this café because it was away from the busy promenade and all its dawdling, annoying tourists. It was normally a quiet haven and exactly what he needed. He would have something to eat, a cup of tea, a cigarette and a mull over things. Over the course of the afternoon he had been feeling a little more confident about Mickey, deciding he was just going to front it out until a better idea presented itself.

He walked into the café.

"Hello, love," said the lady behind the counter, pouring a cup of tea from a large urn. Wiping her hands on her apron, she turned and went to the counter. "Usual, is it?"

"Please," replied Stanton.

The women shouted through the kitchen hatch. "Betty, double chips and a round of bread and butter, please." Then to Stanton, "Take a seat, love, and I'll bring it over."

Stanton momentarily toyed with sitting outside. But he thought better of it, choosing instead to sit in a quiet corner. As he took his jacket off, he noticed he was the only person in the café. Grabbing an already brimming ashtray from the next table, for the first time today he began to relax. In fact, he actually felt quite good. It might be fleeting, but for now he was back to feeling like the King of the Seaside.

Feeling hot, he pulled his t-shirt over his head and threw it on the chair opposite.

The woman brought over his food, along with a mug of steaming hot tea.

"There you go, love."

Stanton smiled. He lit a cigarette and waited for the food to cool.

He turned to gaze out of the window and across the bay. It was high tide, the sea having been pulled like a grey curtain across an estuary that was as flat as the glass he was looking through. Outside, the only sound was the rhythmic putt-putting of a few fishing-boat engines, followed as they were by raucous seagulls.

But this bay could kill and it often did. A sea that could be so gentle and weak in the summer it hardly had the strength to wash the sand from your feet. Yet, in winter, so fierce it could roll in and snap your spine in half before retreating back around the headland, taking with it your limp and broken body. The locals said that if the sinking sands didn't get you and the currents didn't drown you, the cold would finish you off for sure. It would grab you by the throat and squeeze your chest so that you gasped and panted, and each pant and gasp would allow the sea to get inside your mouth and down your throat and practically freeze you from the inside out.

Stanton stabbed at some of his chips and took a large mouthful of tea, his throat thankful for the quench of thirst. Glancing back out of the window he noticed something, but thought no more about it as he shook his head and laughed to himself while greedily jabbing at more chips. With his other hand, he lifted his cigarette and took a long drag. But, try as he might, he couldn't stop his eyes drifting back to what was happening outside.

On the deserted jetty, a girl was acting strangely. Stanton had seen her walk past a few moments before but assumed she had walked to the end and then left. But she was still there, pacing agitatedly up and down. He carried on observing her, watching as she stopped to hang her schoolbag on the statue of a fisherman.

Stanton slowly put his fork down, perplexed as he watched the girl pick up an empty drink can and throw it into the sea. She stood there for a while, watching as it bobbed and floated with the tide.

Stanton drank some more tea and stubbed out his cigarette before reaching for the fresh one behind his ear. None of what he was seeing made sense. He strained in his chair to see if the girl was with anyone but there was no one else there.

He looked back toward the railings.

"What the fuck," Stanton said, scraping his chair back noisily and banging his mug down hard on the table, spilling its contents in the process. Taking one more look through the window, he grabbed his lighter and headed quickly outside just as the girl started to climb over the railings.

FIVE

"WHAT THE FUCK ARE YOU DOING?"

The girl spun round at the shock of hearing a voice from behind, strengthening her grip of the railing as she pulled herself in.

Standing confidently in front of her, was an older boy. He was tall and bare-chested, smirking with a barely lit cigarette clinging loosely between his lips. Her cheeks reddened under his confident, unblinking gaze.

Sensing the immediate danger had passed, Stanton took his time.

"I said," pausing while he breathed out some smoke, "What the fuck are you doing?"

The girl seemed lost for words as she looked down at the sea, shuffling her feet more securely on the jetty's ledge. It was obvious she was scared and Stanton decided to play it cool rather than make the situation any worse.

"You see, I was sat drinking my tea, minding my own business. I look up and see you walking around out here. One minute over there; next minute, over there," he pointed with his cigarette. "The next minute, you're jumping over the railings." He pointed to where the girl was standing. "Just seemed a bit, you know, weird."

The girl looked over her shoulder at the gurgling, fast-running sea slipping away below her. As she looked back, Stanton could see she was crying.

It caught him off guard. There was more to this than he had first thought.

He softened his voice and delivered his most engaging smile. "My brew's getting cold."

"Sorry about that," said the girl, finding her voice through the tears.

"Ah, so it does speak. I'm not sorry, it tastes like piss. Still, I've paid for it, so I'm going to drink it."

They both stood looking at each other, a silence falling like a curtain between them. There was nothing but the noise of a seaside town, humming gently in the background.

"How about this," Stanton said, breaking the tension. "Why don't I buy us both a brew?" He had nowhere else to be and besides, the busier he was here, the less chance there was of bumping into Mickey.

"I've had better offers," the girl joked weakly, dabbing her cheeks with her sleeve, wobbling slightly as she took one hand off the railing.

"Careful, these are new boots. I don't plan on getting them wet."

The silent curtain fell between them again.

"What if I throw in some cold chips as well? I'm all heart. Come on then, they'll be closing soon."

Stanton turned and walked back towards the café. "Don't forget your bag," he shouted without looking back.

As he headed inside, he checked in the window of the café. He could see the girl climb slowly back through the railings and unhook her bag from the statue.

"I'm over there," he said, indicating a table in the corner where his jacket and t-shirt hung over the back of a chair. Weaving around the closely arranged maze of tables and chairs, the girl sat down and waited.

"Here." Stanton put down two mugs of steaming tea, sitting opposite her so that she had no choice but to look directly at him. He felt a bit sorry for her, she seemed lost and confused, but he couldn't help but be curious about what was going on.

"So," he said after a while, "out there by the railings, what were you doing? Walking up and down. All looked a bit suspicious to me."

The girl didn't reply and instead looked behind him at the door.

Stanton followed her eyes. "You're free to go if you want, no skin off my nose," he said, laying his head back and casually blowing smoke rings up at the ceiling. "Oh, in case you're wondering, my name's Stanton."

He held out his hand which the girl ignored, so jokingly, he moved it closer.

"Heather," she finally conceded. "And do you mind not being so nosey?" She moved her chair a little further away. "It's got nothing to do with you, so mind your own business."

Stanton smiled and drew on his cigarette. "Makes sense," he said, laughing.

The girl looked properly at Stanton for the first time. "What does?" she asked, frowning.

Stanton knew he was an intimidating figure. He was tall, with heavy boots and shaved hair. It crossed his mind whether she might be scared of him.

"Want a drag?" He offered her his cigarette.

"No thank you."

He followed her eyes towards the door again, trying to read her mind. "No, not at all, or no, not just yet?"

Stanton stopped himself from saying anything else. He leaned back slowly; he knew he was teasing her unnecessarily. If he carried on this way, he would still be no closer to knowing what was going on.

"When I said it makes sense, I meant I reckon you don't even know yourself what you were doing out there. Am I right?"

Heather's eyes filled with tears again.

"Here, you've not touched your tea." He gently handed her a mug.

Heather held it and took a few sips, the steaming hot tea feeling good in her dry mouth. The drink was exactly what she needed, and it made her feel slightly better. She put the mug back on the table.

"So, you sit in cafés all day long and spy on girls, do you? That's the kind of thing the police might want to know about."

Stanton smiled. "Not really, not all the time, not since the court case." He put two large teaspoons of sugar in his tea and stirred it.

"That's far too much sugar. You won't have any teeth left. Your mum will have to feed you baby food when you get older!" Heather laughed at her own joke.

"Yeah, well, it's what makes me so sweet," Stanton winked. "So, were you?"

"Sorry?"

"Were you about to jump in the sea? You can keep ignoring the question, but I'll only keep asking it until you tell me or until you get up and leave."

He nodded his head confidently towards the door.

Heather was in no rush to answer. She didn't think this handsome boy could be much older than her and yet he seemed so self-assured and worldly wise. Everything that she wasn't.

"I don't know," she said truthfully after a lengthy silence.

Stanton took a drink.

"I think you would've jumped."

"Maybe," Heather said, lowering her head.

"No maybe about it, I could see it in your face when you first walked past. If I hadn't turned up to save the day, right now the crabs would be eating your legs."

Stanton had meant it as a joke but Heather lifted her head quickly as he said those words, horrified by what he was saying and by the fact that he might be right.

Stanton handed her a napkin.

"What's this for?"

"For you, when you start crying again."

"Who says I will?"

"Me, and I'll tell you why." He leaned forward with his elbows on his knees. "Whatever put you on the wrong side of those railings is still out there. You might pretend to yourself it's not, but it is. You might decide to run away from it and if you do, the door's just there. But whatever it is, I guarantee it will be outside waiting for you. If that's what you want, you can take your bag and leave." Stanton picked up her bag and handed it to her. "Don't worry about giving me money for your brew. That's on me."

Leaning back confidently, he waited for his words to settle in.

"Or," he said, pausing for a reaction.

Heather put her bag down. "Or?"

Stanton leaned forward again. "Or you tell Uncle Stanton all about it, after which he'll tell you exactly what you need to do to make life better so that he doesn't have to come back down here and save your arse all over again."

Stanton's perfect smile drew Heather in. He looked like

trouble but, at this moment, he seemed about the only person in the world who knew she existed. Heather picked up her mug, trying as best she could to stop her sadness showing through any more than it already had.

"I never meant to actually to do anything. Out there. At least, I don't think so. You've got to be pretty brave to kill yourself, and I'm learning today that that's not me, I'm not very brave."

Stanton had one arm draped over his head and was smoking with his free hand, his blonde underarm hair hanging like spindly cobwebs.

"I think you're brave."

"Really?"

"Yeah, for a start you're drinking that awful tea."

Heather gave a genuine and heartfelt laugh.

"Yes, perhaps the sea would have tasted better after all." She breathed out deeply, her shoulders rounding as though they were breaking under the pressure. "It's all such a mess."

Without her thinking, or pausing, words started to tumble from Heather's mouth.

"My family's falling apart. My parents fight and argue all the time. No one actually talks to each other anymore and it's like I'm not there sometimes. It's like I'm invisible. I don't have many friends, I'm stuck in the middle of class, in the middle of my parents who don't love each other. I am in the middle of everything and all the time busy going nowhere."

As Heather began to unburden herself, Stanton sat back and listened. He was a stranger to her and yet she was telling him the problems she had in her life right now. Stanton listened impassively when she described spying guiltily on her dad crying at the breakfast table, thinking he was on his own. Heather told him about school, and about how she couldn't stop feeling sad all the time. She told him about a silly schoolgirl crush she had on someone from afar and how he didn't even know she existed but had totally humiliated her at the school disco that lunchtime.

Stanton sat motionless, listening intently throughout, his face refusing to betray any judgement or reaction to what he was hearing. There was a lot of information coming his way, far more than he'd been expecting when he'd first asked her if she wanted a cup of tea.

When Heather finally finished talking, he scanned her face. He might be cynical and from the wrong side of the tracks, but he knew a troubled soul when he saw one.

"Look, if it's any consolation, that crush, Shane was it?"

"Sean."

"Well whatever his name, he sounds like a right arsehole to me."

Heather laughed before quickly composing herself.

"But at least I didn't cry: you were wrong about that, Mr-Know-It-All."

"Yeah, well done. See, I'm already making you tougher, all part of my charm. Do you know what you need?"

"Please don't say another cup of tea."

Stanton leaned forward and dropped his cigarette in Heather's half-finished drink. "That should make it taste better."

"I was still drinking that!"

Stanton grasped the momentum and the change in sentiment.

"Not now you're not. What I think you need is some sunshine on those freckles."

"Sunshine?"

"You've had a shit day. I'm going outside to sit and catch the last of the sun and think about me taking over the world. Coming?"

It would have been so easy to say no but instead Heather answered quickly and before she could change her mind.

"Why not. But I should really ring home and—"

"—No, you shouldn't," he shot back. "Fuck 'em. Come on, I'm in charge of you for the next hour or so, not them."

Stanton picked up the cigarettes and loose change off the table and pulled his t-shirt back over his muscular body, his tight torso inches from Heather's eyeline. Putting on his jacket, he brushed past her and headed for the door.

SIX

IN HIS STURDY BOOTS, STANTON MADE EASY WORK OF MOVING
effortlessly over the rocks. Behind him, Heather tripped and
stumbled as she went more cautiously in her school shoes. It
was still warm, but cooler than the airless café they had left.

"You could have waited," she said when she finally reached
the large boulder that Stanton had chosen to recline on, hoping
to catch the late afternoon sun.

"Thought you'd gone home," he said, lying back, resting on
his elbows, his ankles crossed.

"It might have been quicker."

Heather sat primly, hugging her knees, the screams from
the fairground travelling on the breeze. She looked away. Ever
since he had asked it, Stanton's question had been bothering
her. Would she have jumped? Even now, she didn't know the
answer. Thinking back, she couldn't remember walking down
the jetty, let alone stepping over the railings.

"I hate this town," said Stanton, interrupting her thoughts.

Heather looked across. "Really?"

"Yeah." He sounded almost defeated by the thought of it.

"Me too, I'd love to escape. I thought it was just me."

"Maybe I'll take over some day, put it all right."

"But then you'll have to stay here forever."

Stanton grimaced at the thought. Lacing his fingers behind his head, he lay back and closed his eyes.

They stayed like that for a while. Heather watched the children playing in the shallows, occasionally stealing a glance at Stanton and wondering whether he had fallen asleep.

"What don't you like about it?" she asked, half hoping he would sit up and talk to her.

He didn't reply.

Heather turned her gaze back to the beach, watching as a small child built a sandcastle, proudly decorating it with lolly-stick flags and seashell walls.

"It's different for people like me," said Stanton from behind closed eyes.

"How do you mean? How is it different for people like you?"

"Just is." Stanton opened his eyes and sat up.

"There's nothing stopping you getting away from here."

"Very funny. No qualifications, no money. Just problems, that's all I've got." He threw a small pebble into a nearby rock pool. Rolling up his jacket, he made a pillow and laid back down. "Besides, someone needs to look after Margaret."

He had said it so casually, almost as though he were saying it to himself, that Heather wasn't sure she had heard him right.

"Margaret?"

"My mum. She's a cripple," he replied cruelly.

The wet sand twinkled in the sunlight. Although late afternoon was passing into early evening, there were still plenty of children playing on the beach, running through salty puddles, scavenging for driftwood and treasure. Hungry seagulls stalked the shoreline, pecking on the detritus that bobbed in the wash, occasionally flapping their wings to escape a child with a spade. The colourful lights, strung like bunting along the promenade, turned sharper against the dusky sky.

"My mum used to work there," Heather said, absently.

Stanton sat back up with interest. "Where?"

"Over there, the bingo hall, the big building with red paint."

"I know that place. What'd she do there?"

"I don't really know, something in the office upstairs. But there was a kiosk at the back that served food. They used to put us in the storeroom next to it to keep us quiet and out of the way. Just shoved us in there, turned the lights on because there were no windows and then closed the door saying, 'Don't touch the rat poison on the floor.'"

Heather laughed at the memory and the absurdity of it.

Stanton laughed as well. "What the fuck? They actually said that. 'Don't touch the rat poison'?"

"Yes, they put us where they kept the food and it must have attracted rats. So they smothered the place in this white powder that looked like flour. It was everywhere, like it'd been snowing. Then they shoved us in and shut the door. Hilarious. They would give us some bingo cards and those giant felt-tip pens they used, and we'd play along with our ears to the walls to see if we could hear the numbers."

Stanton couldn't help but laugh as Heather told her story.

"The pens were toxic as well. It was like sniffing glue, not that I've sniffed glue, and we were locked in this little windowless room inhaling these pen fumes and surrounded by rat poison."

"Wait, they locked you in?"

"Oh yes, we were locked in. They said it was to keep us safe."

"Keep you safe, surrounded by rat poison? That's funny. Grown-ups are just fuck-ups, in my opinion. That's mental."

Heather looked wistfully at the bingo hall. "She's having an affair."

"Who?"

"My mum."

"How d'you know?"

Heather sighed. "I don't really, not for sure, but it's obvious when you add the little things together. Arguing all the time with dad. She's always out, probably out this evening. She'll be dressed up, which is totally pointless in this stupid town unless you're meeting someone worth meeting. I answered the phone the other day and whoever was there put it down without saying anything when they heard my voice."

"Wrong number?"

"Right number, wrong person."

"Like I said, grown-ups for you," Stanton said philosophically. "They all lie. You have to be like me, authentic, otherwise what's the point?"

Heather turned her face in to a welcoming breeze as they fell back into a comfortable silence.

The shadows all around were fractionally longer now, marginally sharper, a little darker overall. Heather hugged her knees tighter, her chin resting on them.

It was Stanton's turn to speak randomly. "I've been on the stage in that bingo hall."

His words snapped Heather away from her malaise.

"Really?"

"They used to do talent shows during the summer holidays. Some knackered old comedian in a stupid hat used to do them."

"That's right! Teddy Page was his name. He sang *happy birthday* to me once. They were kind enough to let me out of the dungeon for that. What did you sing?"

"I didn't, I told a joke."

"What was it? Can you remember?"

"Not really, but I do remember no one laughing."

"I'd have laughed."

"No you wouldn't, you were being suffocated in that room."

Once again, they both laughed easily, each momentarily escaping the parts of their lives that were hurting them.

"It's going to rain," Heather said, as she looked over at the clouds building up across the bay.

"Don't be stupid, it's too hot."

Stanton lay back and closed his eyes.

"Do you know there are dead bodies buried up there?" Heather turned to look directly at him, her breath catching slightly in her throat.

"Up where?" Stanton asked, without opening his eyes.

"The Whale." Heather was trying to recall the joke that Mr Jenkins had told the class today in Geography. At the time she had sat mesmerised, believing the story all the way through to the punchline, but now she was worried she had started something she couldn't finish.

Stanton didn't respond.

Heather tried again. "Dead kids."

Stanton turned his head and opened an eye. "Dead kids?"

"Yes, there used to be a church around here hundreds of years ago full of Devil worshippers."

Stanton sat up and looked across at The Whale in the distance.

"It was like an orphanage, and poor people would bring their children to the church for them to look after."

Stanton opened his other eye.

"My dad told me when he was drunk." She stopped, waiting to see if Stanton was willing to play along.

He sat up on his elbows. "Go on."

A broad smile stretched across Heather's face as she leaned closer toward Stanton. "Well, the priests and the nuns would take the children in, feed them and look after them. But really, they were like a satanic cult or something, only no one knew that, and once the parents were out of the way they would butcher the children in their sleep and tear their organs out and eat them."

Stanton squinted against the bright setting sun. "Your dad told you this?"

"Yes. Like I said, he was drunk. Came into my room and woke me up to tell me because he said he had to tell someone."

Stanton tensed his brow as he listened to the story.

"The priests and nuns all danced naked around the dead bodies, offering them as sacrifices to the Devil. But then they realised they had to get rid of the evidence. So, in the dead of night, they would pile the bodies on a cart and take them up into those hills."

Heather pointed behind her, Stanton looked over her shoulder.

"That's where they buried them. That's why it has that shape. They say The Whale is a hundred feet higher today because of all the dead children buried up there."

Stanton hardly moved.

"And do you know something?" Heather asked.

"What?" Stanton replied without moving, his eyes piercing Heather's.

"They say that all those bodies they buried up there are now one of the main contributing factors in the cause of relief rainfall in the local area."

The gap between the teacher telling the story and the class joining up the dots to groan in unison had already passed. Stanton's eyes remained fixed on Heather. It felt as though time stood still on that rock.

"What rainfall?" he asked eventually.

It hadn't occurred to Heather that he wouldn't actually know what she was on about. She blushed and looked away, reminded that this boy was still a stranger from another part of town.

"Doesn't matter."

"So that a true story, then?" he asked, confused.

"Yeah, I think so."

"Weird," Stanton shrugged.

Heather hugged her knees tightly again for comfort. She really should go home. She hadn't phoned, left a message or said where she'd be.

Stanton sat up suddenly. "Fuck, the time."

They both looked over at the clock tower. It was nearly 6 o'clock. They'd been so absorbed doing nothing on the rocks that they had lost track of everything else.

Stanton jumped quickly to his feet. "I need to go."

Heather looked up. "Do you need to be somewhere?"

"I just need to sort some shit out."

Heather could see that his face had changed. He seemed more serious now, more aloof.

"Besides, I can't hang around all day saving schoolgirls from jumping in the sea." A hand slowly appeared in her peripheral vision. "I'll walk back down to the promenade with you."

Heather took his hand and pulled herself up. She was surprised at how soft and delicate it felt before Stanton let go and set off over the boulders. This time he went slowly, thoughtfully waiting for Heather at every big rock they jumped onto.

As they made their way back down the jetty, toward the promenade, the sharp screams from the fairground carried easily across the evening air.

"I used to work on the fairground," Stanton said out of the blue. "It was a great job."

Heather looked away. She didn't need reminding.

"Which way you heading?" Stanton asked as they reached the busy promenade.

"Oh, it doesn't really matter to me, left or right or straight on. I'll get home eventually. What about you?"

He jerked his head. "That way."

"I'll go this way, then." Heather nodded in the opposite direction.

But neither of them moved. Despite who he was or seemed to be, Heather wanted to carry on their connection which had already become, to her eyes at least, the most meaningful thing that happened to her in years. She was intrigued by Stanton and would have happily stayed on the rocks with him until the moon had swapped places with the sun.

"Thank you," she said.

"What for?"

"Just, you know, earlier." She looked down toward the far end of the jetty. It seemed a long time ago. Smiling weakly, she turned to leave.

"What you doing tomorrow?" Stanton shouted as she walked away.

Heather stopped and looked back. "Tomorrow?"

"Yeah, tomorrow. The day after today. What are you doing?"

She took a few small steps back.

"I've got school." She immediately felt stupid. "It's the last week before the holidays. Hardly seems worth going in."

"Well, don't."

Heather frowned. "Don't what?"

"Don't bother going to school."

She laughed. "Don't go to school? What do you mean? I can't just not go to school."

"Bunk off, give it a miss. Didn't do me any harm." He smiled at his own joke.

"What would I do if I didn't go to school?"

Stanton moved a little closer.

"Hang out."

"Hang out where? With who?"

"Me."

"You!"

Could she really just not go to school? Could she spend time with a boy, almost a man, whom she barely knew?

"Tempting. Very tempting. But not everyone can glide through life as easily as you. Besides, some of us need to get an education otherwise we won't be able get a job in the supermarket and work there for the rest of their lives." Heather thought of her mum as she spoke those words.

Stanton laughed. "Fair enough. Tell you what, then. Meet me here after school tomorrow, same time? You can buy me back that cup of tea. Least you can do for me saving your life."

He gave Heather time to think but she had already made up her mind. She had rolled the dice today when she stepped back over the railings and went to the café with him. So what was the harm in rolling it again?

"Okay," she said.

Stanton gave his cocky smile. "See you here tomorrow, same time, same place. And try not to kill yourself before then." He winked, turned and walked away, leaving Heather to watch as he moved quickly through the holidaymakers swarming the length of the promenade.

She stayed there for a moment, hoping he might look back. But he never did and was soon lost among the crowds.

SEVEN

An hour or so later, the rain arrived. At first, the clouds tumbled slowly into the bay, before the wind whipped them on towards the town where they chased Heather all the way home, nipping at her heels but never quite catching her.

Dropping her school bag by the door she looked at her reflection in the hallway mirror and wondered, as she always did when she looked at herself, if anyone would find her pretty. But she didn't think anyone would. Heather was quite small for her age with chestnut hair that dropped around a lightly freckled face. She could have been the most beautiful girl in the world, but she would still have felt the same. Ugly on the inside, ugly on the outside.

Last week, she had turned sixteen. There had been no party, no celebration, just some cake and an awkward giving of presents. It had been like that ever since her little brother Robert had died. It was as if her family were stuck in a never-ending nightmare from which none of them could awaken. They seemed cut off from everything, not just each other. Their house used to be fun and vibrant, but these days hardly anyone visited and they rarely spent time together as a family. When they did, it was functional and lacked empathy or love.

Heather was slowly becoming erased from the world, and no one could do anything to stop it from happening. She was in a world of pain, only nobody knew, and if they did, no one seemed to care.

"Heather, is that you?" her mum called from the kitchen. "Dinner's ready."

Heather went into the kitchen.

"Where've you been?" demanded her mum. "Five more minutes and you'd be soaked to the bone."

Heather sat down quickly at the table as her mum plated up the food. "Sorry."

"Hello, love," said her dad. "You got home just in time."

Heather smiled as she sat down across from him, her mum presiding over them both at the head of the table. The space opposite remained empty and silent as it had since Robert's death. No placemat, no plate, not even a chair anymore – that had been quietly removed to the garage. Out of sight, out of mind.

They began to eat in a deathly quiet, Heather taking small mouthfuls of food, sneaking glances from under her fringe at her mum's heavily made-up face. Her new hairstyle made her look younger and she'd lost weight over recent months. Lowering the fork, Heather looked quickly across at her dad. He seemed older now, his skin grey as though sifted with dust. Heather couldn't even remember the last time she'd heard him laugh.

Silence was the force that reigned in their lives, weighing them all down; oppressive, suffocating, all-encompassing. They couldn't bring themselves to talk about what had happened, so the words remained lodged in their throats.

Heather gripped her knife and fork, the grating of her parents' cutlery on crockery travelling through her body like fingernails running down a chalkboard. She longed to scream, to shake them from the collective grief that was drowning them all, yet the only sound Heather could hear was the tap, tap, tap of steel on porcelain, and each tap felt like a hammer striking Heather's skull. If she didn't say something, her head was going to explode from the pressure of it all.

"Robert," she said quickly, the only word she could think of to say.

Her parents looked up at Heather from their plates, waiting for her to say something else.

"What?" her mum asked coldly.

Heather looked down at her knife and fork. She was grasping them so tightly, she thought they might bend in her hands.

"I'd...I thought because it would be his birthday soon..."

She knew immediately that she should have kept her mouth shut, watching as her dad's head dropped onto his chest, her mum glaring at her so intently it felt like she was burning a hole in her face. Without saying a word, Heather's mum went to the bin where she furiously scraped food off the plate. She didn't return to the table and instead went to the sink, pulling on washing-up gloves.

Heather knew she had to continue, she had to gouge out this cancer that was eating them all alive.

"I just thought we could do something for him?"

Her mum began washing up.

"You have school and in case you've forgotten, me and your father have work. Nothing to be gained from taking time off unnecessarily."

Heather glanced across at her dad, who looked as though he had aged another five years in the past two minutes.

"Unnecessarily?" repeated Heather.

"Colin." Heather's mum demanded his plate.

Heather tried again. "But don't you think we should do something, maybe take some flowers?"

With her back to the conversation, her mum turned both taps on fully.

Heather dropped her gaze to study her folded hands in her lap.

"It's just that I've never been. I'd like to. I'd like to see—"

"—Heather!" Her mum spun round. "See what, exactly? There's nothing *to* see. Now hand me your plate."

Heather slowly got up and took small steps toward the sink. "Mum, I didn't even go to the funeral. I've never even seen Robert's grave. Why?"

"*Why?* Because thirteen-year-old schoolgirls don't go to funerals and sixteen-year-old schoolgirls don't go to graveyards, that's why." Her mum reached out to snatch Heather's plate. But her soapy gloves couldn't grip the porcelain and it slipped from her fingers, crashing to shatter on the floor.

Heather bent to pick up the broken pieces.

"Leave it, Heather! Just leave it. I'll sort it, like I do everything around here. Go upstairs. I'm sure you must have homework to do. You need to start making an effort next year, instead of moping around here." Her mum's face was red, a finger pointing accusingly at Heather, soap suds dripping slowly onto the floor.

Heather turned back to the table. "Dad?" she implored.

He'd hardly moved, frozen like an ashen statue. "Do as your mum asked, Heather," his voice sounding as broken as the plate.

"But Dad—"

"—I won't tell you again, Heather. Go to your room."

Heather ran out of the kitchen as tears welled up in her eyes, trying hard not to sob aloud.

~

Heather turned up the volume on her record player, leaned on the windowsill and looked out.

Their house was set up on a hill where the roads were wider and the gardens much bigger than those in the rest of the town. Heather could see strings of street lamps shining and reflecting on countless wet roofs belonging to neighbours and strangers. She could see the railway line and the park at Billy Hill. But no one was out in the rain tonight. Other than occasional cars, their headlights permeating through the gloom, the town was motionless. The weather had put everything to sleep.

On the horizon was a glimpse of the black sea that had filled the bay, and behind that, sat among the dark brooding hills, was the sloping ridge of The Whale, its image reminding her of the joke she had tried to tell the boy on the rocks a few short hours ago.

She looked over in the distance at the fairground where the rollercoaster and the big wheel stood in the gloom, etched and silhouetted against the sky. It only made Heather feel sad so she pulled the curtains closed, shutting out the town, the night, and the memories.

Heather turned the record over. As she did, she heard angry shouting from the living room and curiosity got the better of her. Tiptoeing onto the landing, Heather listened from the top of the stairs to the argument erupting below.

"Just leave it, Colin, please," her mum hissed in a vexed voice, the only tone she used these days.

"I'd bloody love to, Jackie. I'm sick of it all!"

Other words were spoken, but Heather couldn't hear what was said. More muffled voices, more words spat through clenched teeth, unclear shouts of mutual hatred tossed carelessly like verbal hand grenades.

"Yeah, I get it, another night out. You spend more time with other people than you do with your own family!" Her dad stormed out of the living room and into the kitchen, pursued by his wife. Heather ducked quickly back behind the banister.

The argument simmered on, but Heather could no longer hear. She stood up and walked softly back to her room, stopping briefly at the closed door of her brother's bedroom. She reached out and gently touched it, once again trying the handle, even though she knew it would be locked.

Climbing into bed, Heather lay for a moment, tired but knowing sleep would not come quickly. The record was still playing its love songs, the volume just loud enough to distract from what was happening below.

Closing her eyes, she allowed her thoughts to drift away to the words from the songs circling her head. She was on top of The Whale. The sun was high, the sky was cloudless. The boy from the jetty was there, holding her hand, keeping her safe, making her feel she was the only person in the world.

EIGHT

S<small>TANTON</small> <small>FOUND</small> <small>HIMSELF</small> <small>BACK</small> <small>IN</small> <small>THE</small> <small>PHONE</small> <small>BOX</small> <small>ON</small> <small>THE</small> promenade, frantically feeding money into the slot. This time, it was Roper who answered.

"It's me."

"Stanz, what's happening?"

"Nothing."

"Mickey?"

"Nah, staying out of his way."

"You turned invisible? He knows all our places."

Stanton looked out of the phone box and past the raindrops that raced each other down the panes. Through the gloom, he could just make out the stone jetty as it was slowly enveloped by the late evening murk.

"Not all of them. Let's meet tomorrow. Just us two, no need to get the rest involved, not yet anyway."

"Okay."

"Can you get any money? Your old girl got anything?"

Sarcastic laughter came down the line. "Nicked that ages ago."

"Has she got anything we can sell, any jewellery?"

"Yeah she's still got a couple of massive tiaras after my old fella ran off. Don't be stupid, Stanz. She's more skint than we are. Margaret?"

Stanton sighed. "I'll have a look, she'll have a bit but nowhere near what we need."

He put the phone down and stepped out into the rain, zipping his bomber jacket up to his neck and thrusting his hands deep into its pockets. There was nothing much to do in this town when it wasn't raining, let alone when it was. With hunched shoulders he headed home, his boots marching effortlessly through the puddles.

Today his head had been full of questions, tomorrow he needed to start coming up with some answers.

WEDNESDAY

NINE

By morning, the storm had broken the humid air which had sat heavy over the town for the last few days. Now the blue sky was broken only by rivulets of thinning clouds. The surrounding hills hugged the bay with a patchwork quilt of green and brown. The Whale looked down on everything and everyone.

The puddles had gone, the promenade baked dry once again, and Stanton was sitting on the bench under the clock tower, staring at the ground deep in thought. He was beginning to wonder if he would ever sleep well again. Every time he'd thought sleep would come, a flash of lightning had lit up his room, closely followed by a growl of thunder. He looked across at the stone jetty. It still wasn't clear to him why he'd suggested meeting the girl later today.

"Been here all night?"

Stanton looked up to see Roper. He was pleased to see his loyal friend but not the person he had standing next to him. He stood up aggressively.

"What the fuck is he doing here?"

Roper gently held his friend back.

"No Stanz, don't worry, he's got something to tell you."

"He's a fucking weasel, I wouldn't trust a word that comes out of his gob."

"I'm being serious. Jackson, tell him what you told me."

Jackson shuffled nervously from one foot to the other. He was a shambles of a man with a hollowed-out face. His clothes were dirty, his hair greasy and matted. Stanton and Jackson had history that went back a couple of years. You only ever crossed Stanton once, there were no second chances.

Stanton slumped back down on the bench. "Hurry up then, he stinks."

"Well you see, Stanz, I collect my giro every second Thursday."

Stanton folded his arms and looked bored.

"You know how I'm always skint?" Jackson laughed to try to ease the tension, revealing a mouth of sporadic teeth.

Stanton looked away.

"Hurry up," Roper ordered Jackson.

"Yeah well, that money don't go far in two weeks. A lot of the time I can't afford to wait for the giro to clear."

"Stop sniffing glue then, you toerag," said Stanton cruelly.

Jackson looked to Roper, who nodded for him to carry on.

"Well, you see, there's a corner shop over the west end of town, not far from the digs, it's an Asian bloke what runs it."

Stanton was getting frustrated. "What's this got to do with anything?"

"Just hear him out, Stanz, trust me. Hurry up, dickhead."

Jackson nodded his head quickly. "Well, me and few of the others go in there and sign over the giros to them, they clip a bit off for themselves and give us cash there and then."

Rising off the bench, Stanton had heard enough.

"Why are you telling me this? I've got better things to do than listen to a day in the life of a junkie."

Roper was getting bored as well, so took over the story.

"This is where it gets interesting. Jackson said last time he was in there, he saw how much money was in the till. Fucking loads, Stanz, they could hardly close it. You know what tomorrow is, don't you?"

Stanton ran through the days in his head.

"Second Thursday in the month," he said quietly to himself.

"Problem solved," said Roper.

"Do you know where this shop is?"

"I do now, it's about a mile that way."

Stanton rubbed his chin. This might just be the break he'd been looking for.

"We good now, Stanz?" asked Jackson, hovering like a loose bag of nerves.

"For now."

"Cool, cool. Any chance of…" Jackson indicated the box of cigarettes on the bench.

Stanton couldn't deny the information had been useful, and reluctantly offered him the box.

"Cheers, Stanz. I always…"

Stanton brushed past him, indicating that Roper should follow him down the promenade.

"What do you think?"

"Seems like an option, maybe the only one we have."

"But Jackson's a rat, I don't trust him."

"He is, but he's gained nothing from telling us apart from a few fags."

"That's true. Come on."

"Where we going?"

"Bin day, the alley'll be full of rats."

The two friends jumped over a small wall and marched through the ornamental flower beds that stretched along the promenade, heading in the direction of Stanton's house.

TEN

A BELL RANG UP AND DOWN THE EMPTY CORRIDORS.

"Pack up quietly please, it's only the summer holidays coming up, not Christmas morning."

"Sir?"

"Yes, Stephen?"

"Merry Christmas."

Mr Graeme playfully threw a piece of chalk. "Idiot. Now then, I won't see you again until September. Good news for us all, I'm sure you'd agree?"

"Hurray!"

"Yes thank you, Stephen. Next term, we'll be starting with *The Grapes of Wrath* by John Steinbeck, a fantastic book set in the Great Depression. It's a book about economic hardship, the exploitation of man, poverty, adversity, and an important piece of work about how greed can corrupt society. Such is the depth of Steinbeck's writing you can almost taste the dust of the mid-west plains. The intelligent among you will take time to learn more about this over the summer. Now get out of my classroom and allow me to start my recovery."

"Goodbye, Sir."

"Goodbye, Sophie."

"Have a good summer, Mr Graeme."

"And you, Peter, see you in September. Good work this term, by the way."

"Thank you, Sir."

The pupils splintered into their favoured groups as they left and the classroom emptied quickly.

Heather, ambling and lost in thought, was the last to reach the door.

"Heather, do you have a minute?"

Heather stopped. "Yes, Sir?"

Mr Graeme raised his eyebrows. "We're not in a Dickens' book, Heather. I thought we agreed you could call me Simon when we were away from the rabble?" He jerked his thumb at her departed classmates. "Unlike you, that lot couldn't tell the difference between a Balzac and the *Beano*."

Heather smiled. "They probably think Dennis the Menace is the one Sherlock Holmes is always trying to catch."

The teacher threw his head back and laughed. "Very good, Heather, very good."

Mr Graeme went to the door and closed it before returning to his desk, sitting on its edge directly in front of Heather. "So you read the book, then? What did you think?"

"I loved it, Sir."

"Ah," he said, scowling and pointing a finger at her.

"Sorry. I loved it, Simon. I really enjoyed his stories and the characters he created."

"Indeed. Conan Doyle was a fantastic writer. What he did with Moriarty was brilliant. He created an evil character that didn't actually do much evil work. Instead, he got everyone else to do it on his behalf. Sounds a bit like the Department of Education." He chuckled at his own joke. "Have you ever watched any James Bond films, Heather?"

Heather thought for a minute. Her dad loved them, but she

56

couldn't remember sitting through an entire film. She shook her head.

"Okay, well that's a shame."

Heather could see the disappointment on Mr Graeme's face. "I could go to the library at lunchtime and see if they have any in there," she said eagerly. "Although it's a pretty rubbish library."

Mr Graeme rubbed his chin slowly.

"You're right, Heather, it is a rubbish library. I tell you what. I'll bring some Fleming books in for you next term. Or perhaps we could meet for a coffee during the holidays if you're free? Fleming copied the Conan Doyle idea but made it bigger. He created a whole secret organisation, SPECTRE, which was run by a psychopath. Sounds a bit like this place." He rolled his eyes as they shared the private joke. "I won't say any more, I don't want to spoil it for you. You can tell me what you think after you've read them."

"Thank you. I love reading."

"I know you do, that's why you're my star pupil. But can I ask you something, Heather?"

"Yes. Of course."

"We'll keep it private. It can just be between us, but is everything okay? These last few weeks you've seemed very, how should I say, distracted? And today, it was almost as though you were here, but not here at all."

Heather thought for a moment, searching for a quote she knew would impress him. "The greatest secrets are always hidden in the most unlikely places."

"Yes! Roald Dahl, you remembered, well done."

Heather liked Mr Graeme, he had always been kind and encouraging to her. She recalled the trip to Stratford earlier in the year when he had walked with her to Shakespeare's grave whilst everyone else had swarmed around the gift shop.

"So, is something the matter?" he asked as he moved a little closer along the desk so that his leg touched hers. "You don't have to tell a silly old teacher like me but is there a problem at home, maybe?"

At this moment in time, Heather felt that everything was the matter and there were just not enough words to begin to explain it all. She looked down at her shoes and nodded gently.

"I thought so. Look, it's not easy growing up. Trust me, I've been there, although it was far too many years ago now." Mr Graeme smiled. "It can be lonely out there sometimes. People don't always understand you. They think you're different, so they treat you differently, and guess what? You become different. Sound familiar?"

Heather nodded again, it sounded all too familiar.

Mr Graeme looked at his watch.

"Damn, I need to go to the staffroom before the next lesson starts. This was our last lesson before you break up on Friday." He appeared to be sad as he leaned a little closer in and put his hand on her shoulder.

"Heather, from one misfit to another, trust me, there is nothing wrong with you. You have simply opened doors in your head that the others don't even know exist. Do you know who else did that?"

"No," she replied, as his eyes looked directly into hers.

"These people." He leaned behind him and picked up a book. "The world's greatest authors. They're just like us. They didn't fit in, either. Here," he said, handing her the book.

Heather looked at the cover. She loved the feel and smell of books.

"Orwell," said Mr Graeme. "Simply one of the best. Enjoy it, Heather. Now, I really need to get moving." The teacher was so close to Heather that when he stood up, their whole bodies were practically touching. He moved awkwardly past her and went behind his desk and started to pack his briefcase.

"Heather, you are quite brilliant. I'm very lucky to be your teacher. There are so many great books and writers that I want to introduce you to. I'm not sure we'll ever have enough time to get through them. That's why I put my number in the book. Please don't tell anyone. You know how people are. But I won't be going anywhere over the summer if you want to learn more about literature and maybe help with my book, you remember the one I told you about in Stratford?"

Heather nodded, smiling at the memory. "Have you nearly finished writing it? I'd love to read it."

"I'm stuck a bit on the plot actually, I need some fresh eyes on it. Would you like to help me?"

"Really?" Heather struggled to hide her elation. "I'd love to."

"Well, you have my number now so if you want to meet up just give me a call. Okay I need to go, I've got 5C next. Wish me luck," he shouted as he dashed out of the classroom.

"Thank you," Heather said. "Have a nice summer."

Closing the door behind her as she went, she stood in the hallway and opened the book.

On the inside cover, Mr Graeme had written 'Home' followed by a telephone number and a kiss. Smiling to herself, she put the book in her bag and headed down the now deserted corridor.

"Causes and effects of the First World War. As instructed, you should have all read that from last week, so now we'll test you." The teacher was met with a sea of groans.

Heather looked at the back of Sean's head and then absently out of the window. He hadn't so much as looked at her since the disco yesterday when he'd made a fool of her in front of his friends. In that respect, she was lucky. She didn't have any.

~

At half-past three, the bell rang and a thousand pupils poured out through the wrought-iron gates to make their way home.

Heather took her usual seat on the top deck of the bus, but not before casting a clandestine look for Sean. He was normally upstairs being loud and funny with his friends. But today the bus was quiet. With only two more days before school finished for summer, everyone was off doing other things. But no one had asked Heather to stay behind and do something or go anywhere.

As the bus pulled away it caught some low-hanging branches, causing them to rattle the windows and wake Heather from her daydream. She had been lost in thought, wondering what she had to do to make her life exciting. Only sixteen and already it felt like life was passing her by.

The bus moved lethargically through the town centre, becoming stuck as it always did at the traffic lights opposite the hospital, leaving it exposed to the sun which burned through the windows, blinding those on the top deck, tormenting them like ants under a magnifying glass.

The heat was stifling. Heather blew her fringe away from her face, brushing her dry lips with her tongue. She undid a button on her blouse and shifted uncomfortably in her seat.

The bus crawled through heavy traffic. Stop start, stop start. Heather looked down at the cars below, their windows wound down, bare arms hanging outside, passengers fanning themselves with whatever was to hand.

Opposite the cemetery, the bus came to a complete stop and a pang of guilt hit Heather in the stomach as she recalled yesterday's conversation with her parents. Whenever the bus drove past here, Heather would always morbidly scan the graveyard for fresh flowers or grieving families. One time, she had seen a woman sinking to her knees and, clearly in distress, lay a teddy on a small but perfectly kept grave. Heather had felt guilty about watching, but couldn't stop herself, and she wished she could have gotten off the bus to watch a little more.

But the cemetery was quiet today and the only person Heather could see was a man pushing a wheelbarrow through the grounds. She pressed her head to the glass. Robert was in there, somewhere. But where?

The traffic gave way and the bus moved off, heaving itself up the steep hill, from the crest of which you could look down over the town and the bay. As her stop approached, Heather pressed the bell, made her way downstairs and got off. She crossed the road and made her way to the quieter end of the promenade, where the small family hotels mingled with the nursing homes. She preferred this part of the town, away from the amusements and the stench of fast food. You couldn't hear the screams from the fairground, either. Heather felt happy when she was sat here, alone with her thoughts. Taking out her cassette player she put on her headphones, pressed play and closed her eyes.

Lately, Robert's death had been plaguing her. Her brother was never far from her thoughts, but for the past few weeks he was the last thing she thought of when she went to sleep and was still in her thoughts the next day as soon as she awoke.

When her parents had sat her down and explained that her little brother was dead, Heather fell deep into herself and never fully returned. There was no coming back from news like that, not just for her but for all of them. It was like her family were a sandcastle and the tragedy was a wave that crashed in and washed them all away. The hurt, the shock, the continual pain all conspired together to turn Heather into collateral damage, her parents seeming to have forgotten about her as they battled to keep themselves alive.

When it all became too much, as it had recently, Heather came and sat here. This green-painted, weather-worn peeling bench was her haven, a sanctuary where she could just be with her thoughts. It was always a place where she could find some peace for herself, however brief.

Opening her eyes across the beautiful bay, the murderous tide had been and gone. The water receded, taking with it the detritus of the day, hauling it back out to the bigger sea and then beyond into an ocean somewhere on the other side of the world. But it had left behind sparkling wet spots of quicksand across the flattened estuary. If you didn't know what you were doing, that sand could kill you. Only last week, Heather had thought about walking out there, imagining the sand taking her, pulling her down and out of sight, forever. The impulse had been fleeting, but she had felt it nonetheless.

She looked up at the red warning flag that hung limply in windless air and then down towards the clock tower.

ELEVEN

Heather saw him standing by the railings where she had climbed over yesterday.

"Thought I'd wait here, just in case you tried to jump."

"Very funny."

Heather put her school bag down and peered over, imagining the millions and millions of gallons of grey-green sea that would have passed by, taking with it fish and crabs, effluent and rubbish, away out past the headland, to be swallowed whole by the horizon, never to be seen again.

"I wouldn't have got very far anyway, the tide's out."

Stanton looked over. "I wouldn't have been here to save you anyway."

They stood awkwardly, equally conscious that the momentum from yesterday's drama was missing from today.

"How was school?"

"Boring as ever. What exciting things did you do today?"

"Shot some rats."

"Sorry?"

"Yeah. You've never shot a rat?"

"I've never shot anything. What do you mean, you shot some rats?"

"It's Wednesday," replied Stanton, as though that would answer the question.

"And?"

"It's bin day. The alley behind my house is where they put them out. Stinks on a hot day like this, so it brings the rats out as well. Me and Roper take turns shooting them from my window."

"Roper?"

"Mate of mine."

"Roper, that's his first name?"

"It's what I call him."

"Why don't you call him by his actual name?"

"You can ask him yourself in a bit, thought we'd go and have a game of pool on the pier."

Heather looked across at the pier, its brilliant white structure shimmering in the afternoon sun.

"I thought you wanted me to buy you a cup of tea?"

Stanton grinned. "You can, tomorrow."

"Tomorrow? I might be busy tomorrow."

"Are you busy tomorrow?"

"As it happens, no."

"Knew it."

"I've only just got here today and already you're talking about tomorrow."

"That's how I roll."

"Tell me your name. I'm not calling you by your surname, that's silly. What's your first name?"

The question caught Stanton by surprise.

"What's wrong with Stanton for a name?"

"Nothing, nothing at all."

"You might end up as Mrs Stanton and then we can both call each other Stanton," he teased.

"No thanks."

"Guess."

"Guess?"

"Yeah, guess. Guess my name."

"I don't want to guess your name. Why can't you just tell me? I'd really like to know."

Stanton felt guilty like he had in the café yesterday when he knew his teasing had gone too far.

"Some people call me Jimmy," he said quietly.

"Jimmy? As in James?"

"No, idiot. Jimmy, as in Keith."

They laughed at the silliness of what Heather had just said, reminding them both of how they had laughed together on the rocks.

"James is a nice name. I'll call you that from now on."

"Come on, then. Pier today, brew here tomorrow."

Stanton pushed himself off the railings and headed off down the jetty, leaving Heather with no choice but to pick up her bag and run to catch him up.

They walked toward the pier in a comfortable silence, zigzagging through the increasingly busy crowds.

"Everything ok when you got home last night?" asked Stanton. "You know, after…"

"Yes," Heather said, down to her shoes more than to him. "They were arguing all night again, though. Mum's such a bad liar, and she lies a lot. If you lie to your partner, you can't love them very much. I didn't realise how many girls were in the admin team and all of them having leaving drinks in the past few months, apparently. Do you remember the other pier?" she asked, wanting to change the subject.

"Yeah," he said, smiling at the forgotten memory.

"That fierce storm that washed it away!"

The winter storm had blown in that year with such a force that the locals still talked about it as the worst they could remember. It had ripped up the roots of the town's second pier as though they were flimsy weeds and bent the structure practically in half. Wrought-iron stanchions were snapped like toothpicks as wave after wave crashed up and over the pier in a relentless battering that lasted for hours. As the light faded that day, the pier had still been there. But when the town awoke the following morning, it had practically gone, shattered and snapped, a third of it clinging to land like a broken tooth, the rest just a mass of tangled iron and wood. The end had been ripped away, claimed by angry waves. A midnight smash-and-grab; the storm like a giant octopus creeping up, clutching the pier tightly, and pulling it back down beneath the waves.

"I went down the day after the storm with a few mates," said Stanton.

"You did? I was there as well."

"Felt like the whole town was there."

"When did you go down? Can you remember?"

"No idea, Margaret heard about it on the radio, and me and a few mates rode down there to see what was going on. There was a slot machine on the shore and we tried to drag it up to the promenade, but it weighed an absolute tonne. We tried to kick it open to get the money out, but a copper started shouting at us, so we legged it."

"Don't you think it's strange that we could have walked past each other that day? You know, I saw you, you saw me, but we just didn't realise, and yet here we are today?"

Stanton looked at Heather. "Not really."

"Just think about it. Do you believe in fate? That the stars can align to make things happen. Do you believe in astrology?

I bet I can guess your star sign. You're quite guarded. You don't like to let people in."

"Especially weirdos like you," he said, defensively.

"But you're independent, and very, very serious. I'm going to go with, Virgo! You're a Virgo. Yes, I bet your birthday is between August and September?"

"What are you, some sort of witch?"

"No, just very intuitive. So, am I right? I bet I am."

They reached the entrance to the pier and went in. Almost straightaway, Stanton felt invincible. He loved it in here, the musky smell, the dimly lit room, the sounds that rang out in a cacophony of laughter, squeals and games being played.

He pushed a way through the tourists for Heather and himself, heading for the pool tables at the back, the crowds thinning out as they got closer, a welcome breeze ushering in through the open side doors. Approaching the tables, he could see the gang hanging around and looking bored.

"Alright, you took your time, we were just about to start." Sally picked up a cue from the table and held it out.

It was only in that moment that she and the others spotted Heather.

"Didn't think you were coming," added Bin Bag.

Stanton took the cue and pointed it at Bin Bag's head. "Why would you think that? If I say I'm going to be somewhere, I'll be there."

Bin Bag dropped his head and went back to setting up the table.

Sally couldn't keep her mouth shut. "So where've you been, Stanz? Out making friends?"

Heather looked down at her shoes, feeling embarrassed.

"Who's with who? Winners stay on," shouted Jez excitedly.

Sally picked up another cue and went to stand next to Stanton. "Sounds good to me. Come on, Stanz. We can beat anyone."

Blanking her, Stanton went to another table, picked up a cue and handed it to Heather. "Played before?" he asked.

Heather started to confidently rack the spots and stripes in their correct positions, leaving the black ball which she flipped into vacant hole in the middle of the pack without even touching it.

The others looked on impressed, except Sally who brushed past Heather and went to join Kat at another table.

"Know her?" she whispered to her friend.

"Nope," replied Kat. "Perhaps he's kidnapped her from school."

Sally shouted over to where the other two were standing, "So Stanz, who's your new girlfriend?"

Stanton knew he was pushing the girls' noses out of joint.

"Why don't you ask her?"

"Okay, I will." Sally moved and stood directly in front of Heather. "Who are you, then?"

Heather could feel Sally's animosity oozing from every pore.

"I'm Heather," she finally volunteered.

"Not got a surname then, Heather?"

"Give it a fucking rest, will you," said Stanton.

Sally had played her cards too early and everyone knew it. Stung by the betrayal, she walked back to be with Kat at the other table.

"Hi Heather, I'm Roper."

Heather smiled, she liked Roper straightaway.

"Ignore her, we all do. That idiot is Jez, and that fat idiot is Bin Bag."

"Come on," interrupted Stanton. "We haven't got all day. We'll take on Roper and Bin Bag. I'll break."

"What about me?" asked Jez weakly.

"You can watch and learn," said Stanton as he bent down, his strong arms tense on the baize, his long legs balancing his body, his thin delicate fingers splayed like spider legs on the table. The cue ran slowly across his thumb, his middle finger tapping rhythmically on the cloth. He knew all eyes were on him so he held the moment just long enough before pushing the cue through powerfully to send the white ball smashing into the pack, spinning the balls haphazardly off in all directions.

"Stripes," said Heather excitedly as she checked to see which balls had been potted.

Stanton raised himself up slowly and chalked his cue.

"Me again then," he said, winking at Heather. He bent back down but this time overhit his shot and the white ball rattled in the jaws of the pocket.

"Unlucky," laughed Bin Bag as he walked around the table, slowly assessing his options.

"Hurry up, we're not playing snooker," said Stanton to laughter from the others. It was enough to distract Bin Bag from his shot and he missed.

"Go on," said Stanton to Heather. "Show these losers what you can do."

"You put me off," pouted Bin Bag.

"You put yourself off. You bored your arms so much they fell asleep, like the rest of us. Go on girl, clear up."

Heather looked at the table. Her dad had taught her to play many years ago and they'd played nearly every week. But not anymore. They no longer did the things they had once taken for granted. She gently massaged the chalk slowly over the cue tip, before gently blowing the dust away.

Sally watched from the other table, simmering.

"This place closes at 11.00."

"Oh sorry," said Heather. "I thought we were playing snooker."

Stanton folded his arms and grinned.

"Brutal," laughed Bin Bag.

Heather pushed her school tie around her neck. Her eyes ran down the cue, past the white ball and onto the ball she was aiming for. She jabbed the cue and everyone's eyes followed as the ball rolled gently towards the pocket and disappeared out of sight.

"Get in!" shouted Stanton, doing an exaggerated dance. He turned his cue around and held it to his shoulder, pretending it was a gun and aiming it at the others.

"Piaow…Piaow."

Sally rolled her eyes and looked away.

Heather bent down to take another shot. The whole gang were watching this game and ignoring their own. Heather attempted an ambitious long pot into the corner pocket and managed to pull it off.

"Nice job," said Roper. "Hang on, where's the white going?"

They watched as the cue ball inched toward a pocket, before it dropped into the void.

Sally now had a big smile on her face. "Oh dear, that's a shame."

"I'm sorry, James," said Heather, without thinking.

"Oh for fuck's sake," said Bin Bag, laughing to himself and turning away.

Stanton went and got the white ball out of the pocket and handed it to Roper. "Two shots to you."

Roper took it from him and put it on the table before bending down to play his shot.

"James now, is it?" said Sally. The words had barely left her mouth, when from the front of the pier a commotion erupted. They couldn't see anything but they could hear shouting and loud bangs.

A solitary syllable punched out into the air, half pleading, half demanding. "Stanz!"

The shout made everyone jump and they turned in unison see where it had come from.

Stanton had been around enough trouble to know what it looked like and when it was coming his way.

"What's up?" he asked Kenny, the pier manager, who was only about five yards away and who was talking quickly as he approached.

"Richie, Foxy and a few others are here, they're all glued up and looking for a ruck."

Stanton stood on his toes and looked down the pier. "Where?"

"About thirty seconds behind my arsehole," said Kenny poetically. "They've done one of my guys in, we're outnumbered."

Stanton saw them now, marauding and menacing as they moved up the pier, pushing through anyone who got in their way. Just another day, just another fight, a seemingly unbreakable cycle repeating itself. The punks and the skinheads, steel cap toe to steel cap toe.

But there wasn't time to stand and ponder his life choices, he needed to get Heather away from here.

Stanton grabbed a pool ball and threw it hard, just missing the punk out in front. It was a sign for the others to start doing the same, and soon a barrage of pool balls launched through the air, slowing down their attackers' advance.

Using the opportunity, Stanton pushed Heather physically through the side door and outside onto the gangway.

"What's happening?" she asked. "Who are those people? Are you in trouble?"

Too many questions and not enough time.

"Welcome to my world. It'll be alright. You need to go home now. I'll see you tomorrow at the café, same time. Bring your purse, you still owe me that brew."

"But…"

Stanton had already dashed back inside, closing the door behind him as he disappeared into the dark.

∾

Counting to three, Heather leaned in and pushed. But the door didn't open. She tried again, before ringing the bell and stepping back. But there was no answer, no one was home.

And why would they be? There was nothing to be home for, her parents were simply doing what she had tried to do.

Heather went around to the side of the house and moved the bin to get the spare front door key. With it, she let herself in. The house was eerily quiet, even quieter than normal, as though it were feeling the grief on their behalf and in their absence.

Going into the kitchen, she saw a note on the table. Before she'd even picked it up, she knew it had been written by her mum.

Dad's out. I'm doing an evening shift, someone was ill. Plenty to eat in the fridge. Dad home about 9 pm. I'll be back late, we're stocktaking. Don't wait up.

Leaning against the kitchen table, Heather looked at the letter in her hands.

Her parents might regard Robert's memory as something disposable, but Heather wouldn't. Why couldn't they have sat around the table tonight and talked about him rather than skulk around the truth and refuse to accept he was dead and never coming back?

She scrunched the letter with her fists before ripping it to shreds with her fingers, her face reddening with anger as the pieces became smaller and smaller as they fell to the floor like confetti.

It was becoming too much, she couldn't stay here, she was going to die if she did. The end of the jetty hadn't been an accident, she had meant it, she had meant to put herself there.

Wiping away her tears, she stooped to pick up the pieces from the floor to put in the bin.

Don't wait up.

Don't worry, she thought. I won't.

TWELVE

Stanton was at his bedroom window, looking out onto a cloudless, pitch-black sky awash with pin-prick stars.

Since coming back from the pier he had prowled around his room like a caged tiger, smoking incessantly and playing records. Occasionally, he would get his air rifle back out and take pot shots at seagulls innocently resting on the apexes of the terraced roofs. He was never short of targets, they lined up almost willingly, practically inviting Stanton to turn them into clouds of white feathers.

He wasn't tired, just bored, and he went and lay on the bed.

Sometimes, when looking in the mirror, he didn't recognise himself, as though the corporeal him was a whole different person from the one in his head. He flicked the bedside lamp on and off, watching himself present in the light one moment, and gone in the dark the next.

It was at times like this, when on his own, that his mind would haunt him with memories. The flashbacks would be vivid, and often he would struggle to sleep. Once he did, the screams, when they came in the night, were his.

Stanton had a recurring nightmare that made him feel like

one of the puppets he used to enjoy watching as a child at the fairground. In the dream, people whose faces he couldn't see would come out of the shadows and cut away at the strings holding him up, so that every time he wanted to run away his legs wouldn't move, and those chasing him would smother him. Just as they enveloped him he would invariably wake with a start, feeling like he couldn't breathe as his heart thundered in his chest.

His life had changed so many times in so many ways that now, looking at his face come and go in the mirror, he felt like he was nothing more than a collection of mistakes. His past had done a poor job at giving his future any hope.

But Stanton wanted more, he wanted to be better, he knew he didn't want this life that he had been given. Change was coming, he could feel it. The issue with Mickey was a distraction he didn't need, but he also knew it was a sign. A sign that said something needed to be done.

He got off the bed and turned the volume down on the stereo as he sat at the small table. There was a fleeting sense of guilt at the thought he had used some of the stolen money to buy it. But there was no point feeling guilty for long, surrounded as he was by ill-gotten gains. New boots, new albums, new clothes, new rifle. Roper's room was the same. Neither of them had been shy about getting rid of the money.

He picked up an album and looked at it closely before removing a piece of paper from the sleeve. On the paper he was carefully holding, was a half-finished drawing of the singer whose voice and lyrics were coming out of the speakers.

Stanton picked up a pencil and sharpened it, pausing to recall that this pencil sharpener was the first thing he could remember stealing, having first got the taste of taking things that didn't belong to him on a school trip when he was seven or eight. On a blustery winter's day, after moping around some ancient ruins, he had, out of sheer boredom, gone to the gift shop and filled his pockets with whatever he could. He thought he had got away with it, until he was dragged off the coach and humiliatingly made to hand everything back. But Stanton managed to conceal the pencil sharpener in the shape of a Roman villa. It had been a small victory at the time, but an important one. Turned out that some of his classmates had seen him stealing and told a teacher. From that day on, he stopped trusting people.

Stanton blew the pencil shavings away and took a drink of tea, grimacing at its cold bitterness on his tongue. He spat it back in the mug and carried on with his drawing, pencil in one hand, cigarette in the other, the smoke casting a wispy shadow on the wall in front of him as he forced his mind to focus on something other than his troubles. He liked to draw and, looking back, he wished he could have taken school more seriously. But school hadn't bothered to take him seriously and so both skirted each other until he was old enough to be expelled.

So absorbed had Stanton been in painstakingly copying the album cover, he hadn't noticed the needle was no longer on the vinyl and that the music had stopped playing. He looked down at what he had drawn. Even he had to admit this one was good. He carefully put the drawing back in the sleeve and went and looked at himself in the wardrobe mirror.

His pretty face stared back at him. His hypnotic eyes and smooth porcelain skin meant he could have whatever and whoever he wanted. Yet he wanted nothing and no one. Because, whenever he looked in the mirror, it never felt like him looking back on himself. Peering into the mirror, he examined the red mark on the side of his head which he had sustained in the fight on the pier. It was a fight that no one had really won, the result rolling over until the inevitable rematch in the next day or so.

Leaning his head back, Stanton gathered the saliva at the

back of his throat before leaning forward and spitting heavily at his own reflection. He watched the trail run slowly down the mirror for a few seconds before stopping it and using the spit to clean the graphite dust from his fingers

He might hate the town and the people in it, but on days like this he hated himself even more.

The room was totally silent. Only the television downstairs could be heard. Margaret would already be in a gin-laced sleep and so it would stay on all night, because Stanton had no intention of going down and turning it off.

Instead, he went and pushed the window as wide open as it would go before lying back on the bed. Tomorrow, he would need to move fast. There was no room for error. The gang knew something was happening but only Roper knew what.

Stanton turned the lamp off for one last time, allowing the moonlight from the clear sky to pour in, turning his room monochrome. He liked this time of night, when one day ended and another began. It meant that every night before he went to sleep, he could dig a grave and bury his past and then start all over again.

Outside, a distant church bell echoed over the rooftops.

Midnight.

THURSDAY

THIRTEEN

STANTON'S PLAN WAS SIMPLE. HE WAS GOING TO LEAD HIS GANG into robbing the shop that Jackson had told him about yesterday and get back some of the money he owed Mickey. He doubted he would get it all, but if he could get enough to keep the wolves at bay, it would buy him something else that was in short supply. Time.

But he had a problem and that problem was slouched languidly on the benches under the clock tower. The confidence drained from his body.

"Fucking state of you lot," he said, unable and unwilling to hide his disappointment.

"Charming as ever, Stanz," said Sally. "You on your own today, then?"

Stanton ignored the dig.

"What's happening, Stanz?" asked Bin Bag. "What's all the urgency?"

Fleetingly, the thought crossed Stanton's mind to just turn around and go home, but he didn't have the luxury of choice.

"We need to get our hands on some money," he said.

"Tell us something new," mocked Sally, rolling her eyes in Kat's direction.

"How much money?" asked Jez.

Stanton had debated on the walk over here how much he should tell them. He didn't want to scare them off by making the job seem too difficult.

"All of it, whatever that is."

No one said anything. A couple of them exchanged quick glances, while others shifted uncomfortably on the bench. They were okay at shoplifting and doing some gentle mugging, but this already seemed bigger than anything they were used to.

Sally waved around the cigarette she was smoking. "What's the plan, then? Want me and Kat to dress up as schoolgirls?"

Kat elbowed her friend in the ribs and turned her face away as she laughed.

Stanton's heart sank. He knew this lot were simply not good enough. But he had to try.

"We're going to go and rob a shop. Who's in?"

"Me," Roper said, without hesitation. He went and stood with his friend.

"Count me in," Jez said eagerly.

Roper looked at Bin Bag. "Fatso?"

"Sure, may as well. Fuck all else to do."

Sally and Kat looked at each other. "Whatever, but we're not getting into any rough stuff."

"You won't need to. Leave it all to me. Come on, it's about a mile away, we can't hang around."

Stanton turned and walked quickly away, followed by Roper. The rest peeled themselves lethargically off the bench and fell in behind.

Fifteen minutes later, the six of them were huddled on the corner of a quiet, residential backstreet.

"Roper, look round the corner. Tell me what you see."

Peering his head around the wall, Roper assessed the situation. "Looks like a little food shop to me. Got some fruit and veg outside, door's open, can't see anyone inside, but it's dark, so can't be sure."

Stanton collected his thoughts. Having marched them here and endured their complaints about the heat, he needed a moment to play it through his mind. This was a perfect location. It was quiet, there was no one around and, more importantly, it was about as far away from the police station as you could get.

"Right, here's what we're going to do. Apparently an old Asian bloke runs it. He'll be on his own. I'll be the only one going inside, so I need you lot to distract him. Bin Bag, you wait here and keep an eye out. Last thing we need is you having a heart attack in the middle of all this. The girls will go in first and buy something cheap. When you come out, if it's clear, give me a sign."

"Like what?" asked Sally.

"Use your brain. Buy something to eat. We're good to go if you come out, take the wrapper off, and drop it on the floor. Then come back here and wait with Bin Bag. Got all that?"

"Yes, Sir," Kat gave a mock salute and turned to Sally. "May as well have joined the army."

"Roper, Jez, I need you to cause some havoc and get the old man outside and away from the shop."

Roper nodded.

Stanton looked at the two girls. "Well get on with it, then."

They watched as the girls crossed the road, arm in arm, and disappeared inside the shop.

In the distance, a car moved up through the gears as it

drove away. Other than some birds chirruping in the trees, the road was completely silent and deserted.

It felt like the girls had been in the shop for hours

Stanton bit his nails. "Come on, what are they doing in there? Shouldn't take this long."

"Girls for you," said Roper, shaking his head.

"Here they come," said Jez excitedly. They all scrambled to peer around the corner and could see the girls walking back out of the shop, each holding an ice lolly. They unwrapped them before discarding the paper on the floor. Looking across at the boys, Kat sucked on the lolly suggestively and giggled.

"Right," said Stanton. "You two ready?"

Roper nodded and he set off with Jez from their hiding place and quickly reached the shop.

Stanton felt tense. This may well be a quiet part of town but that didn't escape the fact that it was still broad daylight. He watched as Roper picked up an apple from the stall and began to eat it. Then, he picked up a banana which he started to peel.

Within seconds, the shopkeeper was outside.

"What the bloody hell? Hey! You pay me for that, you bloody bastard." In his hand, the shopkeeper had a lump of wood. He raised it above his head and marched toward Roper and Jez. Roper saw him coming and picked up as much fruit as he could carry and started to hurl it at the advancing shopkeeper.

Jez picked up the first thing he laid his eyes on, a free-standing metal sign advertising ice cream. It was much heavier than he'd anticipated, but he picked it up anyway and tried to run away with it.

"What the fuck's he doing?" said Stanton, watching Jez stagger clumsily away with the advertising sign.

"Come on then, you old bastard," an elated Jez shouted, as he tried running as best he could with the metal flap of the sign banging against his legs.

"Bring that sign back and pay me for that fruit, you bloody bastards."

The shopkeeper threw back some of the fruit and set off in pursuit of his sign.

Out of sight and safely concealed, the others watched excitedly at the unfolding drama. Except Stanton, who closed his eyes in despair. He felt like he was watching a cartoon.

But he didn't have time to worry about that. The chaotic plan had worked. The shop was empty, and he had work to do. Stanton set off at speed towards the now unguarded shop, arriving before the others even knew he had gone, only catching a glimpse of his back as he ran in through the door.

Jez had now grown bored with carrying the heavy sign and had abandoned it in the middle of the road, and Roper was running low on fruit.

"I'm calling the police on you," the shopkeeper shouted as Roper and Jez disappeared around the corner. "I've seen both your faces."

Back inside the shop, Stanton quickly went behind the counter and tried to open the till. But there was a problem. He didn't know to operate it. He tried pressing a few buttons before desperately trying to open the drawer with his fingers. But it soon became obvious that the till wasn't going to open.

"Fuck!" he screamed, more at Jackson than anything. He knew he shouldn't have trusted him.

Stanton was contemplating just taking the whole till with him, when the shopkeeper's wife appeared through a side door that Stanton hadn't seen. Once she saw him behind the counter, she started to scream loudly.

"Shut the fuck up," Stanton shouted, but his aggression only made her scream even louder as she shouted back at him in a language he couldn't understand.

"What? What are you saying?" he shouted back. "Speak English and open this fucking till now!"

This was all talking too long. Stanton tried some different buttons on the till but they only beeped and the till refused to open. In a final act of desperation he tried to lift the till, but it was fixed to the counter and wouldn't budge.

"Fuck!" He punched the till with his fist. "And fuck you," he screamed in the face of the woman, who was sinking to the floor. Stanton had no choice. He gave up and headed for the front of the shop, pushing aside the shopkeeper who had just arrived back, sending him sprawling into a display stand.

Back outside, he sprinted across the road.

The rest of the gang, now back together, watched him approach.

"Leg it!" he screamed as he ran past them.

No one needed telling twice.

Stanton didn't know how long he'd been running for but eventually began to slow down, hoping he'd put enough distance between him and the shop. He hadn't paid much attention to the direction he'd gone in; he just knew he needed to get away. Realising he was in an unfamiliar part of town, he slowed to a brisk walk. Occasionally he checked behind to see if anyone was back there, but he was on his own. He'd worry about the others later; in the meantime, he needed to worry about himself.

The robbery was always going to be a long shot, but Stanton hadn't anticipated it being an abject failure. He couldn't blame any of the others, although Jackson would regret the day if he ever bumped into him again. Stanton knew he'd panicked when the shopkeeper's wife appeared, and he cursed himself for not at least grabbing as many cigarettes as he could. The whole thing had been a waste of time and there was no way he could get the money by tomorrow.

Stanton wasn't thinking straight and that is when mistakes happen, and far too many mistakes were being made. He was angry with everyone and everything. This town, his stupid gang, the old Asian shopkeeper. He was angry with time for running out on him, and he was angry at his life for conspiring against him.

Stanton had been here many times before, his back against the wall and the world lining up in front of him. When his anger manifested itself deep inside like it did now, he knew only one way out. To fight. To challenge. To face down whatever was staring at him, to never blink first. If there was one thing Stanton was good at, it was fighting.

It was in this festering state of mind, mired in dark thoughts, his temple throbbing with anger and frustration, that he spotted something up ahead. Or more accurately, someone. On the opposite side of the road, at a bus stop, sat slouched and half asleep, a cheap bottle of cider on the floor beside him, was a punk.

Given the mood he had worked himself into, this was too good an opportunity for Stanton to miss, and he quickly crouched behind a car.

Whoever it was, slumbering across the road from him, they weren't from last night's fight on the pier. But to Stanton, they all looked the same. He'd hated them all with a vengeance ever since they attacked him when he was younger and stole his bike, albeit one he'd stolen himself. From that day, they had been his collective enemy. With their stupid clothes and stupid hair, stupid piercings and stupid studs, not to mention their stupid music.

Stanton checked his surroundings. It was quiet, it was just him and the lad in the bus stop. Again, he couldn't waste time. If a bus came along or the punk woke up, another chance would be gone.

He set off in a straight line, his eyes never deviating from his target dozing unaware.

The punk at the bus stop didn't stand a chance when Stanton arrived unannounced, flying in and smacking him firmly in the mouth with a full, powerful swing of his arm.

"What the f—," was all the punk could manage before Stanton was standing over him, pummelling him in the face. Left punch, right punch, left punch, right punch. The only thing going through Stanton's mind as he felt the cartilage shatter in his victim's nose, was that this was the best he had felt all week.

But the punk was no slouch. Up close, he was bigger than Stanton had realised and he had to press home his advantage while he could. Although his opponent managed to land a blow back, it was weak and ineffective.

"You lot think you're fucking hard, eh? Look at you down there, pathetic." Stanton started to use his boots on the body huddled at his feet, leaning with both hands on the Perspex and kicking hard.

"Hey, you! Stop that. I've called the police."

Stanton snapped his head around at the sound of the voice from behind. From a doorway across the road, an old woman was shouting in his direction.

"They're on their way. I've got a good look at you. They'll be here any minute."

"Oh fuck off, you old bag," Stanton yelled back.

But the brief interruption had broken the spell. Stanton paused for a moment, panting after all the physical exertion. He couldn't take any chances. The interfering old woman probably had phoned the police, she certainly looked the type.

With the energised blood coursing through his veins, Stanton had to end it now. He needed to finish this, to liberate all the tension that had been building throughout the week.

Stanton kicked the punk again and again. He was out of

control, his anger had long exceeded the point he was trying to make, that he was better than them, better than everyone. But he couldn't stop himself. If he carried on, he was going to end up killing him.

"They're almost here, the police. I've seen everything. I'll recognise you again."

Once more, Stanton turned round and shouted at the woman across the road. "Will you just fuck off, or I'll come over and do the same to you."

The woman put her hand to her mouth and quickly closed the door.

Stanton needed to get this finished. Picking up the cider, he poured it all over the prone and motionless body on the floor. He contemplated one more kick to the face, but thought better of it. Right now, he couldn't take any chances with the police, choosing instead to walk casually away, as though he had simply been checking to see the time of the next bus.

But as soon as he turned the corner, once again he was running for all his life was worth. The malaise he had been recently suffering from seemed to drain from his soul the faster he ran. Lately, life had made him sluggish and slow, but now he felt as though he could run to the other side of the world. Nevertheless, his elation was tempered with the knowledge he really needed to be careful. In just the space of an hour, he had given two people very good reason to call the police on him. He was meant to be keeping a low profile but was achieving the exact opposite.

Mistake after mistake; instinct told him to get where it was busy, to the promenade, so he could disappear amongst the meandering crowds. Turning down a random side street, he soon found his way back to familiarity and blended in amongst those who were out and about in the late afternoon.

He looked down at his hands. His knuckles were caked in dry blood. The busy promenade that was meant to throw a cloak of anonymity over him now made him feel paranoid, as though everyone was looking at him. He needed to get cleaned up before someone started asking awkward questions.

Making sure he kept his hands in his jacket pockets, Stanton made his way towards the public toilets. Going in, he went straight to the sink and turned on the taps whilst looking at his face in the mirror. The cold water felt good after all the running and he used soap to get the last stubborn smears of blood off his skin, watching as the scarlet water swirled away.

He leaned on the basin and stared at himself in the mirror. Would the past ever leave him alone? Along with danger and violence, would these things ever stop following him? He couldn't live like this forever.

Stanton splashed cold water over his face to stop the questions in his head and went back outside and into a phone box.

Roper, already back home, got straight to the point. "Now what?"

"No fucking idea. Let's meet."

"Where?"

"Need to keep away from the pier after last night."

Stanton thought about some places they could go and where trouble might not find them.

"Let's meet in the precinct later this evening."

"Not sooner?"

Stanton looked over at the stone jetty, resplendent in the sun.

"No, I need to be somewhere else. See you later."

Stanton replaced the receiver and headed down the promenade.

FOURTEEN

<small>TODAY HE HAD CHOSEN TO SIT OUTSIDE THE CAFÉ IN THE SHADE.</small>

"Still alive, then? That's three days in a row. Knew you wouldn't be able to resist seeing me again."

"I can easily resist you, it's the tea I can't live without."

Heather pointed to the red mark on Stanton's face. It wasn't as angry as it was last night, but it was still visible. "What happened?"

"Banged it."

"On what?"

He laughed. "Someone's fist."

"Last night on the pier?"

Stanton gave a shallow nod.

She sat down opposite and put her bag on the chair next to him.

"How was it today?"

"School? Same as every day. Boring mostly, lonely for the rest of it." Heather looked over to the pier. "Who were those people yesterday? Did they hurt you?"

Stanton scoffed. "Takes more than one of those dickheads to hurt me. We fight all the time, doesn't mean much, gives us something to do so we don't have to get a job. Or go to school."

"Wish I didn't have to. Perhaps I can join your gang?"

"Can you fight?"

"No."

"Right, you can't join then. But I tell you what, get me that brew you owe me and I'll think about it."

His enigmatic smile drew one from Heather and she went inside to get their drinks.

Pulling a vacant chair closer to him, Stanton stretched out his legs on the seat, before leaning back and looking up at the sky. Closing his eyes, he took a moment to enjoy not having to think about anything.

"Here you go, we're quits now." Heather set down two mugs of hot tea.

Opening his eyes, he sat back up.

"Sorry, did I wake you?"

"No, I was getting some rest in before you started nagging."

Stanton unzipped his jacket and took out his cigarettes.

"What's that?" asked Heather, sipping her tea.

"What's what?"

"There on your t-shirt, is it blood?"

Following Heather's eyes, Stanton looked down and saw a fresh blood-splatter on his crisp white t-shirt. He hastily zipped the jacket back up.

"From yesterday," he mumbled.

They sipped on their tea, both of them content to just sit for a moment and do nothing. Stanton pulled out a cigarette.

"You smoke a lot," said Heather.

Stanton shrugged as he leaned into the match.

"How long have you smoked for?"

He thought for a moment. "Dunno. Seven, maybe eight, years."

"And you're how old?"

"Nineteen." He held the match and her gaze as the flame flickered toward his fingers.

"Nineteen!" Heather exclaimed. "You've been smoking since you were twelve?"

He shrugged.

"We had a talk in school about smoking and they showed us pictures of people's lungs who died from cancer. It was disgusting. Those things will kill you."

"Good." Stanton flicked the dead match and watched it cartwheel away.

They went back to their tea.

"Did you get in trouble?" Stanton asked.

Heather was confused. "Trouble?"

"When you got home last night. Were you late?"

"Not really. Besides, I couldn't get into trouble because no one was in. They were both out avoiding each other. She left another note for me with another lie written on it."

"Weird," said Stanton, shaking his head.

"What is?" Heather shifted uneasily in her chair.

"Your mum and dad. What's the point of hanging around if you don't want to be there? My old man didn't."

Stanton drained his mug and quickly stood up before Heather had a chance to ask him about what he had said.

Heather squinted, shading her eyes from the setting sun. "Are you going?"

"No, of course not. I haven't done teasing you yet. Another one?" He picked up Heather's near-empty mug.

He stopped at the doorway and turned back. "Oh, just so I have this right. You don't have a boyfriend. You don't smoke. I assume you don't drink, and it seems like your mum's the only one having any fun around here? Maybe I should have done you a favour and let you jump the other day, after all."

The grin he gave before heading inside the café was enough

for Heather to know he was only making fun of her. But the bitter reality was, he was right. Her mum was having all the fun while it seemed like Heather was carrying all the guilt and taking all the blame.

She looked out across the bay. This time yesterday the tide was out, but today the tide was still coming in. If she had chosen today to jump, she would have been dragged further up along the coast, towards where the banks of prickly grass stretched for miles, destined to never truly escape this place, even in death.

She watched Stanton leaning with his back against the counter, his arms crossed against his chest, his long legs roaming forward, clad in tight blue denim as they had been every day she had known him. Heather noticed his pristine leather boots. He made out that he didn't care about anything, but deep down, perhaps he did.

Stanton glanced up directly at Heather, just as she still gazed directly at him. She abruptly looked away, hoping he hadn't seen.

He came back outside with their drinks.

"Checking me out in there, were you?"

He had seen, and now he could see her cheeks begin to flush.

To Heather, Stanton seemed a lot older today. He was more confident, he had a moodiness about him she hadn't seen, or at least hadn't perceived before. Intentionally or not, he was making her feel childish and immature. She hadn't spent much time in his company, but she knew she didn't want to be anywhere else right now, even if it meant he was the cat and she was a ball of string. Heather wanted to impress him, to show him she was worthy of his time, to keep him there as long as possible. Most importantly, she had stop him getting bored of her.

Remembering the book in her school bag, she reached in

and took it out. "Have you read this?" she asked, putting it on the table.

Stanton reached out but ignored the book and instead picked up his mug. "What is it?"

"It's a book!" Heather laughed.

Stanton showed no further interest and took a mouthful of tea, despite Heather urging him with her eyes to pick it up and open it.

"Do you read?" she asked, nudging the book a little closer to him.

He gave the cover a cursory glance before leaning defensively back in his chair. "A pig?"

"Yes, Napoleon."

"Stupid name for a pig."

"Not really. There's another called Snowball. But Napoleon is now the leader of the farm, and he's just given a brilliant speech where—"

"—A speech?" Stanton scoffed. "It's a talking pig, is it?"

"Yes, but—"

Stanton was laughing harder now. "—A pig that talks. Can it dance as well? If it can, they should get him up on stage over at the bingo hall."

Heather slumped back in her seat. "Simon gave it to me."

Stanton slowed his laughing as curiosity got the better of him. He gingerly picked up the book, turning it slowly in his hands.

"He looks weird," he said, noticing the author's picture. "Is that Simon?" he added, without looking up.

"No, that's George, he wrote the book."

"So who's Simon, then?"

Heather chose her words carefully. "Oh, just a friend."

Stanton slowly opened the book without taking his eyes off Heather. "There's no pictures?"

It was Heather's turn to laugh. "It's a book, not a comic, silly."

Stanton pulled a face; he wasn't used to being the one that was teased. He flicked through some pages until he ended up where Heather had wanted him to start, the inside front cover. He saw the message written on the page but said nothing.

"Where do you know him from?"

"Who?"

"This Simon boy."

"School."

She hadn't lied, exactly.

"Got a kiss, though?" There was a hint of jealousy in his voice. "That the one you have a crush on? You said the other day you'd had enough of the boys at school. From what you were saying, it seems they're just dickheads, all football and rugby wankers. But if that's what you're after." He tossed the book dismissively back on the table.

"No, Sean isn't like the others."

"Sean?"

"No, Simon, Simon isn't like the others."

"The other day you said he was."

"Who was?"

"You said Sean."

"No. Sorry. I was confused then."

"Seems you're confused now."

"I'm not. It's just that, it's been a long day and—"

"—What's changed, then?"

Heather started to feel like she was being interrogated.

"Nothing, nothing has changed, not really," she replied weakly.

"I heard about a Sean, but you never mentioned a Simon."

"I'd forgotten and—"

"—You've gone from not having a boyfriend to having about ten. Maybe you're not as innocent as you make out?"

He hadn't said it aggressively, but the accusation wounded Heather. She had only wanted to show him that she was more than just that vulnerable schoolgirl he had stopped from jumping in the sea. She only wanted him to like her.

"Mr Graeme thought that—"

"—Another one! Who the fuck's Mr Graeme?"

"He, he's Simon."

"Who's Simon?"

"Mr Graeme is Simon."

Heather slowly stirred her tea, watching it swirl around inside the mug like her own meandering words. Stanton leaned forward, took her mug of tea and sniffed.

"Someone slipped something in there?" He laughed and handed it back. "If Simon is Mr Graeme then the obvious question is, who the fuck is Mr Graeme?"

"Simon, Mr Graeme, he teaches English and—"

Heather didn't need to say anything else. Stanton had already made the connection.

"—He's your fucking English teacher?" Stanton looked inside the book again. "This his number?"

Heather nodded.

"His home number?"

She nodded again.

"And you call him Simon?"

"Only when we're on our own." She looked up quickly, realising her mistake.

Stanton tossed the book on the table and stood up as though he were about to leave.

"Has he—" but he couldn't finish the sentence.

Heather's eyes widened. "—What? No, not at all, nothing like that. He's not like that. He's been helping me, that's all."

She couldn't form any coherent sentences, her thought process dissolving in the heat of the moment.

"It's just, I'm sorry, he's been – very nice to me. I'm sorry."

Heather wasn't sure if she was apologising to Stanton or to Mr Graeme. Realising she couldn't hold it in anymore, Heather let go of the hurt that had been building within her over the past few days and broke down. Putting her arm on the table, she collapsed her head into its crook and sobbed heavily while Stanton towered over her.

"Are you fucking stupid? Messing around with a teacher? They're all perverts."

She lifted her head slowly to look at him, her eyes full of tears, and she saw in him a face she hadn't seen before, one that had been reshaped by disappointment.

"I'm not, I haven't, it's not like that, it's really not."

Heather put her head back down and cried, the emotions crashing over her like storm waves. The trauma of the week had finally caught up with her and there was nowhere left for her to go. Crying heavily, she remembered Stratford and the walk by the river and then the talk on the bench. She had told Mr Graeme about the locked bedroom door, or at least she had tried to. She recalled the touch of his hand as he pushed her hair behind her ear and the empathy that shone like a beacon in her dark world. Above all, she remembered feeling special, the belief that she was the one he had chosen.

But then she also remembered the furtive glances whenever they talked, the silent stares from across the classroom which were always followed by a smile. She remembered when Mr Graeme ignored her for weeks, making her feel as though she had done something wrong. She had even written him a note, although she never gave it to him. Then, the next day, he surprised her with a poetry book, and it made her feel important again. Finally, she remembered the secrecy. It was all a secret, everything. No one could ever know.

"Here."

Heather looked up, startled by the voice.

It was Stanton, she had assumed he had gone. She wouldn't have blamed him if he had.

Her eyes were red from crying, her cheeks wet from the tears, her fringe a mess from lying on her arm. Stanton was holding a serviette that he had gone inside to get and now he was handing it to her. Sniffing, she gave a weak smile and took it from him and used it to clean her face.

"I'm going," he said.

The words were received as brutally as they were delivered.

"Really? Do you have to?"

"Yeah."

He turned and headed off towards the promenade.

"Will I see you again?" she asked weakly, her voice barely carrying beyond the edge of the table.

Either Stanton didn't hear her or he chose not to as Heather watched him go, imploring him with her eyes to turn around and come back. But she soon lost him in the crowds.

FIFTEEN

STANTON HELPED HIMSELF TO A BEER FROM A CARRIER BAG ON THE floor. It was a sign that the others could now drink and some took a can for themselves.

"Where you been, Stanz?" asked Jez.

Stanton drank thirstily. "What's it to you?"

"We were wondering, that's all. You know, after the shop and that, when we all split. Just that you never met up after. Some of us went to the arcades."

"Sit down and shut up," said Roper, pushing Jez back and forcing him to sit on the wall. He'd been stuck with them for most of the day and no one was more pleased to see Stanton than him.

When Stanton arrived in the precinct, he could see them sitting around smoking. He hadn't wanted to come after what had happened on the jetty. He had thought about going straight home. But he didn't want to be there any more than he wanted to be here.

"Fag?"

Stanton took one from Sally, who sat on his knee and lit it

for him, draping her arm around his neck and kissing his cheek, pleased he had arrived on his own.

"How funny was it watching Jez running around with that ice cream sign," she laughed.

"Yeah, you looked a right spaz," said Bin Bag.

Stanton didn't laugh. The image of Jez only served to remind him he was no closer to getting hold of any money. All in all, it had been a wasted day. Standing up, causing Sally to fall onto the bench, he nodded his head at Roper, who followed him away from the others.

Sally shouted after him. "Don't mind me, sorry to have got in your way."

Standing with their backs to the others, Stanton and Roper moved their heads in close.

"Heard anything?"

"Nothing. You?"

Stanton breathed his cigarette smoke greedily in, glancing over at a group of young kids who were kicking a football against a wall. In the enclosed space of the precinct the sound echoed relentlessly, and the continual thudding of the ball on concrete was starting to annoy him.

"Oi, keep it quiet you little shits."

He looked back at Roper and shook his head.

"The others thought you might have got nicked. There were loads of old bill sniffing around town this afternoon."

Stanton rubbed the bridge of his nose and closed his eyes for a moment, his head pounding from the humid air. The pressure had been building all week and it seemed as though the walls of the precinct were closing in. Everything was going wrong all at the same time.

Again, he snapped at the kids behind him. "Oi! Stop kicking that fucking ball or I'll come over and kick the shit out of you."

Sheepishly they did as they were told, scared by the

intimidating presence of the gang and the authority in the voice that had shouted at them.

Stanton turned back to Roper. "Doesn't matter where I was," he said curtly. "Let's assume hearing nothing from Mickey means he's not looking for us and that's the good news we need right now. If you see Jackson again, tell him I want a word with him."

"It was always a long shot, Stanz, but at least we tried."

They carried on smoking while behind them the kids had gone back to kicking the football again, the ball bouncing off the walls, the thuds spearing like a bullet into Stanton's brain.

"Let's just try and keep our heads down for a couple of days. I'll go see Mickey at the weekend and give him some money. Hopefully that'll keep him quiet."

"What money?"

"I'll think of something."

The football smacked loudly off the brickwork, the kids chasing it around, yelling and laughing as they ran. Stanton looked over, the anger building up inside him, his temples swelling, his teeth grinding in his mouth.

"What about tonight?" Roper asked. "We could try another shop?"

Stanton's eyes fell on Sally, who was talking animatedly to Kat. Stanton was tired, and not just physically. He was tired of having to keep one step ahead of his past. He was tired of those he was looking at right now and he was tired at the thought of having to live in this town a minute longer. The football rebounded off the wall, bringing him back to his senses.

"I'll hang out down in Sparrow Park for a bit," he said.

Roper smirked; the implication clear.

"Dirty dog. Fair enough, I'll see if those idiots want to finish those cans off down on the beach."

They were about to go back to the benches when the

football bounced loudly off a bin, and flew narrowly past Stanton's head, missing him by inches. It was enough to finally break his patience.

Stanton marched angrily toward the kids, his heavy boots making short time of the space between them, his face contorted with rage.

"I fucking told you and you didn't listen."

"We're sorry—"

"—Fuck off." Stanton pushed one of the kids aside and picked up the football, putting it under his arm, and walked over to some nearby railings, the kids standing frozen to the spot. Without hesitating, Stanton lifted the football above his head and brought it down hard on one of the sharp metal spikes. The ball punctured, the air hissing sharply as it escaped.

Stanton walked triumphantly back past the kids standing open-mouthed and joined the others over by the benches.

"Making friends as usual I see, Stanz," said Sally.

He looked at Roper, who took the hint.

"Come on, let's go. Not much else happening tonight so we may as well get drunk." Roper picked up the carrier bag.

Stanton suddenly felt compelled to offer the gang something. After all, they'd done what he'd asked of them, even if they hadn't done it very well.

"Let's all meet under the pier tomorrow evening, half six, we can have a laugh and a proper drink."

Roper put his thumb up and he and the others walked away.

Stanton and Sally were now alone and nothing needed to be said. Stubbing her cigarette out on the bench, she hurried after Stanton who had already started to walk away. When she caught up with him, she put her arm firmly around his waist and leaned her head in.

Stanton casually dropped his arm around her shoulder,

smiling as they walked past the deflated corpse of the football impaled on the railings.

~

It was late when Stanton put his key in the lock. He closed the door as quietly as he could behind him and stood outside Margaret's room, listening carefully for any signs she was awake.

He had stayed with Sally in the park, lying on their backs, smoking and looking at the stars above. Not because he'd wanted to, it was no romantic gesture on his part. The truth of the matter was, he had needed to make sure Margaret had drunk enough so that she would be unconscious by the time he got home.

Through Margaret's door, he listened intently at the familiar deep snoring of a woman so riddled with gin that a brass band could not wake her. Stanton gently pushed the door open and went cautiously in.

The curtains were drawn and the room was dimly lit, Margaret having fallen asleep with a small table lamp still on. He didn't want to stay in the room any longer than he needed to, so Stanton moved quickly round to the side of Margaret's bed. He pulled open a drawer of the side table and, keeping one eye on his sleeping mum, he pushed his hand to the back and felt for something.

Margaret stirred briefly in her sleep and Stanton froze, waiting a few seconds until she settled back down again. In his hands he was holding an old tin, which he opened and looked inside to see it was crammed with bundles of notes. There must have been hundreds of pounds, money that Margaret had put there from her pension or from when she had won a bet. Stanton carefully counted out one hundred pounds. It might just be enough to buy some time while he and Roper worked out how to get the rest. Pushing the money into his jeans, he put the tin back and shut the drawer.

Margaret stirred again, mumbling drunken words in her sleep, only one of which Stanton recognised.

"Bill."

Even now, after all these years, after all that pain, he was still haunting her dreams. Poor cow, Stanton thought to himself as he bent down to pick up the broom handle that had fallen over. He put it back against the wall so that she would be able to reach it easily when the time came for her to summon him in the morning. Looking down at the physical wreck he called his family, Stanton thought briefly about putting the money back. But there was no time for sentimentality. Blood was thicker than water, but money was thicker than anything.

Tip toeing quietly back out of Margaret's room, he went into kitchen and made himself a cup of tea before taking it up to his room.

Lying on his bed, Stanton smoked his last cigarette of the day. He had put the money in his bedside drawer for now and he would take it to Mickey on Saturday. It was the best he could do and he hoped the loyalty he had built up with him over the years would be enough to give him some breathing space.

Bare-chested on top of the sheets, he stared at the ceiling, one arm crooked behind his head. His eyes tracked an errant cobweb dangling in the corner of the room, watching as it moved in the breeze. As he drank his tea, blowing smoke that rose above his head toward the cobweb, he realised it wasn't just Mickey he didn't know what to do about. It was also the girl he had been meeting at the end of the jetty.

He dropped his half-finished cigarette into his mug, turned off the light and lay back on the pillow, the moonlight shining through the window turning his already pale skin the colour of snow.

FRIDAY

SIXTEEN

NOT WANTING TO FACE THE WORLD, HEATHER LAY LIKE A CORPSE on a mortuary slab, unable to move, as though her duvet were made of lead and her body of feathers.

Last night Heather had sobbed herself to sleep, soaking her pillow with tears. All she could think about was the boy on the jetty, his confident eyes etched in her mind, and how he had walked away and left her.

Somehow finding the energy, she dragged herself up and got dressed, going downstairs to find her parents sitting in abject silence at the table.

"Hi," said Heather softly.

Her dad looked up from his newspaper. "Morning, love. Last day of school today, you must be pleased?"

Heather's mum stood sharply from the table. "You're going to be late, dawdling like this. You won't have time for anything to eat."

"It's okay. I'm not hungry."

"Don't be silly, Heather. You can't go to school on an empty stomach. I'll put some toast on."

"Mum, it's fine. I'll get something from the shop."

"You can't skip having a healthy breakfast. Girls your age put weight on easily if they don't eat properly. You need to start taking an interest in yourself, have some pride in your appearance. I was fighting the boys off at your age."

"Your mum went to a blind school, Heather."

Her dad lifted the paper quickly to his face. Heather had to bite her lip to stop from laughing.

"Oh shut up, Colin. If anyone's blind around here, it's me."

Lowering the newspaper, her dad sighed. "Just leave her alone, Jackie, she's old enough to decide if she wants some toast or not."

"She needs to eat properly, and breakfast sets you up for the day." Heather's mum put some bread in the toaster.

"It's her last day of school, for God's sake. She's not going to starve to death."

"Don't start taking sides, Colin."

"I'm just saying she's old enough to know whether she wants a slice of bloody toast or not."

Her mum slammed a drawer shut

Rolling his eyes, her dad folded the newspaper. "Here we go again."

"Here we go again, Colin? What do you mean by that?"

Heather tried to speak. "Mum, dad, I—"

It was pointless, the incremental volume of her parents' arguing pushed her back against the wall.

"Just cut her some slack and calm down. Why's everything a fight with you, Jackie?"

"Because you both bring me to this point. It's always the same with you."

"What's that supposed to mean?"

"I'll tell you exactly what that means, shall I Colin?"

"Please do, I'd love to hear all about your troubles because no one else has any, according to you."

He started to get out of his chair.

"Is that so? Any more sarcastic comments you'd like to add before I start doing the washing up, again?"

Heather picked up her bag and quietly left, hearing them still arguing as she closed the front door, neither of them even noticing she had gone.

She walked slowly to the bus stop knowing full well, with only six hours of school left before the summer break, everyone was going to be understandably feral. When it arrived and she stepped on, getting shoved as she did by excited kids, she went straight upstairs where it was quieter and took her usual seat near the front. She took out the book Mr Graeme had given her, looking at the tear-smudged phone number on the inside and the kiss sitting next to it. She read the cover and the author's biography and sniffed the paper for that familiar smell. After yesterday, she wasn't sure she should even open it but she didn't want to sit alone with her thoughts either. Turning to where she had left off, she started to read.

Barely any time later, Heather was already in love with the book and its characters. Mr Graeme was right; this author was one of the best and Heather already knew she was going to devour all of his books once she had finished this one. She was so absorbed in the story that Heather hadn't realised the bus was now parked outside the school, and she was the only person still sat there. Quickly closing the book, she hurried downstairs. Instead of going through the school's main entrance, Heather turned right and walked a little further up the road and entered the grounds via a small side gate. She wanted to be on her own. In fact, she was starting to feel like she wanted to be on her own forever.

Heather moped around school for the rest of the day, tortured by the joviality and excitement that was building amongst her fellow pupils. For a while it seemed that the academic day would never end. The lessons were laborious and pointless, even the teachers themselves were overly friendly as they went through the motions for a few more hours.

Finally, the misery came to an end, the bell ringing for the last time until September, and to the sound of cheering and laughter everyone poured out through the school doors into sunshine and freedom.

"Have you got a felt tip pen?" asked a girl from Heather's class as she walked toward the school gates.

Heather stopped to look in her bag. "Yes I think so, here you go." She handed it over with a smile.

The girl took it and turned to her friend. "Vicky, sign my shirt and I'll sign yours."

Heather stood awkwardly as the two girls laughed and giggled, drawing on each other's pristine white shirts. But they didn't ask her to join in.

"Thanks, see you in September," said the girl, giving back the pen and running off to catch up with another group.

"Maybe," replied Heather quietly to herself. She put the pen back in her bag and slowly walked towards the waiting school bus, her head down, barged and knocked by delirious kids running around.

The crowds of excited pupils thinned away. She made sure to keep her eyes down and avoid any more interactions. As she neared the school gates, she instinctively looked up and what she saw stopped her in her tracks. Leaning confidently against the school railings as though he owned the place, was Stanton.

SEVENTEEN

"What are you doing here?" Heather hissed as she made her way over to him.

"Miss me?"

Heather was secretly pleased to see him, especially after how yesterday had ended. But an aggressive looking skinhead couldn't just turn up at the school gates and it go unnoticed. There was already a small crowd of kids who had stopped messing around and were looking over.

"I've come to save you," Stanton grinned.

"Save me? Save me from what?"

"That teacher."

"What? Why would—"

"—Is that him?"

Stanton was looking over towards the staff car park at a man getting in his car.

Heather looked over.

"No! He's about ninety. For goodness' sake James, you can't turn up here threatening teachers."

"I can. What about him?"

Heather didn't even bother to turn around.

"No, not him either. What do you mean, save me? What did you plan on doing, exactly?"

Stanton pulled his hand out from one of his jacket pockets to reveal he was holding a flick knife. He clicked the release and a shiny blade sprung out.

"I'm going to cut his bollocks off."

More pupils were now congregating close by. Heather scanned over her shoulder to see a teacher closing the boot of his car and looking over. If she didn't get Stanton away from here, it wouldn't be long before someone would come interfering.

"You are doing no such thing," she said, pushing his hand back into his jacket. In the same motion, she linked her arm in his and pulled him away from the school gate and headed toward the town centre.

"You were the last person I was expecting to see today," she said as they crossed the road, heading toward the bus station and away from prying eyes.

"Nice surprise?"

"Seriously James, you can't just turn up to a school with a knife."

"I wasn't going to do anything, I was only going to scare him."

"I bet you would have!"

The further they moved away from the school, the more they relaxed and started to laugh at the absurdity of the situation. A bus was pulling up just ahead of them and Stanton ran ahead and jumped on.

"Come on then, I've got a plan."

Heather ran to catch up. "Fine, so long as it doesn't involve any knives!"

"May as well give you two the keys to this place," said the lady from the café as she collected their empty mugs. "Having another? You've time before we close."

Stanton gave a barely perceptible shake of his head.

"No thank you," said Heather.

"We'll be dead if we drink any more of their tea," said Stanton when she'd gone.

"I know," laughed Heather. "It really is awful."

The book that Heather had been given remained on the table between them.

"Got any plans?" he asked.

Heather shook her head. "Not tonight or any other night."

Stanton narrowed his eyes on Heather's face.

"Look," he said, after a while. "Seems like you've had a shit few days. I don't think I should leave you on your own, I mean the railings are only over there. Problem is, I need to go. But I don't want to leave you here. Do you fancy a laugh? A bit of fun?"

"What do you have in mind?"

"Like I said, fun."

"Is it even possible to have fun in this town?"

"It is if you're with me."

"Okay, why not?" she replied quickly and before she could change her mind. "I need to call home, though. I better let them know where I am, I'll think of an excuse. I've got away with it a few times, I might not be so lucky this time."

"Fair enough," he said, standing up. "There's a phone box down at the end of the jetty. But you're going to make two calls."

Stanton put the book in his jacket pocket.

"Two?" Heather questioned.

"Two. We're ringing this fucker," said Stanton, tapping the book. "Well, you are. Don't worry, I'll tell you what to say."

"I can't—"

"—You can and you will, come on."

His smile and confidence pulled Heather slowly up out of the plastic chair like a magnet and they headed back down the jetty, walking side by side.

EIGHTEEN

THE PHONE BOXES WERE ON THE PROMENADE CONCOURSE JUST BY the entrance to the jetty.

"Right, ring home first and then we'll do the other call."

"No, please, let me just ring home—"

Stanton opened the door and pushed Heather gently inside before going to sit on the wall opposite. "—I'll wait here," he shouted over.

He kept an eye on her as Heather leaned into the phone with her back to him, her ear to the handset. She looked to be talking, someone must have picked up.

Stanton felt a momentary pang of jealousy – he had never rung home; he didn't even know his home number. There was an olive-green phone next to Margaret's bed, but she was the only one that used it and only then to ring scattered family members, pick up local gossip or place the odd bet. He had never needed to ring home. He had never, ever, felt the need to tell Margaret, or anyone else for that matter, where he was, how he was, what he was doing, where he was going or what time he'd be back. Usually, that sense of freedom would appeal to Stanton, but sitting on the baking concrete of a small wall in a small seaside town, thinking these small thoughts, it bothered him.

There was something damaged about the girl he was looking at, something that appealed to him, not in a masochistic way, but in a way he had never felt before. Like he wanted to help her, to fix her. Perhaps, in doing so, he might start to forgive himself for the mistakes he had made in life.

The phone box door swung open and a hot and bothered Heather stepped back out.

"All done?" he asked, walking over to her.

She nodded.

Stanton pulled the book back out of his pocket.

"Good, now this arsehole."

"No, please," she pleaded, reaching out and grasping the hand Stanton was holding the book with. He frowned.

"Look, can't you see what he's doing here?"

Heather dropped her hand.

"If it's not you now, it'll be someone else tomorrow. These people are sick and they need to be lined up and shot. You can't see it, you've been pulled in. Let me guess, he said you were special? Said no one else was like you? You were different?"

Her silence was enough for Stanton to know he was right.

"That lot are all the same. Come on, I'm going to prove to you he's another conman, another fucking fraud walking around. Why did he put his number in the book for you? What was the reason?"

Heather's head was whirring with the events of the past few days, and she was struggling to think straight.

"He said he wasn't doing anything over the holidays, and if I wanted to meet up, we could."

"And?"

"And?"

"And what else, meet up to do what?"

"Maybe read some books."

"Bullshit."

Then Heather remembered.

"Maybe to read his book, he said he had written one and wanted me to help him with it."

"Right, that's it, that's how we'll hook the egotistical prick."

Stanton pulled open the door to the phone box and pushed Heather back in. It was too small and too warm for the both of them to stand comfortably, so he kept the door ajar, one leg in, one leg out.

"Right. You need to be confident. A rat can smell a rat. I need you to ring him and get him to meet you tomorrow."

"Meet him?" Heather said, shocked.

"Don't worry. I'll be with you. I'm just going to talk to him."

Heather was worried. "I'll get into trouble. You can't just meet a teacher outside of school."

"Well that didn't stop him suggesting it, did it?"

The cold logic was impossible to argue against.

"But where shall I meet him?"

"I dunno, anywhere you can think of that won't have many people around."

Heather quickly ran through some locations and then nodded her head.

"Ok, I know somewhere. Why should I say I want to meet him, though?"

"Bloody hell, may as well just ring him myself. Play to his ego and his stupid book, tell him you want to read it. Arrogant pricks like him won't be able to help themselves. He'll be here before you've even put the phone down."

Stanton reached into the pocket of his tight jeans, pulled some coins out and fed them into the phone. He opened the book at the inside cover and started to punch in the phone number, flexing his jaw muscles and shaking his head as he did.

"Are we sure we—" Heather started to speak but Stanton had already thrust the phone to her ear and she could hear it ringing. He moved his head next to Heather's, so close she could smell the soap on his face.

The phone continued to ring.

Click.

A man's voice answered.

"Hello?"

Heather's eyes opened wide. It was easier to call home than it was to call a teacher.

The voice spoke again. "Hello?"

In panic, Heather put the phone down, the unused money clattering into the tray below.

"What did you do that for?" Stanton asked.

"Sorry, I just…I got scared."

"Well, don't be. I'm here. All the time you're with me, you're safe."

Scooping out the coins, Stanton fed them back into the phone and punched in the numbers before once again handing the already ringing phone to Heather.

Click.

"Hello?"

Heather fell mute, Stanton urging her with his face to say something.

"Who's this?" the man's voice asked.

Heather finally found some courage.

"Mr Graeme?"

"Speaking," the voice replied defensively.

"Simon, it's Heather. From school."

The line went quiet. Stanton and Heather watched as the timer ticked away their money, the man on the other end of the line remaining agonisingly silent. Finally, he said something.

"Heather?"

She looked up at Stanton, who encouraged her to carry on.

"Yes, I called your number from the book."

The teacher relaxed his voice. "Well, this is a surprise, although a nice one, might I add. Was there something you wanted, Heather?"

She looked up at Stanton, who nodded his encouragement.

"Yes, I was...I was wondering if we could meet as you suggested. I've nearly finished the book you gave me."

Again, the line went quiet. Stanton could sense the teacher was building the pressure on Heather, forcing her to dictate the direction of the conversation. He looked at her and mouthed the word "book". Heather gave a small nod of her head.

"Also, I'd like to hear about the book you've written."

The stop-start nature of the call was eating into the money they had, and Stanton didn't have much change left.

"When were you thinking of meeting, Heather?" asked Mr Graeme.

"How about tomorrow?"

"Tomorrow? That's short notice."

Heather's confidence surged. "Okay, if it's a problem, it can wait until next term."

Instantly, there was now some urgency from the other end of the line.

"No, no, don't worry, it's fine. I've something booked in for tomorrow, but nothing I can't move. In fact, you'd be doing me a favour."

Heather, feeling pleased with herself, smiled at Stanton who mouthed the word "wanker", causing Heather to almost give the game away.

The teacher's tone changed.

"Is everything okay, Heather? Is someone with you?"

Heather thought quickly.

"No, it's just some skinheads messing around outside the phone box."

There was another pause at the end of the line while Heather bit her lip, waiting to see if he'd taken the bait.

"What time tomorrow, Heather?" he asked.

Heather looked at Stanton, who held up his fingers.

"10 o'clock?" she replied.

"It's early, but it should work. Where do you want to meet?"

"We could meet at the clock tower and walk along the promenade. There are some benches up towards the end. It's always quieter up there."

There came a last lingering silence in which doubts were assuaged, and guilt filed away.

"Sounds good, Heather. I'll see you tomorrow. Oh Heather, before you go?"

"Yes?"

"Remember the rules. Always best to keep these things between us for now. Bye, Heather."

The line went dead, and Heather replaced the handset. No money was returned, they had only just got away with it. Stanton could see Heather's hands were trembling and the blood had drained from her face.

"Well done," he said. "You did great."

"Now what?" Heather asked.

"We'll worry about that tomorrow; silly sod believed every word. Right, come on, let's go to the pier."

"The pier? But what if those people are there again?

"We're not going on the pier; we're going under it."

They stepped out of the airless phone box and fell in with the gathering crowds shuffling their way along the promenade.

NINETEEN

Stanton's gang were already gathered under the shade of the pier. Nearby, a few families rock-pooled but most had already taken the decision to move away. For a town used to summer fighting and bank-holiday brawls, it was sometimes more trouble than it was worth to stand your ground.

A stone landed and splashed in a small pool near where Jez was standing.

"Watch out, dickhead!" he shouted at Bin Bag, who had thrown it.

Bin Bag ignored him and picked up another rock. This time he aimed up at the rafters of the pier at the resting seagulls, launching the stone high into the meshwork of iron. It clanked and clinked off the metal, but missed the intended target.

"Useless," said Jez.

"You have a go, then."

"All right, I will. Can't do any worse than you."

Jez looked around for a suitable-sized stone to throw at the seagulls. He found one and scanned the pier above his head. Gauging the distance and the trajectory, Jez steadied himself on the uneven surface and leaned back to give himself as much leverage as he could. Arching his arm, he flung the stone forward.

The rock flew out of his hand and spiralled miserably away, hitting one of the iron pillars rooted into the seabed before bouncing off some larger rocks and almost hitting a nearby child scavenging through rock pools.

"Oi! Watch what you're doing!" shouted the kid's father.

Bin Bag started laughing. "Nice one, Stevie Wonder," he shouted across at Jez.

"Dickheads," Roper said to himself as he went and sat with the girls.

They all wanted a drink but knew better than to start until the whole gang were together.

"There he is!" Jez shouted.

Bin Bag stopped throwing stones and went over and stood with Jez. The girls stood up to look in the direction Jez was pointing. Only Roper remained where he was, but he looked across and he could see Stanton making his way toward them.

"He's got that bird with him again," said Bin Bag.

"You're joking!" said Sally, putting her hand up to shield her eyes against the sun. They watched in silence as Stanton and the girl made their way toward them and the vaulted, cavernous space beneath the pier.

Sally couldn't help herself as they joined the rest of the gang. "Didn't know it was bring a kid day, Stanz?"

Heather stood nervously, like a child on her first day at school. Stanton hadn't mentioned anything about the others being there, and he certainly hadn't mentioned drinking. She looked down at her school shoes to see them sinking slowly into watery sand. She moved and stood awkwardly on some bigger stones.

Roper handed his friend a beer. Stanton opened the can and took a long, satisfying drink, downing half without stopping. When he was done, he wiped his hand across his face.

Jez and Bin Bag went back to throwing stones at seagulls.

Out of the corner of her eye, Heather could see that Sally was paying her a lot of attention. She was careful not to look directly at her. With a half-shaven head, and a jacket adorned with angry-looking badges, she looked trouble.

"Come on, Kat, let's have a drink." Sally linked arms with her friend and they walked off toward the sea wall.

As the others moved away, Roper grinned and handed Heather a can. A flash of terror flickered in her eyes but she stepped forward and took it, feeling the cold droplets of condensation sliding down the side.

"Thank you," she said quietly.

Heather wondered whether this was a test. Taking the can had been the easy bit, but now she had to drink it. She tugged the ring pull. Foam spewed from the hole and ran down her hand.

Roper and Stanton laughed as Heather bent down and lapped at the foam to prevent any more escaping. The lager tasted cheap and bitter, but she was thirsty and eager to please so gulped a few more greedy mouthfuls before stopping and wiping her mouth. But she had drunk too quickly, and before she could suppress it, the gas bounced back from her stomach and she belched loudly.

"Nice one," Roper said, laughing. "That's nothing though, watch this." He took a long drink from his can and then steadied himself as he let go of a deep rumbling belch that seemed to last forever.

"Class act, you two," said Stanton, swigging from his can. "Come on. Let's sit in the shade." He turned and walked off to where the girls were now sitting.

Heather took another drink before looking over at the sea wall, Roper following Heather's gaze and reading her mind.

"Don't worry about them. They're just not used to having other girls about."

"I don't think Sally likes me."

"Don't worry, she doesn't like me either, but she's alright, once you get to know her."

Heather tilted her can and drank quickly, pretending she liked the taste.

"Come on, you can sit next me."

Heather carefully followed in Roper's footsteps as they crossed the slippery stones and went to sit with the others.

The girls were sat to the left of Stanton, who was leaning back on the cool wall with his eyes closed and his legs stretched out in front of him. Roper went and sat next to him and Heather did the same.

"Any plans for tonight, Stanz?" Roper asked.

Stanton replied without opening his eyes. "Nope."

Heather continued to sip guiltily from her can, missing the intimacy of when it was just Stanton and her. She didn't want to be here with the others. She wanted it to go back to being just the two of them.

Stanton drained his can and threw it out in front of him before picking up some stones and beginning to throw them at the target. Roper joined in. A couple of stones landed close by but missed and only served to push the tin slightly further away.

"Bastard!"

"Come on Heather, have a go," Roper suggested.

Heather put down her can. Picking up a pebble, she aimed carefully, feeling Sally's eyes on her as she threw the stone, which delivered a satisfying, tinny thud when it hit the target first time.

"Get in!" shouted Roper. "First throw, as well."

"Beginner's luck," said Sally, picking up a stone and throwing it toward the tin, only for it to miss and bounce away and spin off into a rock pool.

"You're worse than Jez," Stanton mocked. "Chuck us another beer."

Roper reached into the bag and pulled out another can and also offered one to Heather, which she took.

"Here, give me your tie," Stanton said to Heather.

"My tie?" she said, loosening it and handing it to him. "Why do you need it? Are you going back to school?" She was pleased to hear Roper laughing next to her.

"They wouldn't have him back!"

Stanton took the tie and bent forward so that Heather could smell the intoxicating mixture of beer and smoke on his breath. He put the tie around her head before knotting it firmly so it would stay in place.

He stepped back. "There you go, you're now Rambo."

"Yes, Stanz! That's brilliant. Cheers to Rambo!" Roper raised his can.

Sally whispered to Kat, "Ten minutes here, and she already has a nickname."

"Fag?" Stanton said, offering one to Heather.

Heather assumed it was another test. She had never held a cigarette before, let alone tried to smoke one. Putting the cigarette between her lips, she allowed Roper to light it for her and she inhaled deeply but the fast-moving smoke caught her by surprise as it hurtled into her lungs, causing her to cough violently as her body tried to reject it.

"Not as easy as it looks?" Sally said sarcastically.

Heather picked up her drink and gulped from the can, trying to wash away the taste of burning smoke in her mouth and throat, the bitterness of the drink just about preferable to the acrid taste of nicotine.

They all relaxed again in the shade as the afternoon heat beat down, smoking and drinking and content to watch the world go by. The peace and quiet was broken when they heard a loud, excited shout.

"Fuck me! I got one. I got one! Did you see that?"

They looked over to see what the commotion was all about. It was Jez. He was scrambling over the rock pools under the pier.

"What's he done now?" Stanton shouted over at Bin Bag.

"He got one!" he shouted back, pointing excitedly. "He fucking knocked one clean out!"

"I think he's managed to hit a seagull," Roper said, standing and heading off to see for himself. Stanton, as curious as anyone, followed him.

"Oh my god!" Jez shouted, bending down. "Look at it!"

"Come on Kat, let's go and look. Besides, it smells of shit around here." Sally swung her bag over her shoulder, intentionally catching Heather with it, and they too got up and walked over to see what was happening.

Left to sit alone, Heather was unsure what to do. Taking a final drink from the can she stood up, steadying herself slightly. She decided to follow the others but she couldn't keep up, her school shoes slipped against rocks covered in seaweed. She was also starting to feel the rapidly encroaching effects of strong lager on a hot day and an empty stomach, and stumbled occasionally as she went. Again and again she slipped, one time quite badly, and she had to put her hands out to stop herself from falling headfirst into some water. Standing back up, she was wiping the sand and mud from her hands when a shadow fell across her. Standing in front of her, just a few yards away, was Sally. She'd dropped back from the others and made a point of waiting for Heather.

"Need to be careful. You could have broken something," she said coldly.

Heather gave her a wide berth and carried on walking slowly towards the others.

"You're wasting your time."

Heather stopped. "Sorry?"

125

"Him." Sally nodded her head ambiguously, although they both knew who she meant. "He'll let you down. It's what he does with everyone, reels us in, then throws us away. How come he's never mentioned you before? I mean, if you're so pally and all, how come we've never heard of you until now? Basically, what I'm saying is, who the fuck are you?"

Heather remained rooted to the spot, so far out of her depth she felt like she was drowning on dry land. The menace with which Sally spoke felt threatening, so she forced herself to slowly move past her, making sure there was enough space between them, concentrating on where she was walking, looking up occasionally to see how close the others were, how near Stanton was.

"Where the fuck are you going? I'm talking to you."

Heather stopped. "I'm just a friend."

"Bullshit."

"No, honestly, just a friend."

"A friend from where?"

"Well, we just sort of—"

Roper looked over and shouted, "Hurry up, you two. You need to come and look at this!"

Sally ignored him. "—I don't know who you are or what's going on here, but don't think you can just walk in here and think you're staying."

Heather moved away and quickened her pace, taking the chance that falling was safer than staying.

No one noticed Heather arrive quietly nor Sally soon after, they were all too absorbed with the seagull Jez stood proudly over like a game hunter. The unfortunate bird was lying at an awkward angle, its wing bent back, its eyes darting back and forth, ca-cawing as it tried in vain to move.

"Boom! One hit!" Jez boasted.

"If you ignore the other fifty attempts," said Bin Bag dismissively.

"You're only jealous you never did it."

"Innit big?" said Kat, bending down to peer closely at the bird.

"What you going to do with it?" asked Roper. "You've knocked the poor bastard down here, so what's the plan?"

Jez hadn't really thought about that. "Can you eat them?"

Roper laughed. "What are you going to do, take it home, stick it in your mum's freezer, and wait for Christmas dinner to come round?"

"Its wing's broken," said Stanton.

"So?" Jez replied.

"So it's fucked. It's not going anywhere."

Jez started to feel a bit guilty. "Can't we fix it?"

"Yeah, stick it in a plaster cast and when it dries, we can all come round your house and sign it," Bin Bag joked. "Stanz is right. It's fucked."

They looked down at the poor bird, spread out across the rock pool, its head twisting in desperation.

Jez's crowning moment was disappearing around the headland faster than the tide. He sulked and put his hands in his pockets.

"Two things will happen," Roper suggested. "The crabs will come out later tonight and start to eat it alive. If they don't manage to do that, the tide'll come in tomorrow and drown it."

"Aww, poor thing," crooned Kat.

"Well, I don't know then," said Jez as he poked the bird with his foot, the bird turning its neck to peck defensively at the boot.

"I do," Stanton said, turning away.

The gang and Heather stood silent, all of them unable to take their eyes off the poor seagull, so transfixed by the scene they didn't notice Stanton return holding a big rock.

"What are you going to do with that?" Kat asked, startled.

"This."

Stanton raised the rock high above his head with both hands, steadying himself with one foot on either side of the unfortunate bird. The others looked on open-mouthed, too dumbstruck to intervene. Once he was fully stretched and his arms started to burn from the weight of the stone, Stanton allowed it to start falling, aiming it directly at the seagull's head.

"Stanz!" Kat screamed, but it was already too late. The heavy rock landed with a bone-crunching thud, smashing directly onto the bird's head before rolling away with its own momentum to leave behind nothing but blood, feathers and brains.

"Oh fuck," Bin Bag said, laughing and turning away. "That's gross."

"I'm going to be sick," Kat said, hiding her face behind Sally.

Stanton showed no emotion as he looked down at what was left of the bird.

Heather wasn't too sure what she had just witnessed, but she couldn't help but look at the bloody pulp that was now spread across the rocks at her feet. As she stared, she started to feel as though her legs belonged elsewhere, like they were slipping away from her on the seaweed.

"Did you have to do that?" Kat asked tearfully.

Stanton looked at her. "If there's one thing this town isn't short of, it's fucking seagulls. Anyway, it wouldn't have lasted the night. I did it a favour."

Heather's chest felt tight, her breathing shallow, as she looked at the seagull's mangled body. Its blood was filtering into the rockpool, swirling around as it went, exactly how Heather's mind was feeling.

"I'd do the same to any one of you," Stanton said. "If you were suffering, I'd cave your brains in too. In fact, get me another rock, I'll finish Jez off now and do us all a favour." He laughed, as did Roper and Bin Bag.

"Animals, all of you!" Kat shouted, storming off.

Jez bent down to peer at the mess.

"I don't feel well," said Heather. The combination of heat, drink, smoke and tiredness mixing with the bloody gore of the seagull was making her nauseous and dizzy.

"Shame," Sally said.

Heather felt self-conscious that everyone was now staring at her and it was making her feel even worse.

Stanton went over to her. "Are you okay?"

Heather shook her head. "I think I need to go."

"Okay. Come on, I'll walk you to the bus stop. I need to go anyway. We'll call it a night."

"What?" Sally said sharply. "It's Friday, we can still go the pier like we normally do."

"You go if you want," Roper said, intervening. "I'm going to sit back down over there and finish these beers. You and the rest can join me, or you can fuck off. I'm easy either way." He headed back towards the sea wall.

"Sod you, then." Sally ran to catch up with Kat.

Jez shrugged and followed Bin Bag, who had already caught up with Roper.

"Sorry I've ruined your night," Heather apologised.

"Not really, you've done me a favour. Come on then, Rambo, you look like you've seen a ghost. Let's get you home."

TWENTY

They waited patiently at the bus stop. Heather could have walked home, it wasn't that far, but it was far enough and Stanton insisted she take the bus.

"Thank you," she said softly.

"For what?"

"For today and the last few days. For looking after me. For the bus fare."

"Yeah well, don't tell anyone. I've a reputation to keep. Here comes your bus."

He stood up and held his hand out.

"Are we still meeting tomorrow?" Heather asked.

Stanton frowned. "'Course we are. Keep the day free if you can. Once we sort that teacher out tomorrow morning, we can —," he hesitated. "—Do something. Meet me at the clock tower at half-nine?"

He wasn't sure why he was saying what he was saying. He'd managed to avoid Mickey for three days. He couldn't expect that luck to last much longer and he wasn't sure he had the time to hang around with girls he hardly knew. But he liked the idea of just messing around town, especially with someone different, someone he didn't really know and who, more importantly, didn't know him.

The bus slowed to a stop and the doors opened.

"I enjoyed today," said Heather.

"Yeah, was fun."

"Are you getting on or not?" shouted the bus driver.

"Hold on," Stanton said, before turning back to Heather. "I'll speak to that teacher tomorrow. We'll figure it out."

Heather looked down at her battered school shoes, covered in slime, sand and mud. "Okay."

"I'm closing the doors," said the driver.

"You're fucking not," and Stanton gave him a look that pushed the driver a little lower into his seat.

After the drama of the week, Heather didn't want to make another scene. "I better go."

She stepped onto the bus, bought a ticket and walked to the back, sitting in an empty window seat. Stanton had followed her from outside, so that he was standing looking in as she was sitting looking out. The doors closed, and the bus pulled away from the kerb. Heather smiled, half lifting her hand to wave goodbye. Stanton remained motionless and expressionless, concentrating on his own reflection in the darkened window as it moved away, no longer sure he recognised the person looking back at him.

Kenny was sitting side-saddle on a coin-operated ride at the entrance to the pier. His thinning black hair clung to his scalp like grease on an unwashed plate, his fingers nicotine orange from incessant, chain-smoked cigarettes. Around his neck hung a metallic garland, a chain of a thousand keys, each one locking and unlocking the myriad of coin-operated machines that ran the length of the pier. He was still dozing off yesterday's hangover. It had been a long day and the hot weather had brought a constant stream of people in through his doors.

"Kenny."

He had barely closed his eyes before he was opening them again. When he did, it was to see Stanton staring down at him.

Kenny sat up. "Ah, there he is, the dead man walking."

After Stanton had watched Heather's bus move off and disappear over the brow of a hill, he'd felt at a loss about what to do. He didn't want to go back and meet the others. Aside from Roper, he was growing tired of their whinging and inability to think for themselves, always relying on him to decide or come up with the ideas, something else that had crept up on him over the past few months and helped further shrink this town, making it feel even smaller and more claustrophobic. So when he had walked up the incline to the pier, Stanton somehow felt different. Something had changed, and he was worried it might be him.

Kenny hoisted himself off the amusement ride and offered Stanton a cigarette, which he took and lodged behind his ear for later.

"What did you mean just then?" Stanton asked.

"What?"

"When you said about the dead man walking."

Kenny looked cautiously around. "Come here," he said, moving off to the side.

Stanton followed him over to the railings.

"What you been up to, Stanz?" Kenny asked, as he kicked cigarette butts over the side and watched them disappear.

Stanton was confused. "What do you mean?"

Kenny seemed agitated, totally on edge. He was looking everywhere but directly at Stanton.

"A couple of hours ago, some people came around here."

"And?"

"They were looking for you."

"So what? I'm popular," Stanton half joked, but Kenny wasn't in the mood for laughing.

"I can tell you now for nothing, you weren't popular with these guys. They didn't come just the once, either. They came back again. Proper nasty-looking fuckers, and I've been around enough to know what a nasty fucker looks like. See this?" Kenny pointed to a lump on the side of his head that Stanton hadn't noticed. "Let's just say I didn't have that when I left the house this morning."

Stanton was struggling to make sense of what Kenny was saying. "They came back again?"

"Yep, second time they got rough."

"Weird. Why'd they come back?"

"They didn't have balloons or a card, so I'm assuming it's not your birthday. Look, Stanz, I like you. I'll have your back, you know that. But whoever they were, they're not fucking about. They'll be back here. They told me that before they gave me this." He pointed to his head again. "They made a right mess of one of my guys as well, I've had to send him home."

Stanton knew that Kenny and the other pier workers could handle themselves. For Kenny to be scared meant that whatever this was, it was serious.

"I've put some feelers out for you. Not heard anything back yet."

Stanton tried to catch up with everything Kenny was saying. "How many of them were there?"

"Six, maybe seven."

Stanton's face dropped. "That many?"

"Yup."

"What did they look like?"

"What did they look like? Trouble, that's what. There were a couple of punks with them to make up the numbers, but the others were proper nasty looking. Nah, this is something else, Stanz, something different. This whole thing didn't feel right.

I'm going with my gut on this. Whatever it is, it's fucked, and you need to stay low for a bit."

It wasn't in Stanton's character to run. He never had before, and he didn't plan on starting now. People were always looking for him around this town and quite often justifiably; it came with the territory.

"Was Mickey with them?"

"Mickey?"

"Yeah, was he there?"

"Didn't see him. But why would Mickey be there?"

Kenny was right, Mickey wouldn't do the dirty work. But if this was about the money, it had escalated far quicker than he'd hoped.

"Okay, cheers Kenny. Pool tables free?" Stanton nodded at the pier.

"Jesus Christ, Stanz. You haven't time for a game of pool. Get home, get off the street and keep your head down. I'll cover for you as best I can, but it only takes one gobshite in there to blab and we'll both be hanging off the end of the pier by our ankles."

Stanton exhaled heavily and leaned against the railings, folding his ankles and arms.

"Where've you been today, anyway? They've been looking for you in all the usual places from what I gather."

Stanton had no desire to explain, but he was thankful now that he had been with Heather at the café and then under the pier with the gang. It seemed those innocent decisions had kept him safe. For now at least.

"Where're the others?" Kenny prodded.

"I've just left some of them under the pier. They're having a drink."

"Roper there?"

Stanton nodded.

"Well, I'd keep him close. He's the only out of that lot you can rely on. I'll get one of the lads to pop down there to give them the heads up. They might be better clearing off home tonight as well. Look don't take this personally, but fuck off home, Stanz. When you get there, lock the door and let whatever this is sort itself out."

Stanton took a minute to consider his options, quickly reaching the conclusion that he didn't have any.

"Yeah, okay. Cheers, Kenny."

Without saying another word, a troubled Stanton turned and walked back down the shallow incline that joined the pier to the promenade.

"Go straight home," Kenny shouted after him. "Please."

Stanton carried on walking, his mind turning the word over and over in his head. In all the time he'd known him, Stanton had never once heard Kenny say the word *please*.

TWENTY-ONE

For the first time in longer than he cared to remember, Stanton took someone's advice and went home. It wasn't the usual end to his typical Friday, but this had been a far from typical week.

Nervously, he took a slightly different route home, his eyes alert as he walked, making sure to stay where it was busy. There was no denying it, Stanton was worried as he walked quickly, his body tense beneath his clothes, crossing roads that didn't need crossing and even doubling back once or twice. His shoulders started to ache with tension and doubt, his fists balled in his jacket pockets, ready to fight an unknown enemy. All the time, Stanton wracked his brain, his brow wrinkled like a furrowed field as he searched for answers to what was happening. Each time he did, he ended back up where he started. He owed money to people and now they wanted it back. Stanton cursed himself for creating another mess in his life; the continual cycle of failure seeming to stick to him like glue.

The conversation with Kenny had been unsettling enough, but that was nothing compared to what he saw when he finally turned into his road. Parked directly outside his house was a police car and two policemen were sat inside. The sight stopped Stanton in his tracks like someone had nailed his feet to the ground. He wasn't intimidated by the police; he'd had enough run-ins with them over the years. But they never came to his house, it was almost an unwritten rule.

The police hadn't seen Stanton, so he took the chance to beat a hasty retreat and duck back around the corner. Carefully, he peered back around the wall of the end terrace house to see what the police were doing. They didn't seem to be in any rush. It was while he continued to keep an eye on them from a safe distance, that Stanton realised he was himself being watched. He turned to see a young kid on a bike looking at him.

"What are you staring at?" Stanton asked.

"Not much," the kid replied.

Stanton went back to keeping an eye on what was happening outside his house.

"Any idea what they're doing there?" he asked the boy.

"That your house, then?"

"Yeah."

"Someone smashed your windows in."

Startled at what he had just heard, Stanton looked quickly at the kid.

"What?"

"Yer windows have been kicked in."

He leaned around the corner to look at his house, but it was on the shaded side of the street and the police car was in the way.

"Who did it?"

"Do I look like a copper?" the kid replied.

"Fuck off, you little shit."

"You fuck off."

The kid turned his bike around and cycled away.

The police car was leaving, fortunately heading the opposite way from where Stanton was hiding. He watched it move off, turn left and disappear out of sight. Waiting thirty seconds to make sure the coast was clear, Stanton set off nervously towards his house, walking rapidly down the street. He could feel the curtains twitching.

"Nosy bastards," he said under his breath.

He quickly reached his house and stopped, the hairs rising on the back of his hands, a shiver moving slowly down his spine. The kid was right. There was no living room window. The one that had been there when he left the house this morning was gone, and the space now boarded up. There was no glass on the floor, it had all been tidied up. It appeared that whoever was looking for him had been doing so for most of the day.

Stanton wasn't sure what was waiting for him behind the front door as he deftly pushed the handle down and went in as quietly as he could, but he had only managed to put one laced boot on the hallway carpet before all hell broke loose. From Margaret's room came a volley of staccato shouts.

"That you? Get in here! They could have killed me. I had to call the police. What've you been doing now?"

Knowing it was pointless to ignore what had happened, Stanton opened the door to Margaret's room and went in. Margaret was propped up in bed, having already made a move on the gin.

He decided to play dumb.

"What you whinging about now?" Stanton asked.

"Bloody look at that!" Margaret shouted, pointing to where her window used to be.

He carried on playing ignorant. "What happened?"

"You tell me," Margaret yelled.

"How can I? I've been out all day."

"Didn't stop your friends coming around here though, did it?"

He looked at the boarded-up window. "What friends?"

"How the bloody hell should I know? I don't know what you do when you leave this house."

"Well, how do you know they were my friends then, you daft cow?"

"Because they were shouting for you. That's how I know."

Stanton swallowed hard. The last minuscule chance that this might be something that would be easy to fix, slithered out of his mind.

"So what happened?" he asked Margaret.

"Like I said, cloth ears, your mates came here banging on the door. I'm shouting at them I'm on the commode. Next thing I know, a brick comes through the bloody window. If the commode were a foot on either side of where it is, I'm as good as dead. My whole life flashed before my eyes."

"Did you see who it was?"

"Did I see who it was? Of course I didn't. Well not properly, I had the curtains pulled for privacy. Some lads from the council came straight round to sort it out, but I won't be getting a new window before next week."

"What d'you call the police for?"

Margaret's dentures rattled in her mouth. "Lord give me strength! Look at the bloody state of my house, Jimmy. First, they were shouting for you through the letter box, then they tried to come through the window by smashing it. Luckily they took one look at me on that, and they ran off."

"Can't blame them," Stanton mumbled. "Be enough to scare anyone."

"That's why I called the police, I was in fear of my life, I could have been murdered."

They tried to get in the house.

"What did the police say, Margaret?"

"Nothing much, bloody useless as ever. They're coming back tomorrow morning to speak to you."

Stanton spun his head quickly to look at his mum. "Me?"

"Yes, you, it's you those people wanted to speak to, and the police want to ask you about them."

"Well, I don't know any more than you do."

For once, he wasn't lying. He needed space to think. He needed time alone. Stanton certainly didn't need the police sniffing around right now.

"You want a brew, Margaret?"

"Aye, go on. Put a thimble of gin in mine, Jimmy. My nerves are all over the place." She lay back dramatically on her pillows.

Stanton went into the kitchen, where he filled the kettle and waited for it to boil. He sat on the table's edge, deep in thought, until the kettle began whistling, momentarily rescuing him from his malaise.

Once he had finished calming Margaret down, Stanton went to his room.

He stretched out on his bed, staring up at the cobweb still dangling forgotten in the corner of his room, and played out the events of the day, his mind working its way through endless threads of doubt, solutions and realisations.

It couldn't be a coincidence that today was the day when he needed to get the money. Clearly, he hadn't been able to do that. Even so, it seemed to Stanton that recent events came across as heavy-handed for a debt that was only a few hours late. Arguably, it wasn't late at all.

Leaning over, he opened the bedside table drawer, took out the money he had stolen from Margaret and shoved it into his pocket. The amount was hardly worth the effort, but he just hoped it would be enough to calm everything down. He needed to get ahead of this and the only way he could think of doing that was by going to see Mickey.

Running down the stairs, he ignored Margaret's shouts from her bedroom. Slamming the front door behind him, he set off quickly down the road. He was tempted to run to the Smugglers and get it over with, but if he'd learned one thing in life, it was that a running skinhead attracted more attention, not less.

He crossed over a road, before crossing back again further on when he saw a phone box up ahead. He wasn't thinking straight. It made sense to ring ahead rather than just turn up.

He went in the phone box, inserted some money and quickly punched in the numbers. After a few rings, the call connected.

"Smugglers."

"Is Mickey there?"

"Hang on. Mickey, phone!"

Stanton heard the barmaid put the phone down as he listened to the familiar sounds of a pub enjoying itself after a long week.

"Yeah," Mickey said gruffly, picking up the phone.

"It's me."

There was some disruption on the line as Mickey switched the receiver around so that he could speak more discreetly.

"What the fuck have you done?"

Stanton closed his eyes.

"I was hoping you could tell me, Mickey?"

"You've got a problem, Stanz. It's a big problem, a big fucking problem. Word is, you're a dead man walking."

The temperature inside the phone box dropped as Stanton heard those words for the second time in only a few hours. He put his head on the cold surface of the phone box and tried to straighten out his thoughts.

"Look, Mickey, about the money. I've got some of it here now. I just need a few more days to get the rest sorted—"

"—You don't know, do you? You've not heard?"

"Heard? Heard what?"

There was a long pause at the other end of the line while Mickey chose his words carefully.

"Daft bastard. Get yourself down to the office now, I'll explain when you get here. Meet me round the back in the car park, don't go inside."

The line went dead.

TWENTY-TWO

Heather closed the front door just as the phone rang, the incessant shrill echoing around what she assumed was another empty house. She put down her bag and picked up the receiver, expecting to hear one of her parents on the other end.

"Hello."

The line was quiet. She tried again.

"Hello."

Heather concentrated on the breathing she could hear at the other end of the line.

"Who's there?" she asked.

Whoever it was put the phone down and the line went dead, the end of another silent call.

"Who was that?"

Heather looked up to see her mum at the top of the stairs in her bra and with a towel wrapped around her head.

"I was washing my hair. I didn't hear it ring and then I heard you talking."

"Wrong number," mumbled Heather, looking at the phone.

"Really? Okay, well I'm having leaving drinks for Alison from admin tonight, and your dad's at Uncle Terry's."

Her mum disappeared from sight, leaving Heather once again alone with her reflection.

Another girls' night out. Another lie.

Her mum reappeared at the top of the stairs, a quizzical look on her face. "I thought you said you were going to be back later, you said you were seeing Libby?"

"Yes I was, but she was going out so I came home."

Heather looked at herself in the mirror and was disappointed in what she saw. She'd started to lie as well.

Heather lay on her bed, her thoughts wandering back over the last few days and how they'd made her feel alive.

She heard the front door close. Sitting up, Heather peered out from behind the curtains and watched her mum walking down the garden path, all dressed up for her night out. She could almost smell the perfume her mum wore on special occasions, knowing that if she opened her bedroom door now, the aroma would be hanging on the landing like a fog.

Heather continued to spy on her mum, watching as she closed the garden gate. Pushing her head through the gap a bit more, Heather looked down the hill, just making out her mum's mousy-coloured hair bobbing through gaps in the hedges. In about five seconds, she would see her for a few moments as she passed between two houses and then again at the end of the road. After that, she would be out of sight. Her mum reached the junction, where she stopped as though she wasn't quite sure which way to go. Then, as if making a decision, she crossed over and turned left.

Left was away from the town, not towards it.

Heather let go of the curtain and fell back on the bed.

TWENTY-THREE

STANTON WALKED THROUGH THE FRONT DOOR OF THE SMUGGLERS, so distracted by his problems he'd forgotten Mickey told him not to. As soon as his boots touched the sticky carpet, he realised his mistake. The bar fell into an uncomfortable silence. He knew the rule better than anyone. If the place went quiet when you walked in, you weren't meant to be there. He glanced around at people who were staring into their half empty glasses. There were a few embarrassed coughs and continued whispered conversations, but most simply ignored him and looked away.

The tension hung with the smoke in the low-ceilinged salon until Stanton's awkwardness was saved by the barmaid. She lifted the bar top and ushered him through, whispering "car park" to him as he made his way to a well-lit but stark, brick passageway that led outside. He could see the door at the end held open by a barrel and he headed straight for it, the murk of a summer night clashing with the fake neon world that Stanton was about to leave.

Mickey, deep in thought, hands thrust into the pockets of his stolen council jacket, leant on his van under the only outside light that worked. It elongated his shadow over the car park, his quiff accentuated like the ridge of The Whale. He looked up to see Stanton framed by the doorway.

Nervously, Stanton edged a few steps closer.

"You never could listen to instructions," said Mickey as he leaned off the van and walked slowly over, the grit crunching beneath his heavy boots. As he reached Stanton, he stood directly in front of him, his eyes scanning his face as though he were debating where to strike him first.

"Mickey, look—"

Mickey interrupted him, his eyes still flickering.

"—You really are a stupid little prick." He rubbed his neck, looking up at the cloudless night sky. "You've fucked this, fucked it proper."

"How?" asked Stanton.

"I trusted you and this is how you pay me back?"

"Mickey, I don't understand what you're talking about, what do you mean? I've always done right by you, always."

"Bringing him to my office."

"Bringing who? I don't know what you're talking about, honestly Mickey I don't."

Mickey moved in closer and Stanton could feel warm breath laced with cheap Scotch on his face. Feeling the panic rising in his body, he dug his hands into his pockets and pulled out the money.

"Here Mickey, it's all I've got, I can get the rest next week."

Mickey looked contemptuously at what he was being offered before throwing his head back and laughing.

"Always the joker, Stanz."

Without taking his eyes off Stanton's face, Mickey knocked the money out of his hands as he moved toe to toe with Stanton, the caps of their boots kissing the front of the other.

"You think this is about them Moroccan fellas? You're

gonna wish it was them. Besides, I got the date wrong; they're coming next week, not this."

Mickey took a step back and looked at the money on the floor. "Pick that up."

Stanton bent down and made a grab for the notes before shoving them back in his pockets.

Stanton couldn't be any more confused than he was right now. Mickey didn't want the money and yet in all the time he had known him, that's all he ever wanted.

"So what's all this about, then?"

Mickey gave a long pause, almost as though he were too scared to say the word out loud.

"It's Sonny. He's the one looking for you."

Stanton could feel his life tilt across the secluded car park as his mind registered the name. What little blood he had left in his face quickly drained away.

"He came in earlier. I was doing some business in the snug and him and his thugs walked straight in. I always said to you not to bring anything from the outside in there and that's exactly what's happened."

Even if Mickey thought he was the hardest man in town, everyone knew it was Sonny. Everyone knew Sonny's reputation; he was a nasty piece of work. He was never seen wearing anything other than dirty jeans, leather boots, a filthy t-shirt and a filthier denim jacket. On top of his long, greasy hair sat his faithful woolly hat. No one had ever seen him take it off, even the women he slept with. Sonny came from the roughest council house on the roughest estate in the roughest part of town. The police left him alone. There were whispers that he was an informant, the only reason he wasn't in prison. There were rumours of a murder behind a pub on the edge of the estate, but those rumours died quicker than the man did.

"What did he say?" Stanton asked through a dry mouth.

"That they were looking for you. Sonny's on the warpath. I

said I didn't know where you were and that was the truth. Not too sure he believed me, but they slapped the poor sod that I was with around to make sure I got the message. When they finished, they said to pass that message on."

Stanton didn't need to hear those words again.

"What do I do, Mickey? I don't even know Sonny."

"Well, he knows you. I think you need to fuck off out of here, that's my advice."

"Go home, you mean?"

Mickey rolled his eyes. "No dickhead, fuck off out of town, let this simmer down, if it ever does. I've put some feelers out, but I keep getting the same message back. You're damaged goods, no one wants to know you. They don't want a ruck with Sonny, and they'll sell you out rather than risk it. You're on your own here, Stanz."

Mickey lit himself a cigarette while making a point of not offering Stanton one. He walked to the back of his van, opened its creaking doors and took something out before walking back to where Stanton was still rooted to the spot.

Mickey handed him something wrapped in cloth.

"Here."

Stanton was given no option other than to take it and he could feel the weight of something heavy as he held it.

"What is it?"

"An insurance policy. A bit of confidence. You're gonna need it."

Stanton carefully folded back the cloth, its shape taking time to reveal itself in the poorly lit car park. But it soon became clear what he was holding. Stanton looked up at Mickey, wide-eyed.

"Seriously, Mickey? A gun? This is too fucked up, what are you giving me this for?" Stanton tried to hand it back but Mickey kept his arms by his side.

"It's my old service revolver. Hasn't been fired in years. I keep it under the bed, you never know these days. Go home Stanz, stick it under your bed until you sort out what you're doing. You know what Sonny's capable of. If he comes knocking at your door you'll want to be holding that, not your mum's walking stick."

The panic started to rise in Stanton's throat. He tried again to hand the gun back but Mickey was having none of it.

"I'll go and see him. Sort it out with him one to one."

Mickey looked despairingly up at the sky before moving forward and getting right in Stanton's face, his nostrils flaring as he grabbed the collar of Stanton's jacket, pulling him in close.

"I won't tell you again. Get out of here and go home, then tomorrow fuck off until no one knows where you are. Keep moving, stay where it's busy and find places where you have friends, but that won't be easy. I looked in Sonny's eyes a few hours ago and what I saw is the reason I'm giving you this."

Mickey took the gun out of Stanton's hands and shoved it inside Stanton's jacket before zipping it up to his neck.

"I was taught to always have two bullets in the chamber. If someone's coming for you, use one on them. The second one is for you if you miss. There's two in there now. Good luck Stanz, I always liked you."

Mickey tapped Stanton's cheek with his rough calloused hands before walking back inside the pub and leaving him alone in the car park.

At that moment in time, standing in a deserted car park, Stanton had never felt so alone.

Nervously Stanton began to make his way home, finding a phone box en route from which to ring Roper.

"We were talking with Chris from the pier when we saw

them coming. There was no point running, there was nowhere to go. They asked where you were. Stupidly, Bin Bag opened his fat face and told them to piss off. They got him Stanz, they got him bad. We couldn't do anything. They absolutely battered him. They told me to pass on a message if I saw you."

"A message? What kind of message?" But Stanton already knew what was coming.

"That you're a dead man walking."

Third time unlucky. Stanton put the phone down.

He could feel the weight of the gun inside his jacket and realised he was cradling it like a baby. He felt paralysed, not so much with fear, but with indecision. He didn't know what to do but consoled himself with the thought that for tonight at least, he was the safest he would be. They wouldn't come back to the house, not now the police had been there. But tomorrow would be a different matter.

Stanton kicked the door of the phone box open and sprinted the rest of the way home, making sure to double lock the front door when he got there. He stopped to listen in on Margaret snoring in her room before moving quickly upstairs and shutting his bedroom door behind him.

He sat dejectedly on the bed. In the space of a few hours, his life had unravelled. Not long ago he was laughing and drinking on the beach, and now he was sat holding a gun in his hands. The realisation jolted him into action. He put the money back in the bedside drawer before kneeling down and pushing the gun under his bed. He turned all the lights off and went and stood by the window.

It was easy to get used to trouble, especially when it had followed you around for so long. But this felt different, and when people start telling you to get out of town, only a fool would choose not to listen.

So much violence, so much pain, it seemed to be

everywhere in his life, and he could feel it all now, pressing down, conspiring to crush the air from his chest.

He knew he had to run, and he would.

But first, he'd made a promise to Heather.

Whatever was out there in that town, hiding in the darkness beyond those slate roofs, whatever fate was going to be delivered tomorrow, he was going to do something he had never done before.

Stanton was going to do the right thing.

He was going to make sure Heather would be okay.

SATURDAY MORNING

TWENTY-FOUR

Heather looked at the posters fixed on her wall. Yesterday they had hung there as idols, today they just seemed silly. The morning sun streamed in through the fabric of closed curtains, bleaching further the faces of those fading pop stars.

Allowing her furtive imagination to run wild, Heather smiled at the prospect of spending time with the boy from the jetty and the fun and danger he had quickly brought into her life. She ran her hand gently over her stomach, feeling the nervous butterflies dancing deep inside. Heather kicked down the bedsheets to cool her body. Closing her eyes, she ran a tongue over her dry lips as she pictured his perfect face and his eyes that seemed to hold you in their gaze and make you think you were the only person in the world.

"Are you staying in there all day or are you planning on actually doing something?" her mum shouted from the hallway.

Heather opened her eyes and sat up.

"Getting up now," she shouted back, quickly swinging her legs out of bed, her heart thumping guiltily.

Sitting there, Heather couldn't recall ever feeling so much

anticipation about what might lay ahead and she thought carefully about what to wear, deciding on blue jeans and a pretty blouse that she had worn to a tortuous family party a few months ago. Picking up the small vanity mirror on her bedside table, she stared at the girl in the reflection. Did her face look different from yesterday? Did she look slightly prettier? If not prettier, perhaps slightly less plain?

Heather hastily applied some make-up before sneaking into her parents' bedroom, where she carefully opened her mother's chest of drawers. Taking out a small bottle of perfume she quickly dabbed some behind her ears and on her wrists. She was about to put the bottle back when she noticed an ornate box at the back, one that she hadn't seen before. Checking she was alone, Heather took the box out and opened it, staring disbelievingly at what was inside.

Her mum called loudly from downstairs. "Heather! Are you coming down for breakfast?"

Heather carefully put the box back in the drawer and quietly left her parents' bedroom.

Upstairs was the past, locked away behind the door. The present was simmering in silence around a kitchen table. And the future? The future was unknown, but it might start with Heather walking through the front door and going out and finding it for herself.

"Morning, Heather," said her dad. "You look nice."

Heather self-consciously pushed a lock of hair behind her ear. "Thank you."

"I won't bother asking you if you want any breakfast after yesterday," her mum said from the sink.

"Mum, Dad, I'm going to Libby's today to listen to some records, we might stay there all day, I might even have tea there."

"Okay love, have a nice time," her dad said, smiling.

Her mum turned to face her. "Libby? You keep mentioning this girl but I can't picture her. Have I met her before?"

"I'm sure you have, she was new to school this year."

"No, no I don't think so, Heather. Libby, you say. Where does she live?"

Heather could feel herself start to flush.

"I…er…"

"What do her parents do? Why don't you bring her here and we can meet her?"

"Leave her alone for god sake, Jackie. Why does every conversation make you sound like Poirot?"

"Oh shut up, Colin."

"She's sixteen now, old enough to have some independence. Have a nice time with your friend, Heather. Don't forget we're at your Uncle Terry's tonight, he's having a big party for his birthday. Unless, of course, you want to come?" He winked as though he already knew the answer.

Her mum turned away and carried on with the washing up.

"Yes, it'll be a late one, you know how that side like to drink."

"I'm sure you'll keep them company." Once again, her dad winked at Heather.

"And what does that mean?"

"Nothing."

"Then why say it?"

Heather knew what was coming and left the kitchen. She was about to close the front door behind her when her mum appeared, holding up her school shoes.

"Heather? What have you been doing to your shoes? You've ruined them!"

Heather didn't answer. Taking one last look at her mum, she left the house and started to run as fast as she could, down the garden path and out through the gate and towards the promenade.

TWENTY-FIVE

STANTON WAS ALREADY WAITING FOR HER, LEANING AGAINST THE brickwork of the tower.

"Hello again," said Heather, noticing that he seemed distracted, worried even.

Stanton eyed her clothes. "I thought you only ever wore school uniform?"

"Very funny, I do own other clothes, you know!"

Looking up at the clock, Stanton didn't have the luxury of wasted time. "We've got ten minutes," he said, sitting down next to her. "What's that smell?"

Heather blushed and changed the subject. "What are you going to say to him?" She was hoping he had changed his mind about the whole thing.

"I'm not saying anything," he replied. "You are."

Heather's eyes widened. "What? Me? Why me?"

"Because I know a pervert when I see one and I'm not sure you do."

"What if he's just being over-friendly? I could just ask to change classes?"

"There's being friendly and there's..."

Stanton stopped himself, conscious that Heather wasn't the kind of girl that would be used to the way he talked.

"Look, I told you, if it's not you today, it'll be someone else later."

Using his finger he lifted her chin, forcing her to look directly into his eyes. "You trust me, don't you?"

Heather nodded.

"Good. Don't worry about anything. I'll be right with you, but he won't see me. Where are you going?"

"Going?"

"Yes, going. You said to him on the phone there was somewhere you could go that was quieter. There's no way he'll stay here. It's too dangerous for him."

"There are some benches up the end of the promenade, they're always quiet. I go there sometimes."

"Show me."

"You want me to take you there?"

"No stupid, come on, he'll be here in a minute, and if he sees me, it's over. I need to get out of sight. Where are these benches? Come on, quickly."

Heather stood up and pointed down the promenade, Stanton following where she was looking.

"Up by the lifeboat? Okay. Get him down there as soon as you can. I'll be watching you, don't worry. I want to see what he does. You're not alone, remember that. Do you believe me?"

"Yes, I believe you."

"Good, now stand out there a bit more so he can see you. He might think you've got cold feet. Remember, don't hang around when he gets here. I've got stuff to do today."

There wasn't time for Heather to ask what he meant by that as he disappeared quickly around the back of the tower. It would have been too late, anyway. At that precise moment, Heather spotted Mr Graeme crossing the road.

Heather's first thought was how funny it was to see a

teacher outside of school, especially when they were dressed in normal clothes. Mr Graeme was wearing jeans, a jacket and a smart shirt. Heather wasn't sure but he might even have had his hair cut since she saw him in the week.

"Well hello, Heather," Mr Graeme said, arriving at the stroke of ten.

Heather smiled nervously.

"Well, you look totally different outside of school, I must say. You look very grown up."

Mr Graeme swung his satchel over his shoulder as they both looked at each other, neither really sure of what to do next. Heather remembered what Stanton had said. Get him moving straightaway and lead him down to where he'd be waiting by the benches.

"We could walk further down the promenade. It's a bit quieter there."

"That sounds like a good idea, Heather. I'm not a huge fan of busy places. Lead the way!"

They walked slowly towards the quiet end of the seafront, Heather slightly ahead of Mr Graeme, her arms folded defensively as she scanned the horizon ahead.

"Tell me, have you finished the book I gave you?"

Heather had forgotten all about the book. "No, not yet," she replied casually.

Mr Graeme looked directly at her. "But you said on the phone call yesterday you'd nearly finished it?"

Heather couldn't remember the lie she had told but she could feel the teacher's stare burning into the side of her face. She stayed looking straight ahead, scanning the horizon to see if she could see Stanton anywhere.

"Out last night with your boyfriend or something? That's as good a reason as any not to finish a book, I suppose."

He sounded like a disappointed teacher speaking to his class.

Heather quickened her pace. "I don't have a boyfriend."

Mr Graeme feigned surprise. "What? An intelligent and pretty girl like you? I'd have thought they'd be queuing around the block. I know I would have been if I were twenty years younger."

He laughed, too loud and for too long, just as they reached the bench that Heather liked to call her own.

"Shall we sit here?" Heather asked, looking furtively around. There was still no sign of Stanton.

Mr Graeme also took a moment to check their surroundings. "Yes, this is lovely Heather. This is ideal, nice and quiet."

They sat on the bench, Heather crossing her legs away from the teacher while he crossed his towards her.

Mr Graeme stretched his arms along the back of the bench. "So you come here sometimes?"

Heather shuffled slightly forwards. "Yes, sometimes."

They sat there in silence, looking out across the sandy bay.

"It's so lovely here. They say you can always tell how the day will go by the colour of The Whale in the morning. Look at it, magnificent. I can't imagine living anywhere else than here, I'd miss this view."

Heather looked at Mr Graeme as though it was the first time she had ever seen him.

"Really? I hate it, I can't wait to get away."

"Are you okay, Heather?" Mr Graeme asked. "You seem nervous, not quite yourself."

Heather knew she wasn't hiding her feelings very well.

"Would you like me to leave, Heather? I can if you like, we can talk again in September."

Heather tensed her body; she would like nothing more than for him to go. But she knew she needed to keep him here. Looking at him, she shook her head.

"It was lovely to get your phone call yesterday. I was

actually working on my novel when you called. I have it here in my satchel, the book I've been writing."

Heather just wanted Stanton to arrive and take her away from here. She instinctively looked behind, searching the promenade, but they were on their own. There was no one around.

"Would you like me to read some of it to you? You might recognise someone in it. It's a love story, because all the best stories are."

Taking the manuscript from his satchel, he moved a little closer to Heather and dropped his arm so gently onto her shoulder that she hardly noticed.

"Move a little closer, you can trust me. I'm stuck, I need you to help me with the ending of the story."

Heather froze as he pulled her closer to him.

"I hope you don't mind me saying, Heather, but you smell beautiful. May I?"

Before she could answer, Mr Graeme slowly moved his face to the nape of her neck, gently nuzzling her skin.

"Please," Heather said, trying to move away. "No, please, I don't want to. I want to go home."

The teacher grabbed Heather's wrist.

"Please, you're hurting me."

"Don't be silly, Heather," he said, his voice now firmer, like the one used when shouting at unruly pupils. "Let's stop pretending, I've seen the way you look at me, don't tell me you don't feel something?"

Heather tried to wrestle herself free but he was too strong and she felt her small frame begin to buckle under the weight of his body pressing down on her.

"No, please Mr Graeme, please no!"

Where was he, where was Stanton?

TWENTY-SIX

Stanton had already seen enough.

The moment the teacher had leaned into Heather's neck, he had set off at speed from where he had been watching from behind the lifeboat station. By the time Mr Graeme was practically on top of Heather, the shadow of Stanton's body was already falling across them both, casting them in shade and causing the teacher to quickly break away and look up.

"Excuse me—" said Mr Graeme, beginning to stand.

Stanton gave him a look that made the teacher wilt back onto the bench.

"—Sit back down."

Heather had moved herself along the bench, as far away as she could from the teacher.

"Stand up," Stanton ordered.

Mr Graeme started to rise, but Stanton jabbed his chest with splayed fingers and forced him back down onto the bench.

"Not you, nonce chops."

"Look, what is going on here?" Mr Graeme stammered. "Who are you? What right—"

The teacher's face was beginning to redden and perspire in fear and intimidation.

"—I won't tell you again. You keep that mouth of yours shut until I tell you to speak."

Stanton looked at Heather. "Stand up."

She rose slowly, her legs feeling as though they belonged to someone else, a tear falling slowly down her cheek as the reality of the situation started to sink in.

Reaching out, Stanton carefully wiped it away.

"Listen to me. You did great but now I want you to walk back to the clock tower. Once you get there, wait for me. Do not look back. Do you understand? Do not look back."

The teacher tried again to interrupt. "Heather, what's going on? I thought we were going to read my book. Who is this boy?"

"Go," said Stanton forcefully.

Heather shuffled slowly, still in shock, keeping her head bowed, carefully watching the ground as she walked away.

Stanton watched her go before turning back to the teacher. "I'll tell you who I am, shall I? I'm your worst nightmare, that's who I am."

Heather had barely gone ten yards before curiosity got the better of her and she looked back.

"What did I just say?" Stanton shouted at her. "Don't look back! Go to the clock tower now."

This time he watched her go and Heather did as she was told, disappearing into the distance. Stanton turned his attention back on the teacher. Yesterday, his plan had been to beat him up and he'd actually been looking forward to doing it. But yesterday was a long time ago in Stanton's world. Today, he had woken up a different person to the one that had slept restlessly. Things were changing in him faster than he had the strength to keep everything the same.

He leaned in as close as he could. "Consider yourself a

lucky bastard. I had plans for you today, only I haven't got the time now. But know this. If you look, speak or get close to touching that girl again I'm going to hear about it, and when I do, I'm walking into your school carrying the bluntest knife I can find. Then I'm going to come to your classroom and walk in, and in front of everyone, I'm going to chop your cock and balls off. That clear?"

Mr Graeme dropped his head; the game was over.

Stanton grabbed the manuscript from his hands. "What's this?"

The teacher made a desperate attempt at taking it back, but Stanton was too strong.

"Nothing. Please, that's mine. I don't have another copy."

Stanton flicked through the pages. "Important, is it?"

"Yes, very. Now, please may I have it back?"

"Bad news if something happened to it?"

"Yes, now give it back and we won't say anything more about this misunderstanding."

"Misunderstanding? That's what you think this is, a misunderstanding?"

"Yes. You've got this all wrong. Now, if you don't mind?"

The teacher held his hand out expectantly.

Stanton sneered. "You lot are all the same."

Taking out his cigarette lighter, Stanton held its flame to a corner of the manuscript. It took a moment for the paper to begin burning, but when it did, the flames rose quickly towards his fingers. Stanton grinned as he dangled the burning paper in the teacher's face. Mr Graeme tried to stand up again. Once more, Stanton was too strong and pushed him back down, before Mr Graeme made a last pathetic attempt at feebly grabbing the burning manuscript. Stanton laughed as he held it just out of reach. It wouldn't have mattered anyway; the paper was well alight and burning quickly. There was nothing much left to save. Walking over to the bin Stanton dropped the smouldering remnants in, embers of burning black paper dancing around his feet.

Slumped and defeated on the bench, Mr Graeme stared into space.

"Two days ago, I'd have cut your face open," confided Stanton. "Like I said, today's your lucky day. Sorry for any misunderstanding."

Turning on his heels, he set off towards the clock tower. Time was going to be a precious commodity today and he couldn't afford to waste any of it.

Stanton had surprised himself, avoiding violence in a situation that clearly warranted its use. But he didn't want to do anything that could impact Heather. He could walk away from this problem but she couldn't. Striding purposely back towards the tower, he realised something else. You didn't always need to fight what was in front of you. Sometimes you could just walk away and live to see another day.

The clock face said it had just gone eleven o'clock. He had twelve more hours in this town and that would be it. He was leaving today, that much he'd decided.

Heather, small and vulnerable on the bench, looked up as he reached her.

"Sorry," she said, before he could say anything.

"Sorry? What for?"

"You were right about him. I probably knew it all along but my guard has been down for a long time. He must have seen that and used it against me. I'm sorry, I'm such an idiot."

"None of this is your fault."

Stanton loomed over her. He knew he had to tell her he was leaving. After yesterday, his only chance was to keep moving. He also needed money, enough money to last him a few days, enough to buy some time to sort himself out, and he only had twelve hours in which to get some.

He looked nervously back up at the clock and then back at

her. He needed to get going. But he found himself still drawn to Heather, who seemed to be shrinking in front of his eyes. She looked exactly like she had when he'd approached her at the railings a few days ago. Broken.

Stanton had kept his promise to make sure Heather was safe from the teacher, but now he was starting to wonder if it would be enough.

"I've seen that face before," he said, smiling at her.

"Practically every day you've known me," she replied, shaking her head and smiling. "At least I'm predictable."

Stanton was in two minds. Flee, and get on with the urgent matter of saving himself. Or stay with Heather a moment longer so that he could at least say goodbye on better terms.

"Know what you need?" he said.

"What?"

He nodded his head toward the jetty.

"A brew. Come on, before it gets busy. One for the road."

Turning, he walked quickly away before he could change his mind.

TWENTY-SEVEN

Heather sipped her tea from a chipped mug cupped in her hands.

"What happened back there?"

Today, Stanton had sat them on the far side of the café, choosing a table where no one could see them and where no one would think to look. It was just the statue of the fisherman and the railings between them and the empty, waterless bay. Beyond that, The Whale arched across the sky, its humped back sloping down toward the shoreline.

He played dumb. "What happened where?"

"With, you know, him, on the bench."

Stanton took his cigarettes and lighter out of his pocket and put them on the table. "Have you got make-up on?" he asked, grinning.

Not for the first time in his presence, Heather felt the blood warming her cheeks. "No."

"Yes you have, and perfume. Was that for him or me?"

He gently kicked her chair while picking out a cigarette and holding the box out to her. Slowly she took the end of a cigarette and pulled it out, her eyes flicking between the cigarette and Stanton's face. Putting it to her lips, she let it dangle for a second while Stanton reached with his lighter, their eyes locking together as he lit the end of the cigarette and Heather inhaled as deeply as she could.

Once she'd finished coughing, she looked up through watery eyes to see Stanton laughing.

"Idiot. You're trying to suck through too much smoke. No wonder you're choking to death. Look."

With confidence, he showed her what to do.

"Try again, but slower, and when you take the fag out of your mouth, inhale the smoke into your lungs, but take a deep breath. Anything else, and you'll end up coughing and looking like you just did."

Heather tried again, this time taking it slowly, breathing in shallow and inhaling deeply. This time, the smoke went straight into her lungs and settled there.

"I did it!" she laughed, feeling pleased with herself.

"There you go, easy once you know how. You'll be on forty a day like Margaret before you know it."

Heather inhaled again, proud of herself and her newfound skill.

"Why d'you call your mum by her first name?"

"Just do. Didn't feel right calling her mum, seeing as I pretty much brought myself up."

"That's sad."

Heather placed a hand on top of his as they retreated into a comfortable silence, the smoke from their cigarettes intertwining.

"He won't bother you again, that bloke on the bench," Stanton said absently.

"What did you do? You haven't told me."

"I didn't hurt him. I wanted to, but I didn't. So I burned his book."

"No! You didn't?" Heather laughed at the thought of the

look on Mr Graeme's face. "Looks like I'll never be borrowing that from the school library. I bet he's furious."

Picking up her tea with the cigarette still burning in her fingers, she looked at Stanton through the steam and smoke.

"Can I ask you something?"

Stanton smiled. "I don't think I'm going to have a choice in that."

"You don't. But, why are you still talking to me? What I mean is, you could have just left me there once I'd climbed back over the railings."

Heather looked forlornly at the spot where Stanton had intervened earlier in the week.

"I still don't think I would have jumped, but you didn't need to stay. You did, and I'm glad you did. You didn't need to meet me again and you certainly didn't need to meet me again today and set fire to my teacher's book. You don't have to answer the question, but you can...if you want."

Stanton looked out across the bay. He had to tell her he was leaving. Even this conversation was too intimate for him. She was asking about feelings he didn't even know he possessed. He was worried, not for himself but for her. For some reason, he felt responsible although he wasn't sure why. If he left, he knew he was leaving her in trouble. The school, that teacher, this town, her family. She'd simply fade away and never be seen again. But after the events of yesterday, he couldn't stay either.

Stanton arose from his chair and paced nervously around the end of the jetty. He was going to tell her now. Looking absently back towards the promenade, he tried to buy himself some time as he searched for the words he needed. "Look," he began.

But that was as far as he got as the hairs on the back of his neck rose in fear and he found he couldn't catch his breath.

Yesterday, he'd heard about the people that were looking for him. Now, he could actually see them.

There was no doubt it was Sonny's gang. They were approaching quickly along the promenade, their movement dynamic amid the dawdling tourists and dog walkers. Stanton couldn't say for sure how many but he counted at least six. There were a couple of punks in amongst the troublemakers, all were dressed in black and swarming with purpose, heading directly for the jetty. Heading directly for him.

Stanton was trapped, stuck at the end of a jetty with only one way off. Even if he ran as fast as he could, he'd never reach the promenade by the time they reached him. His idea of laying low and ambling around town for the day now seemed naïve.

He stood as immobile as the statue behind him, watching the group move quickly, like a flock of ravens across the horizon. This was no coincidence; they knew he was here; it was no lucky guess. In his panic, he had practically forgotten Heather was there. She was looking up at him, waiting patiently for him to carry on speaking. Whatever Stanton did and said in the next few seconds would dictate not only the rest of the day, but the rest of his life, and possibly hers.

"Look at what?" Heather asked, oblivious to the danger around her.

Stanton was out of time. It was now or never.

"Do you still trust me?" he asked urgently.

Heather frowned and picked up her mug while she thought about the question.

Stanton dashed over to her, taking the mug roughly from her hands, spilling the tea everywhere.

"There's no time for that. Do you trust me?"

Heather looked once more into those intense eyes. "Yes," she said without hesitation.

Grabbing her hand, Stanton forcefully pulled her up, her

chair falling over as he practically dragged her across the table. Without speaking or looking back and still holding her hand, he ran past the statue to the railings, only letting go of her so that he could start to clamber over. Once he was on the other side, he turned and held out his hand.

"Come on. Don't worry, this time we're going over together."

SATURDAY AFTERNOON

TWENTY-EIGHT

TOGETHER THEY CLAMBERED OVER THE RAILINGS, SCRAMBLING down the rocks that had dried in the morning sun, before jumping the last few feet onto the beach and dusting sand and grime from their hands.

It didn't take Stanton long to realise his options were no better down here than they had been a few moments ago. But at least they were out of sight. He looked across at the far side of the bay. It looked close enough but the distance was deceiving, they'd never make it. They'd get sucked down into quicksand before reaching halfway.

"Can I ask, what we are doing?"

Despite two minutes ago having been sat at a table sipping her tea, Heather was now somehow on the beach, surrounded by silt and seaweed.

"I'll explain later. Come on, quickly."

He headed off around the other side of the jetty. Keeping as low and as close to the wall as possible, Stanton rushed over the stones and rock pools, following the jetty's footprint as closely as he could.

Above, the group pursuing him would have reached the café by now.

"Slow down!" Heather shouted.

Stopping, he spun round and put his finger to his lips, his face contorted with concern. One false move and his escape was over before it had started. They carried on in silence, the jetty towering over their heads. Heather managed to keep up although it was tiring, at times putting her hands on her knees to stop and catch her breath. They had to keep going. Stanton knew they weren't safe yet, they needed to get off the beach, they were too exposed.

Moving away from the jetty, they hugged the sea wall closely. The tide would be gone for most of the day, and the beach was filling up with families. They had to get back up on the promenade, back into the town that offered more places to hide.

They stopped by a ladder attached to the wall which led up to the seafront. Stanton weighed up what to do. Right now he couldn't think straight, and if he wanted to get through today, he'd better quickly regain the ability.

"Well, this is fun," said Heather, blowing her fringe from her face. "Now what?"

Since returning home last night, Mickey's words had been circling Stanton's head. *Keep moving, stay where it's busy and find places where you have friends.*

"Come on, follow me up this ladder." He set off quickly, taking two rungs at a time.

"This is crazy. What's going on?" Heather moaned, but again blindly followed him up. "You seem worried and that's making me worried. Are we in trouble?"

But Stanton was already at the top of the ladder and had disappeared from sight.

TWENTY-NINE

Kenny was smoking at the entrance of the pier, watching like a hawk for anything with long legs in a short skirt. As the sun warmed his face, he licked his lips with anticipation of all the fun that a Saturday at the seaside could bring. He was as content as any man could be. That was, until he caught sight of Stanton fast approaching up the slope.

Moments before, Stanton had peered cautiously over the top of the ladder to make sure the coast was clear. Once he was sure it was safe, he turned and helped lift Heather over.

"Stupid bastard," Kenny muttered to himself. He dropped his cigarette and crushed it beneath his shoe as he waited for Stanton to reach him.

"Did you not listen to a fucking word I said yesterday?"

"I've seen them," replied Stanton. "About twenty minutes ago."

"Yeah, well, breaking news Colombo, so have I. They came here first. Seriously, what the fuck is wrong with you?"

Kenny noticed Heather loitering behind Stanton. "Who's this?"

Stanton answered quickly. "No one." He nodded his head

and led Kenny off to the side. "I know who it is that's after me."

"Well that's a start, I suppose. Who is it?"

"Sonny."

Kenny's mouth dropped open. "Sonny! Well, Stanz, that's you well and truly fucked. What've you done? What are you doing business with him for? You know he's trouble." Kenny forced out a weak laugh to try to ease the tension

"That's the problem. I've not had anything to do with him. I've barely spoken to him so far as I can remember, so I've no idea. Seen him around a few times but always steered clear. I went and saw Mickey last night, and he doesn't know either. If I knew what it was, I could try to do something about it."

"Money?" suggested Kenny. "It's always money with him. Do you owe him any?"

Stanton owed money to virtually everyone he knew, but he had never done business with Sonny, or at least he didn't think he had. He shook his head.

"Not money, then it must be a bird. Didn't shag his missus, I hope?"

Stanton looked over to Heather, but she was too far away to hear.

"What did Mickey say exactly, Stanz?"

"Told me to get out of town for a bit."

"Hate to say it, but he's right."

"But I can't go until later tonight, I need to get some money together first."

"Christ, Stanz, you're bringing me a load of headaches."

"I know, Kenny, but—" Again, he looked over at Heather.

"—Who is she?" Kenny asked.

"Long story."

"Bit young for you but you always were a dirty dog."

"Kenny, can you help?"

Kenny rubbed yesterday's bruise on his forehead. "Thought I'd seen the last of you when you walked away yesterday."

Kenny could see his friend was in trouble. Stanton had bailed him out many times before and friendship was thicker than family in this town. He nodded. "Okay. Get yourself and your bird up to the kiddie park at the back of the pier. We've not opened it yet, I'll keep it shut as long as I can. I'll call a couple of extra guys in today just in case. I'll bring you a brew up shortly. I'll see if I can get some money out of the safe, but they're watching like hawks these days. How much d'you think you'll need?"

It was a question that had been swirling around Stanton's mind since he'd woken up. *How much was enough to get away and stay away?*

"Dunno, at least a couple of hundred I reckon."

"Two hundred fucking quid? Where you planning on going, Spain?"

Stanton didn't know the answer to that question himself.

"Needs to be enough to get me away to lay low for a bit."

Kenny scratched his chin. "Okay, I can't do it all but I'll see what I can manage."

The worry visibly drained from Stanton's face. "Cheers, Kenny." He called over to Heather, "Come on."

Heather walked over and they set off toward the entrance to the pier but just as they got there, they heard Kenny shout, "Oh sweet fucking Jesus!"

Stanton looked over in the direction that Kenny was pointing and he almost felt his heart stop. There they were again, the ones he thought he'd just escaped. They were walking quickly down the promenade, away from the jetty, and heading for the pier.

"Run!" Kenny shouted, pushing them both through the entrance. "Fucking run!"

Stanton didn't need telling twice. He grabbed Heather's

arm, almost pulling it from its socket as he dragged her and set off running through the pier.

When Stanton had started running, his only plan was to get as far away as he could from those chasing him. This meant getting to the back of the pier was his only option. He couldn't go forward and now, standing at the back of the pier, breathless and confused, he realised they were in more trouble than they had been on the jetty. There was simply no way off other than the way they had just come.

"What's happening?" Heather asked. "Please tell me, you're starting to scare me." It had almost been fun running along the beach a few moments ago, but this felt different.

"We need to hide for a bit."

"Hide? Why hide? Hide from who? Are you in trouble?"

Stanton spun in a complete circle, looking for inspiration. He ran to the end of the pier and looked down. It was a thirty-foot drop down to the rocks below. It crossed his mind to try to climb down, but Heather would never make it.

"We just need to get out of sight," he said absently.

He knew they were vulnerable being back here, but he couldn't risk going down the way they had just come, that would be suicide. They certainly couldn't risk hanging around out in the open, either. For the second time today, he was trapped. He was just about to give up, when he saw the helter-skelter.

"Come on," he said, running over to it. The door of the slide was ajar. Stanton pushed it open with his boot and peered in. It was empty, just a pile of dirty mats stacked untidily in the corner. "This'll have to do, they'll be here soon."

Heather stood with her arms folded, her face set and unsmiling. "Not until you tell me what's going on."

Stanton didn't have time for this, but he knew he owed her something, so he talked quickly.

"These people are after me, don't ask me why, because I don't even know myself. It all started after I left you last night. That's it, you know about as much as I do. Whoever's coming down that pier right now are here for me, and they won't rest until they've got me. I need to get out of sight, *right now*."

Heather could sense the danger was real as she saw the confidence ebbing away from the boy standing in front of her, his chest heaving behind his tight, white t-shirt.

"Come on then, let's hurry."

Heather dashed inside, followed by Stanton who pulled the door shut behind them.

Inside, it was dark and dank, some token light coming in through two frosted windows on either side of the door. As her eyes adjusted to the dimness, Heather surveyed their surroundings.

"It stinks," she said.

"Yeah, Kenny calls this his sex palace. Wouldn't sit on those mats, if I were you."

Stanton peered out through the keyhole.

The whole place smelt damp; other than the open doorway at the top of the spiral staircase, there was no way for any fresh air to get in.

Stanton couldn't see anything through the keyhole so tried to look through the frosted windows. He could see better, but still not clearly enough. The door had nothing to lock it with, but at least they were out of sight, and right now it would have to do.

"I'm scared," whispered Heather.

"Join the club," muttered Stanton turning to her, making sure to choose his words carefully. "Whatever happens, I promise you I'll look after you. Okay?" He went back to looking out of the window, cursing the speed at which things were happening.

Heather moved closer to him. "I trust you, James."

Stanton went back to guarding their hiding place, cleaning the window with his fingers to try to make it clearer.

"Don't forget you still need to answer my question, though," added Heather.

Instinct told him to ignore the question. But he felt like he still owed her something. She was trapped inside this prison as much as he was, and she wouldn't be there if it wasn't for him.

"What question?"

"You know very well—"

Before she could continue, Stanton pushed his finger firmly on her lips and held it there. With his other hand, he pointed out of the window, his eyes imploring her to remain silent and perfectly still. Peering through as best he could, he looked back shaking his head and slowly dropped his finger from Heather's lips.

On the other side of the door, blurred shadows roamed the deserted pier like three black ghosts hunting for the living. He couldn't hear what they were saying, just mumbled shouts as they moved around the stalls and empty rides. Stanton looked at a small metallic loop on the inside of the door, presumably a remnant of the old internal lock. He could get a finger inside there, but he could never get enough strength to hold it shut if someone was pulling from the other side. He thought about making a run for it, confident he would be quick enough, but doubted Heather would make it twenty yards without being caught. Looking desperately around the hollow shell of their hiding place, it was obvious he'd walked them both into a prison.

Outside, he heard more shouting.

"Stanton! Come on, you little fucker, we know you're back here."

Stanton recognised the voice doing the shouting. It was Richie from the fight on the pier, the one who'd given him the bruise on his face.

"Stanton! You're not going anywhere, show yourself."

In the quiet of the pier, the words echoed around the stalls. Then it went quiet as Richie saw the door in the helter-skelter the same way Stanton had, knowing instinctively that his nemesis was in there, trapped like a rat. He walked over and grabbed the door handle, hesitated and adjusted his stance, checking with the other two that they were ready. He might be outnumbered, but they all knew Stanton's reputation.

Pulling on the handle, all three charged through the narrow doorway, shouting profanities as they went. Once they'd squeezed through, they stood, fists clenched, breathing heavily.

The space was empty.

There was just a pile of mats stacked haphazardly in the corner, as though someone had thrown them there to cover something, or someone. Collectively, they all reached the same conclusion and launched themselves at the mats, frenziedly kicking and stamping at whatever lay beneath.

It had been Heather's idea, pointing with urgent, wide eyes to where the staircase went up into the roof of the slide. He had followed her gaze up into the vaulted roof, and grinned. There was no time to lose. Grabbing two mats he ushered Heather up the staircase so that by the time the punks had barged in through the unlocked door, Stanton and Heather were already quietly preparing to slide down the outside.

They needed to time their descent perfectly, otherwise someone would be waiting for them at the bottom. They needed to go just when those chasing them were making the most noise. Heather was already sitting on her mat with Stanton just behind. If he crouched down, he was able to see part of the downstairs door. He waited patiently until light burst into the darkened room as the punks barged their way in.

"Now," Stanton whispered, gently pushing Heather on the back. She let go and started to slide down. The ride down didn't take long, but it felt like forever. Heather landed on the soft carpet at the base of the slide but she barely had time to get out of the way before Stanton came careering down and fell on top of her before quickly getting to his feet and helping Heather up.

"Come on," he said quietly. "We need to get off this pier now."

"Hold on." Heather crept towards the helter-skelter.

"What are you doing?" Stanton hissed. "Come back. We need to go!"

Heather had already reached the door and could hear voices talking on the other side. Taking a deep breath to steady her nerves, she pushed the door firmly shut and deftly pulled the lock across so that it bolted into place. Those who had been chasing them were now the ones locked in. They were trapped, and Heather and Stanton were free.

"Genius," laughed Stanton. But this would only buy them a few valuable seconds and they still had to get to the end of the pier. He grabbed Heather's hand and they started to run, the punks now shouting and swearing from inside the helter-skelter. But they were still deep in trouble. If Stanton could get to the promenade, they could disappear. The pier was long though, and Heather was slowing them down.

Stanton checked behind to see Richardson was already standing at the top of the slide and looking in their direction, shouting angrily.

Stanton urged Heather on. The pier was still relatively quiet, which meant that they could run in a straight line and there was nothing much ahead to slow them down. Taking another quick look behind, Stanton was alarmed to see that all three of those chasing them were now down the slide, and a mere fifty yards behind.

"Faster!" Stanton implored as Heather did all she could to keep up. "We need to get off here. We can't stop!"

It was Heather's turn to glance over her shoulder. "They're coming!" she shrilled.

They had now made it halfway down the pier, Heather clutching onto Stanton's arm like a weighty anchor as they kept running, getting increasingly closer to the safety of the busy promenade. Stanton took one final look behind. The gap was narrowing. It was going to be close, but he was starting to feel they could make it.

"Nearly there. Come on, one last effort," he shouted encouragingly to Heather, who was starting to tire.

"Why'd they want to get you so much?" Heather said breathlessly.

"Shut up and keep running!"

They finally reached the end of the pier and stepped onto the promenade where Stanton slowed them to a brisk walk, trying to blend in more naturally with their surroundings.

"There he is! Oi, Stanton!"

Hearing his name caused Stanton to stop and turn quickly. He'd been so obsessed with those at the end of the pier, he'd completely forgotten the others would be waiting for them at the front. To make matters worse, the three from the helter-skelter had now caught up. The two groups merged and set off as one after Stanton. Once again, he'd run out of luck.

He grabbed Heather's hand again.

"I'm exhausted, I don't think I can run anymore."

"Yes you can, one last effort," he urged.

In front of the pier, a bus pulled up. Stanton set off towards it, dodging the crowds of holidaymakers in his way. If they made the bus, they had a chance. Heather was tiring quickly and struggling to keep up. The adrenaline which had kept her moving on the pier was all but spent. With only seconds between them and those chasing behind, Stanton hauled Heather onto the bus just as the driver closed the door and started to move off.

Stanton grinned through the door, giving his pursuers the finger, exhausted but relieved as the bus pulled away and he watched them disappear into the distance.

THIRTY

Stanton collapsed on the back seat of the bus, while Heather knelt and looked through the rear window at those that had just been chasing them but were now scattered in the road.

"Well, this is fun! You seriously don't know who those men are?"

Stanton put his laced boot on the seat in front and looked gloomily out of the window.

"Yeah, I know who they are but not why they're after me."

"They chased us off the jetty, then off the pier but you don't know why?" she said, incredulously.

"It's something to do with Sonny."

"Who?"

Stanton left her only too pertinent question hanging, turning to look out of the window as the town swept by in front of him like a movie on fast forward. He wished he were actually in a movie. That way, he could perhaps finally get to the end of it and find out what was going to happen to him.

"What number's this bus? Did you see?" he asked.

"I don't know. Why?"

"Wait there."

He walked down the length of the bus, holding on as it swayed.

"You going to the train station?" Stanton asked the driver.

"Yeah, I am. Now sit down before you fall down, dickhead."

Stanton went to the back but sat apart from Heather. He really was going to have to ditch her, here on the bus. It was nothing personal, but it was getting too dangerous. Heather not knowing who Sonny was, was another reminder of the disparity in their lives. He was doing this not because he didn't like her, but because he did. She was the last person he wanted to see hurt, and he certainly didn't want to be the cause of it. When the bus got to the train station, he'd tell her he was going.

Pushing himself lower in the seat, he cursed his plan for unravelling faster than his ability to fix it. His original idea was to get the last train out of town. It was the idea he'd come up with last night in the dark of his bedroom. Now it seemed absurd. He'd assumed he would at least have until the end of the day, but at this rate, he wouldn't even make it to late afternoon, let alone escape to the next town. Then there was the issue of money. Getting hold of some would give him options and if he had options, he had time. If he had time, he knew he had a chance. But now he was going to have to jump ship and make it all up as he went along.

The bus slowed as it reached the clogged arteries of the town, the engine groaning as it laboured up a hill.

Heather put her hand on Stanton's shoulder. "Is there anything I can do to help?"

"No," Stanton replied coldly and Heather sat back, deflated.

The bus carried on, the traffic easing slightly as it moved away from the centre, both of them sitting with their own thoughts, each locked in their own world of troubles, watching as passengers came and went, the holidaymakers being replaced by the shoppers, the shoppers replaced with the locals.

The train station was approaching. It was a small, end-of-line stop but the only way out of town unless you had access to a car or to money, and right now Stanton had neither. He could see it coming up on the right as the bus began to slow. Pulling himself up quickly, he waited for the driver to come to a stop so he could jump off and get away, planning to not even speak or look back at Heather. She would understand, it was for the best.

Stanton's eyes remained focused on the bus doors, waiting for the moment the driver opened them, coiled like a spring so that he would be down the aisle and outside before anyone had noticed.

The doors finally folded open, but before Stanton could even begin to run, he felt something pulling him back by his jacket. Turning, he saw Heather had hold of it and was pointing with widened eyes for him to look outside.

They were already there. They'd second-guessed his plan and were at the station waiting for him. A smaller group, different from those he'd encountered at the pier, but it was obvious they'd been sent there to wait. The moment he stepped off the bus he would be, as he had repeatedly been told, a dead man walking.

"Quick get down, here," said Heather, pointing to the floor in front of her. One of the thugs outside was already peering in through the bus windows. He had no choice; Stanton quickly dove down on the floor and hid at Heather's feet. They were looking for him, they wouldn't be looking for her.

The driver closed the doors and the bus pulled slowly away. As her window passed the man outside, Heather fixed her eyes dead ahead, feeling the man's gaze on the side of her face as the bus seemed to take forever to accelerate away.

"It's okay, you can get up now," she said, as soon as the coast was clear.

Stanton got to his feet, stooping to peer gingerly through the back window. Resting his head on the back of the seat in front, it all seemed so hopeless to him. He was cornered, on his own, and no one would risk even being seen with him. Mickey was right. He was damaged goods. He wondered if he could simply try to walk out of town, but then again that would only leave him out in the open and vulnerable. It didn't matter how many times he scrutinised the puzzle, or how many times he turned the problem around in his head, no easy solution presented itself. There was still the issue of money and the fact he didn't have any. That had to be where he started getting things right.

Stanton puffed out his cheeks as the bus carried on its journey.

"That was close," said Heather. "Were you planning on getting off there?"

"I don't know what I'm doing. Thanks, though, you saved me. I hadn't seen them there."

Heather smiled. "We're evens now, we've saved each other." Without thinking, she laid her head on his arm.

Ten minutes later, they stepped off the bus and into an unfamiliar part of town. The vehicle disappeared off into the distance and Stanton went and sat on a garden wall, while Heather loitered nearby.

"Do you want me to go?" she asked. "If you've had enough of me, I'll understand."

"I'm in deep shit. That bloke called Sonny, he's nothing but trouble, these people chasing us work for him and they aren't going away. You're in danger just by being here. So I'm leaving."

"Leaving? Going home?"

"No, leaving town."

Heather tried to mask the shock on her face. "Leaving town? When?"

"Now."

"Now, this minute?"

"Well, today, later tonight probably."

"Today? But—"

"—So if you want to go, go. I'll be fine on my own. In fact, it might be better if you do."

"But I don't want to go. I don't, James. I don't want to go home ever, and I don't want you to go either."

She was too tired to try to stop the tear that ran down her cheek.

They hadn't known each other a week ago. Even today they were as good as strangers, though somehow each was deeply mired in the other's life, while feeling without saying, that the other was the only friend either of them had right now.

"I need to get some money."

"I'm sorry, I don't have any."

"I didn't mean it like that. I need to get well away from here and I'm going to need proper money, not pocket money."

"How much do you need?"

Stanton ran through the numbers once again in his head.

"A couple of hundred quid, maybe more."

Heather went and sat on the wall with him. "Two hundred pounds? How are you going to get hold of that much money?"

Stanton didn't see the point in beating around the bush.

"I'm going to steal it."

He held her gaze while Heather hardly blinked. It might sound like madness, but the whole week had been madness when set against the beige and boring life she had lived up until now.

"This man, the one chasing you, Sammy?"

"Sonny."

"What a silly name. Why don't we go and see him? If you don't know what he wants, let's go and find out."

Stanton had already worked his way through that option. Mickey was right again, it would only end up with him in a hospital bed, or worse.

"Nah, I'm getting out. Anyway, this place is a shithole, it's just the excuse I need to go. If I don't go now, I never will."

Those words could as easily have come from Heather's mouth as his, and she put her hand on his arm.

"Okay, then, I'll help you."

Stanton frowned. "Help?"

"Yes, help. I'm here now and I'm not going to leave you on your own. Besides, you've helped me more than you know, and I want to, I really do."

Stanton wasn't sure what Heather was saying, he didn't think he had done anything for her, or for anyone.

He got back to his feet. "C'mon. Let's get moving."

For the next twenty minutes, they made their way through the side streets and backstreets of town, walking and talking as they went, Stanton filling in the gaps for Heather, although he didn't know much more than she did. But he began to feel a little better, unburdening himself of all the problems that had been building up.

"Over here," he said, jogging across the road to a phone box.

He ordered Heather to wait outside as he pulled the heavy door open. Inside, it stank of piss. One of the windows was broken, and there was graffiti daubed everywhere. But there wasn't time to be precious. Stanton punched in the number for The Smugglers. It was the same barmaid who'd answered his call the previous night and he waited again while she went to get Mickey.

"It's me," said Stanton.

There was a prolonged period of silence on the other end of the line.

"Where are you?" Mickey asked.

"Doesn't matter."

"It does fucking matter. It's all kicking off here and I thought I told you to get out of town?"

"I'm trying, I just need to get some money."

"Well, try fucking harder."

"Look Mickey, have you heard anything since last night?"

Stanton glanced out of the dirty window and waited for Mickey to answer. He could see Heather leaning against a wall, half in shadow and half out. The pause from Mickey seemed to be going on too long and it dragged Stanton back to reality. The other end of the line sounded muffled, as though someone had put their hand over the mouthpiece.

"When are you leaving?" said Mickey, his voice clear again.

"Today for sure."

"First sensible thing you've said. Is Roper with you?"

Stanton stopped in his tracks. There was no need for Mickey to ask that question. He tried to buy some time.

"Roper?"

"Yeah, or any of the others?"

Stanton looked again across at Heather.

"No, it's just me."

"Okay, come to the pub, I can give you some money."

Stanton's hopes lifted but then there came another pause, as though Mickey were speaking to someone. Stanton gripped the receiver hard. Mickey came back on the line.

"How are you going to get out of town?"

Stanton relaxed his grip. "I haven't fully worked it out, but—"

He stopped himself. Instinct told him something wasn't right. Ever so slowly, Stanton put the receiver down, the unused money clattering into the tray below. He quickly took the change out of the tray and re-fed the machine, before punching in another number.

"It's me," he said as Roper answered.

"Thank fuck, I thought you were dead."

Roper's calm voice went some way to soothing Stanton's troubled mind.

"I might still be. They got to Mickey."

"Mickey? You sure?"

"I don't know, maybe." He wasn't sure of anything anymore. "How's Bin Bag?"

"He'll live." Roper got straight to the point. "What d'you need me to do?"

With Roper's help, Stanton knew he stood a chance even if it was slim.

"I'm getting out of town later tonight but don't tell anyone, and I mean anyone. I need to get hold of some money. I know you haven't got any but even if you find a tenner, I'll take it."

"I'll try."

"Get the others together. Let's meet at the clock tower at seven."

"You sure?"

"Yeah, safety in numbers and all that. I'm going to try and get hold of some money before then."

"On your own?"

Stanton looked across at Heather.

"I'm not on my own."

"What happens if you can't get to the clock tower? Or we can't? I'm pretty sure they'll be looking for me as well."

That thought hadn't crossed Stanton's mind. Given how quickly everything was changing around him, he needed a back-up plan.

"Okay, where do you think, the pier?"

"Fuck that. That's a death trap. They're all over Kenny."

"Where, then?"

"Needs to be big, lots of open spaces and busy as fuck. Somewhere you can be invisible for a long time. Needs to be the fairground, Stanz."

Stanton swallowed hard. "Really?"

"Yeah, makes sense, everyone knows you, you know the layout. Just—"

Stanton didn't let him finish; he didn't want to hear what he might be about to say.

"—Okay, clock tower at seven. If not, fairground at eight."

He put the receiver in the cradle and went back outside.

"Come on then, we can't waste any time."

"Where are we going?" she called after him.

"You'll find out when we get there," Stanton said over his shoulder, without looking back.

THIRTY-ONE

Neither of them spoke much after that. They didn't need to.

Keep moving, stay where it's busy and find places where you have friends. The first two were easy, it was the latter that was proving more difficult.

Which is why going to the fairground made a lot of sense. If he could hide out there until the park closed at eleven o'clock, he was as good as safe. From there, it was a short jog to the train station, to catch the last train just before midnight. Once away, he'd be on easy street. He could sleep rough if he had to on the first night before catching another train to put him as far from this place as he could get. Then he would find somewhere to stay, get a job and just wait it out or keep moving; either way, he'd never set foot back in this rancid town again.

The only problem with this plan was that Stanton didn't want to go to the fairground.

"Is it much further?" asked Heather, interrupting his thoughts.

"Nope, we're here."

"Where's here?"

Stanton peered round the corner to check there were no police cars parked outside today.

"My house."

"Your house? Why are we going to your house? What are you doing?"

"Stop asking so many questions. I'm checking."

"Checking for what?"

"Checking for trouble. Come on, let's go."

They walked cautiously down the quiet street that was maybe too quiet. Reaching his front door Stanton stopped, swallowed hard and swore under his breath.

On the wooden boards that had replaced the broken window someone had daubed in red paint the words *Dead Man Walking*.

Stanton felt sick. The paint had run down the chipboard like blood and he put his fingers out to touch it, relieved to feel that it was dry. It meant they'd been and gone, but it also meant they could come back at any moment.

"Is this your house?" asked Heather. "Did they do that?"

Stanton opened the front door and pushed Heather through into the hallway. He expected Margaret to launch a verbal assault from the moment he walked through the door, and he wasn't disappointed.

"Jimmy! Jimmy, is that you? They've come back! Your friends! Get in here sharpish!"

Over Margaret's shouting, Stanton intimated that Heather should remain quiet and pointed for her to go upstairs.

Margaret shouted again. "Jimmy!"

Stanton watched Heather tiptoe up the stairs and go out of sight.

"I can't be having all this with my nerves, Jimmy. I'm calling the police!"

∿

Heather found herself alone at the top of the house, looking down at a threadbare carpet that had surely never seen a vacuum cleaner. She glanced through the bathroom door before walking down a narrow hallway and into a bedroom.

Stanton's room.

The carpet in here wasn't any cleaner. The bed was unmade and the sheets needed a wash. On the bedside table sat numerous mugs filled with cold, half-drunk tea, discarded cigarette butts floating in them like dead bodies out at sea.

Heather scanned the room. There was a wardrobe, its door hung limply open, and a table with a fancy-looking music centre on. Other than a chair tucked under the table, there wasn't much else in the sparse and cold room. Aesthetically bereft, purely functional – a dented pillow the only real sign that a human ever came in here. Hearing raised voices coming up through the floorboards, Heather knelt and tilted her ear to the ground to see if she could make out what was being said. The sound was too muffled. She stood back up and wiped the dust and dirt from her hands. The room made her feel sad. There wasn't anything that showed this boy cared about anything, or that anyone cared about him.

Pushing the door of the wardrobe shut Heather looked at herself in the mirror, her image distorted by a smear on the glass. Picking up a discarded t-shirt that had been thrown carelessly on the floor, she carefully rubbed the mirror clean before sitting down at the table, which was as messy and untidy as the rest of the room. Records sat alongside empty beer cans which had been used as ashtrays, and pencil shavings had been pushed into a pile. Heather made a token effort to tidy up and, as she did, noticed some drawings pressed between an album cover. Carefully taking them out she examined them in detail, not quite believing she was holding in her hands very intricate pencil sketches of the musicians whose faces adorned the albums they were copied from. They had been drawn with such care and attention it gave them a likeness that was so real they almost looked like photographs. Browsing through some other albums, she found a drawing inside each one.

"What are you doing?"

Stanton had appeared in the doorway, holding two mugs of tea. His words had an edge to them, a danger even; they made Heather jump and she quickly dropped the drawings.

"I'm sorry. I was just, they're very good. I'm sorry…"

Stanton broke into a grin and gave her a mug of tea. "Here, it's the best cuppa you've had this week."

He carefully put the drawings back in their place.

"It's just some stupid stuff I do."

"They're not stupid at all, they're fantastic, you're very talented. I can't draw anything, and when I do it looks like a dog has drawn it. These are brilliant, James. You should become an artist and then you can draw me."

Stanton sat on his bed and sipped from his mug. "People like me don't become proper artists."

"Don't say that. You're very talented. I'm sure you could be whatever you wanted if you put your mind to it."

He got off the bed and went and stood by the window to check the road was clear.

"Was that your mum downstairs?"

"Yeah."

"She okay? She seemed angry about something."

"She's always angry about something. She'll be fine. I've taken her a bottle in. She's probably already asleep."

Looking up and down the street as far as he could, Stanton thought about what Margaret had said. Even his home wasn't safe. They'd come back, banging on the chipboard, demanding his whereabouts. They hadn't stayed long and Margaret hadn't called the police, but it had clearly upset her and convinced

Stanton, if he needed more convincing, that he had to get as far away from here as he could.

Keep moving.

"Shift," he said to Heather, who got up quickly and moved to the other side of the room. Stanton moved the chair closer to the wardrobe so that he could reach and pull a bag from the top, which he threw down on the floor.

"So you really are going?"

"Not got much choice."

He started to throw random things into the bag without much thought while moving around the small bedroom. Heather kept getting in his way.

"Look, just stand over there, will you?" he said, immediately regretting the outburst. Heather didn't deserve to be shouted at like that. She'd been the most constant and reliable thing in his life lately.

Dropping the bag on the floor, he sat heavily on his bed. "Sorry," he mumbled contritely.

Heather knelt in front of him. "You need my help, whether you like it or not. Sooner you get some money, sooner you can get going, right?"

Stanton nodded.

"Right now, you don't have any money at all?"

Stanton shook his head.

"So let's go and get it. You steal it, I'll be the look-out."

Stanton scoffed. "I can't ask you to do that, this is my problem, not yours."

"Well, let's make it our problem. Come on, teamwork and all that, two heads better than one."

Standing up, Heather walked purposefully to the door and waited.

Stanton knew she was right despite his faux protestations. He needed money and he didn't have time, two heads must be better than one. Picking up his bag, he joined Heather at the door and took one last look around the room.

"Let's go," he said, manoeuvring her out.

Heather carefully made her way down the steep narrow staircase, but when she reached the bottom she turned to see Stanton was still upstairs.

"Wait there," he said.

Going back into his bedroom, he removed one of his favourite drawings from an album, folded it in half and put it in his bag. Next he went to his bedside table and located the money he'd taken from Margaret, stuffing it into the pockets of his jeans. Finally, he dropped to his knees and looked under the bed, stretching his hand out as far as he could before carefully sliding out the gun Mickey had given him. Stanton unwrapped the cloth and slowly turned the gun in his hands. He didn't think he was capable of shooting anyone, but yesterday he didn't think he would be having to leave town either. He put the gun in his bag and covered it up.

He was about to head back downstairs when he saw something on the shelf above the desk. It was the pencil sharpener in the shape of a Roman villa, the one he had stolen all those years ago. He was never sure why he kept it, perhaps as a reminder of a more innocent time, a more innocent Stanton, before life had really got its claws into him. He dropped the pencil sharpener in his bag and took one last look around his bedroom before softly closing the door and moving quickly downstairs.

Checking there was no one outside, he ushered Heather out onto the street and was about to close the door behind him when he stopped.

"Wait here," he said to Heather as he disappeared back inside.

Stanton listened in at Margaret's door before gently pushing it open. She was laid propped up on pillows, her head slightly to one side, arm splayed out. Nearby, an empty glass lay on the bed just out of reach of her fingertips. Momentarily, he actually thought she might be dead, but her sleep apnoea arrived just in time for her to gasp and take a deep breath before letting it out with a long, mumbling sigh.

Stanton picked up the glass and put it on her bed-side table. He then gently pulled the bedclothes up and over her arm and chest, carefully tucking them in at the side. Margaret rasped her gin-heavy breath in and out of her half-opened mouth like a death rattle.

"Daft old bag," Stanton said with half a smile on his face.

He dug his hands in his pockets, took out the money and put it back in the drawer. He didn't know when he'd be back and without him, Margaret would be on her own. This was his problem, not hers. A few days ago he wouldn't have thought twice about taking all the money, let alone putting back what he'd taken.

Without looking back, he closed the bedroom door behind him and went back outside to where Heather waited patiently.

THIRTY-TWO

They moved quickly away from the house, Stanton refusing to look back. He didn't need to. He didn't want to read those words written in blood-red paint where the window had been. He marched the two of them down ever quieter backstreets, explaining what he needed Heather to do, before spotting up ahead what he was looking for.

"This will have to do," he said, holding Heather back and stopping.

"I don't think I've ever done so much exercise," said Heather, sitting down and leaning against a wall.

"Well, don't relax too much, we've got work to do."

It was late afternoon as they both breathed deeply, hearts racing.

Heather grinned. "If my mum and dad knew what I was doing, I'd be in so much trouble."

"Do you care?" Stanton asked, pointedly.

"No, not really."

"Good, because things are about to get a whole lot worse."

Stanton looked through the bag.

"What do you mean, worse? How can it get worse? We're on the run!"

Stanton turned around, having tied a red bandana around his face.

Heather tried not to laugh. "You look like a cowboy."

"Would you recognise me?"

"Yes."

"Tough. I need to get this money. There's a newsagent's over there. This is your chance to get out while you can, there's no going back after this. If you want to go, now's the time. I won't ask you again."

Heather knew she didn't need any second chances and spoke with an assertiveness and confidence she didn't know she possessed. "I'll stay with you until you get on that train. I made a promise to myself to help you. There's no point me going back home right now, so I may as well make it worse before I do."

Stanton's eyes smiled behind the mask.

"Okay, wait here, you're in charge of the bag. Start running that way when you see me coming back around that corner. When I come back this way, I won't be hanging around."

"Okay," said Heather, picking up the bag and gripping it tightly.

Stanton wasn't lying when he said he wouldn't be hanging around, setting off across the road without looking and dashing straight through the shop door without knowing what or who was going to be in there. He was on his own and was just going to have to make it up as he went along.

Inside there was a lady behind the counter, but no one else.

Stanton advanced quickly towards her. "Give me your money!" he shouted.

The woman behind the counter just looked at him and it threw Stanton off guard.

"Did you hear me? I said, give me all the money in the till."

"Sorry, love, I can't hear you with that hanky on your face."

"What?" Stanton said, frowning.

She pointed to her ears. "Can't hear you, love. You're mumbling and I'm a bit hard of hearing."

Only then did Stanton notice her hearing aid.

"For fuck's sake," he said under his breath. He'd hoped to be on his way out of the shop by now, but he was still here and wondering whether anyone had held up a shop using sign language.

A door opened behind the counter and another woman appeared.

"What's all the noise about?"

"This lad here, Kath, I think he wants all our money although I can't hear him very well."

"Is that right? Well, we'll have to see about that," said the other woman, grabbing a heavy stick from behind the counter.

Stanton had seen enough and sprinted back out of the shop.

On the other side of the road Heather saw him running toward her at full speed, the bandana now in his hand.

"Leg it!" he shouted as he grabbed the bag from her. "For fuck's sake, come on!"

There wasn't time to ask any questions as Heather watched Stanton disappearing in the distance, clearly not stopping for anyone.

THIRTY-THREE

HE NEEDED TO RETHINK EVERYTHING AGAIN. THERE JUST WASN'T any time for failure. Stanton took out his cigarettes and lighter, taking one for himself, before offering them to Heather.

"What happened? How much did you get?" Heather asked, still getting her breath back.

"Nothing."

"Nothing?"

She cautiously took a cigarette and put it between her lips while Stanton moved closer and used the end of his to light the end of hers. Holding his gaze she slowly inhaled, coughing slightly but not as much as before.

Stanton laughed. "Easy when you know how."

Heather took another drag of the cigarette. "What now?"

Stanton looked over the road at a woman pruning flowers in her garden who was paying close attention to them.

Keep moving.

"Come on, let's go."

Swinging the bag over his shoulder, he took a final lungful of smoke before arrogantly flicking the cigarette in the direction of the woman. They set off down the street side by side, staying in the shade as the late afternoon sun burned hot.

They soon found another target, another quiet corner shop on yet another deserted street. If he didn't get this right, it would be the third robbery in a row to fail. That was unheard of in Stanton's world and he would soon start to question if he was losing his touch. There was no room for error, in an hour or so most of these shops would close for the night.

Stanton tied the bandana around his neck.

"Isn't this all a bit risky?" asked Heather. "I thought you were trying to lay low. What if the last one rang the police?"

Stanton had been wondering that himself. It was possible the women in the shop had called the police, but he doubted it. No one had got hurt and they were probably still too busy laughing at him to bother. This might be the last chance he was going to get; he wasn't going to make the same mistake twice.

"It'll be okay," he said, after a while. "Same as before. I'll take the bag with me this time and get us some food, I'm starving. Wait for me to come out, then whichever way I run, put your head down and follow me. Got it?"

Heather nodded and Stanton pulled the bandana up over his face before turning and crossing the road. When he was sure Heather couldn't see what he was doing, he reached into the bag and pulled out the gun and jammed it into his waistband. He was leaving here with some money and nothing was going to stop him.

Stanton actually recognised the shop he was approaching. He had bought cigarettes here, but not recently enough for anyone to remember him. Jogging the last few yards, he went inside.

The shop looked different from how he remembered. There

was shelving that ran down the middle with groceries stacked on both sides, a chiller for drinks, a wall full of magazines and papers – and at the back, the counter and till.

Stanton went straight to counter, where an elderly man was filling in some paperwork. He looked up and saw a gun being pointed directly at him.

Stanton got straight to the point. "Open that fucking till!"

The shopkeeper stepped back in shock and was about to do as he was told when his wife stood up from behind the counter with a bundle of newspapers in her arms.

Stanton swore under his breath. This was the last thing he needed.

Then, from behind, a voice. "What's going on?"

Stanton spun round. Someone had entered the shop and was now standing between him and the door. In the time that this was all happening the shopkeeper and his wife moved quickly into the back, locking the door behind them as they went.

Another of Stanton's plans was unravelling before his eyes, it felt as though someone had put a curse on him. But he couldn't fail, not this time, and so he lifted the gun and pointed it at the man behind him.

"Got any money?"

"No, only a fiver, I was about to pay for the papers. Please, that's all I've got." The man held a sweaty five pound note out to Stanton.

"Five quid, is that it?"

The man nodded and a desperate Stanton snatched the money. "Tell anyone about this, I'll find you and pay a visit. Got it?"

By this time tomorrow, he planned on being far away, but this man didn't know that and he took the hint and ran back out of the shop.

Stanton put the gun back into the bag and went behind the

counter. Thankfully, in the haste to escape, somehow the shopkeeper had left the till open – and it was full of money, practically a week's worth of takings. Finally, Stanton was on the receiving end of some good fortune. He grabbed whatever he could and stuffed it into his pockets, some notes fluttering to the floor but he was convinced he had enough; he didn't need to worry about a few lost pounds. Grabbing a couple of boxes of cigarettes and something to drink and eat, he stashed everything in the bag.

He was just about to leave, when he stopped.

In the distance, he could hear the unmistakeable sound of a siren and he had heard enough over the years to know that it was the police. It might not be for him, but the way things were going, he guessed it probably was.

He dropped his shoulders. The repetition of heightened expectation followed by utter disappointment was becoming exhausting. Stanton had the money, he had the bag, he had the gun. But he didn't have Heather and he wanted it all. He sprinted to the door and looked across at her.

She pointed. "James, they're coming down the road!"

At the far end of the street, he could see a police car travelling toward them. But they were in luck, another car going in the opposite direction had inadvertently blocked the narrow road. The police car couldn't get past. But a policeman could and Stanton watched as one got out and started running.

"Come on, James, hurry!" pleaded Heather from across the street.

Stanton ran towards her, grabbing her roughly by the hand and pulling her in the opposite direction, away from the police.

"Now where are we going? We can't keep running," Heather shouted from behind.

"We can, and you'll find out when we get there!"

THIRTY-FOUR

THEY CRISS-CROSSED SIDE STREETS, DOUBLE BACKING ON themselves, running where possible down alleys too narrow for cars to follow and always looking behind. Sometimes they ran fast, sometimes they jogged, often they slowed to a walk when they tired. But Stanton made sure they were always moving. The noise from the sirens diminished over time before finally disappearing altogether, to be replaced with the sound of birds singing on just another normal summer's day.

"Through here." Stanton pushed Heather through a school gate before running again, this time across a playground. They skirted the single-storey building and climbed up a small grassy bank to a wooden fence at the back. Stanton tested a couple of planks before finding the loose one he was looking for, forcing it to one side and leaving a gap just big enough for a person to get through.

"Go on," he ordered Heather.

"Through there?"

"Yes, get a move on."

Heather got down and crawled through, brushing the dirt

from her hands when she stood up on the other side. She looked around and found herself standing in a graveyard.

"Here, take this."

Stanton was handing her the bag through the gap. She pulled it through and waited for him to join her.

"Well, this is glamorous," she joked as his head appeared through the fence. "This where you bring your girlfriends? A dirty old graveyard?"

"Something like that," he replied, standing up.

"So, what is this place?"

"Well, that's a church, that is my old primary school," he pointed behind her, "and that's someone's grave you're standing on."

Heather moved uneasily off the overgrown grave beneath her feet while Stanton lifted his grubby t-shirt over his head. Heather looked away embarrassed while he put a clean one on.

"Here," he said, taking some crisps and bottles of drink out of the bag.

"Thank you."

They sat together on a raised grave, safe for the moment in this secluded corner of the churchyard as the sun drizzled haphazardly through the canopy of leaves thrown over them by a large oak tree. Stanton picked up a twig, absently snapping it in half and throwing a piece away. Standing up, he took the money out of his pockets and counted the notes.

"I've never seen so much money. Is that enough?" Heather asked.

"Almost £250," Stanton replied, zipping the wad of cash safely back in the bag. "Look," he said, turning to Heather. "This has probably gone too far for you."

"Is that a statement or a question?"

Not knowing the difference, Stanton carried on. "You're in trouble just by being here. With school, your mum and dad, now the police. It's too much for you. This is my life; I'm used to it. You don't need this."

Heather put down her drink. "I know all that, silly. I've had plenty of time to think while running around town with you."

Playfully, she tapped Stanton's leg. "We're like Bonnie and Clyde."

"Who?"

"It doesn't matter."

The grave they were sitting on was covered in moss, its headstone leaning heavily to one side, shoved and heaved over the years by the roots of the tree whose shade they were now resting beneath.

"Can we just stay here?" Heather asked, only half joking.

Stanton sat back down and opened a packet of crisps, devouring them noisily as they both recovered from the recent drama.

"That was so exciting earlier, the shop and the running."

"Not really. You get used to it. I always seem to be running," replied Stanton, throwing the empty crisp packet on the floor. Heather looked disapprovingly at him and he picked it up and put it in the bag.

Standing up, Heather peered through the branches and leaves. "Have you been in that church?"

"I don't like churches."

"I do. What do you think happens to us when we die?"

Stanton looked up from eating a bar of chocolate. "What?"

"What do you think happens to us? Is this it, or is there something else?"

He shook his head and laughed.

"No seriously, what about him for example?"

Heather pointed to the grave they had been sitting on. "Gabriel, Gabriel something, I can't read it."

Bending down, she brushed some twigs and leaves away.

"Gabriel Light something." She dusted some more. "Gabriel Lightfoot!"

"That's a stupid name."

"It's a lovely name. Gabriel Lightfoot. He wasn't that old. He was only forty-six."

"Forty-six is ancient, I'll probably be dead by then."

"Don't you dare say such things, James Stanton. You're going to become a brilliant and famous artist."

He laughed gently. "Is that right? Well, I won't if I don't get moving. I might end up dead today for all I know."

Heather knelt down. "Please don't say that. You've got the money now. You're free. When do you think you'll come back?"

Stanton shrugged.

"What about your mum?"

"Nah, I'm leaving her here. She's only got one leg, she'll only slow me down."

It was the moment they both needed to release some of the tension, the pressure leaving their bodies as they laughed and thought about Margaret escaping as well.

Stanton reached in the bag for the cigarettes, this time passing one to Heather without asking, and she took it without hesitation.

"Are we allowed to smoke in a graveyard? We might not get into heaven."

Stanton lit their cigarettes. "That's the last place I'll be going, so I don't care."

"So how do you know about this place? What made you come here?"

"I only remembered it earlier. Loosened those planks myself years ago when I'd had enough, when I needed to get away from them in there. I'd sneak through like we did and just sit here on my own. No one knew I was here. They'd stop looking for me after about ten minutes. No one cared where I was. Probably more pleased to see me gone. But that place did me wrong and I fucking hate it even now. It's all their fault."

He stood up on the grave and looked over at the school. The top of the building was about twenty yards away and just visible above the fence. Picking up a stone, he threw it angrily at the place he hated the most, before grabbing another and stepping back up onto the grave again. Leaning back, he aimed at some of the windows at the top of the building. He missed, but only just. He picked up another stone and threw it towards the school, this time succeeding as they heard a satisfying tinkle of broken glass.

"Fancy a go?" he said to Heather, handing her a stone. "You can pretend this is your school as well."

Giggling, she stepped up onto the grave next to Stanton.

"Fucking perverts, the lot of them," he shouted as he threw another stone that bounced harmlessly off the brickwork.

"Yeah, have that!" Heather shouted as she threw her stone, only just missing one of the windows.

"Fucking perverts!" Stanton shouted, throwing again.

"Perverts!" Heather shouted, throwing, missing and laughing.

"You don't swear enough. You need to swear more. Try it, it might help your aim. Fucking perverts!" he yelled, and launched another missile at the school

Heather was laughing so hard, her sides were beginning to ache. She leaned back and let go of her stone.

"Fucking perverts!" she shouted. They both watched it sail over the fence and heard the sound of breaking glass.

"Bullseye! Told you, it's why you're called Rambo."

"I *am* Rambo!"

They carried on until there were no more stones to throw and no more windows to break, laughing in the twilight of sun and shade, both momentarily unburdened from their troubles.

Afterwards, they sat snapping twigs, enjoying the solitude, the church trees draped protectively over them.

But Stanton knew this peaceful calm could not last. He jumped back up on the grave to peer through the leaves at the church clock.

6.45 p.m.

Keep moving.

He stepped back down and picked up his bag.

"Come on then, if you're coming."

"Where're we going this time?"

Find places where you have friends.

"To meet Roper and the others."

"And then?"

Stay where it's busy.

But he was already gone, walking off ahead through the graves and trees.

THIRTY-FIVE

THE GANG LOUNGED BORED AND LISTLESS BENEATH THE CLOCK tower as the hands nudged seven o'clock, Roper nursing a bag full of cans of cheap lager, the girls sitting slightly apart, while Jez hovered, his nervousness annoying everyone. The only person missing was Bin Bag, and the mood among the group was dour and strained.

"So where's Stanz?" Jez asked.

"Just shut up, will you," Roper replied.

Jez went and sulked on the bench. "You said he'd be here. Everything seems to be turning to shit and no one knows where he is."

"Yeah come on, what's going on?" Sally broke in. "Why all the secrecy? Bin Bag gets a kicking, Stanz disappears, you're not saying anything. Something's obviously going down. Want to go to the pier, Kat?"

Roper had had enough of their whinging. "No one's going anywhere until I say so."

Jez looked down the promenade and watched as a police car pulled up. Two men got out and started heading their way. "Oh shit, looks like trouble."

Roper pushed the cans under the bench. "It's only Armstrong, he won't know anything. Just stop pissing yourselves and keep your mouths shut."

The shabbily dressed detective in an ill-fitting suit with a hint of lunch on one of the lapels ambled over to the benches, a youthful policeman adjusting his helmet as he followed.

"Evening lads," said Armstrong, putting his hands in his pockets and rocking on his heels.

"And ladies," Sally muttered.

Armstrong looked down at her. "If you say so, love. Where's your leader tonight, then? Not gracing you with his presence?"

Roper was the only one to look directly back at him, although they all remained steadfastly quiet.

Armstrong persevered. "Oh, come on. Stanton not coming out to play?"

"Not heard from him, *officer*," Roper said, making sure to use the last word as patronisingly as he could and knowing full well it would rile Armstrong.

"That right? And it's Detective to you, shit for brains. Well, what a shame because it seems your leader has been running around town all afternoon, causing nothing but trouble. So where is he? Any ideas? Perhaps he's gone home for a nap. What d'you reckon? Mind you, we've been to his house and it looks like someone got there before we did."

He was met with more silence

Armstrong took out a handkerchief from his pocket and used it to wipe the sweat off his forehead, mumbling, "too warm for this bollocks."

He was meant to be going on holiday tomorrow. He sighed heavily. "Like I said, he's had a jam-packed day. There's been a spate of robberies around town. Even talk of guns." Pausing to look directly in their faces, he hoped to see some sort of knowledge or guilt reflected in their eyes. But there was nothing.

Roper was curious. "A gun?"

"That's right, Mr Muscles, a gun. Whoever that bird is he's with, they are both running aro—"

Sally looked up sharply. "—Which girl?"

Armstrong looked at her and grinned, his instincts never failed him. "Well it's not you, love, he must have got a better offer. You know anything about this girl he's with?"

Sally went back to staring at the floor.

"Shame. So you're all saying you don't know anything about any of this? Look, just between us, I can't be bothered with any of this myself. Unfortunately, it's my job to be bothered. So when you see him next, you can tell him from me that we're on to him, okay? And if any of you want to have a rumble, you can have one with me down the station and there won't be any witnesses to that either, no one would have seen a thing. Do I make myself clear?"

Those on the bench offered up a collective silence.

"I *said*, do I make myself clear?"

They all mumbled an acknowledgement of sorts.

"Good. Now, if I can suggest you get yourself off home and have an early night. Maybe cuddle up with your teddies and cry yourself to sleep? Maybe wash what's left of your hair?" The last line he directed at the girls.

"Oh, and Mr Muscles, can I suggest you tip that beer down the drain? Otherwise, I'll be back down here again and trust me, next time I won't be in such a good mood."

While Armstrong was talking, Roper was looking over his shoulder in disbelief. He started to rise slowly off the bench, his mouth hanging open.

∽

Stanton and Heather were crossing the road, Stanton's nerves once more on edge as the feeling of being out in the open began to overwhelm him. But, as the afternoon turned into evening, at least he was still alive. The horror he'd felt on the jetty earlier that morning when he'd first caught sight of the enemy felt like a long time ago.

The promenade was rammed with people out for the evening, so neither Stanton nor Heather had seen the police car parked by the clock tower which they were now walking directly towards. Only when he saw Roper rising from the bench with a look of alarm on his face did Stanton sense something was wrong. Sally had also risen off the bench but her eyes were firmly set on Heather. It was then that Stanton noticed the police car as well as Armstrong looking in his direction.

Roper shouted, "Run Stanz, leg it!"

Armstrong was a few seconds behind the action, but now he too spotted Stanton. "You! Stay right where you are!" he bellowed at the tall youth with the shaven head standing out amongst the meandering crowds.

Armstrong had been the bane of Stanton's life and now there he was, standing at the clock tower at the exact same time he had planned to be there. Stanton could feel the noose tighten. This town sure had it in for him.

He turned to Heather and, not for the first time that day, shouted at her to start running as he violently made a path for them back through the thick and heaving crowd.

They crossed back over the road and headed the way they had just come, dashing down a side street and running through the shopping precinct. Stanton wasn't sure where he was leading them, but they somehow ended up in a deserted courtyard behind the library.

It was a dead end, but quiet and away from prying eyes.

Stanton told Heather to wait there as he doubled back to check there was no one behind them.

Heather collapsed to the floor and leaned against the library wall. Stanton slid down the brickwork to join her.

"Please don't make me run anymore," she murmured.

"Don't worry, no one's ever seen Armstrong run. Fat git wouldn't have made it across the road."

"Do you promise you'll keep in touch? Maybe send me a postcard?"

Stanton laughed at the thought. "You wouldn't be able to read my writing. I wasn't very good at all that school stuff."

"I could write to you, then?"

"I can't read very well, either."

He looked away, embarrassed.

"Okay, how about this. When you come back, I'll help you with both."

"If I come back."

"Alright, *if* you come back? And in return you can teach me to draw. Deal?" Heather held out her hand for him to shake.

"Sure," he said, smiling and shaking her hand. "I'll also help beat up all the blokes that keep letting you down."

"We'll both be busy, then. I'm thirsty, is there anything left to drink?"

"Hang on." Stanton rummaged through the bag. "I thought there was one left. I'll get you something when we get there."

Heather frowned. "Get where?"

"The fairground," he replied, zipping up the bag again.

Heather's throat tightened. "The fairground?"

"Yeah, we made a back-up plan just in case, we'll meet them there in about an hour." He closed his eyes and leant his head back on the wall.

"Do we have to go? I don't like fairgrounds."

"You don't have to but I do. Besides, who doesn't like fairgrounds?"

Stanton closed his eyes, he wanted to use the time between now and meeting the others to get his thinking straight. Despite the run of bad luck, he was beginning to think he was actually getting somewhere. Time was his enemy and the more of it he killed, the longer he lived. Once they arrived at the fairground it would be 8 o'clock and there would be only a few hours left to keep out of harm's way. That and the money might just be enough to give him a chance.

In the distance, screams from the roller coaster as it soared into the air drifted on a gentle breeze, its illuminations starting to shine brighter in the darkening dusk sky.

SATURDAY EVENING

THIRTY-SIX

OTHER THAN FOR THEIR SURLINESS, ARMSTRONG HAD NOTHING with which he could detain the gang. Instead, he let them go with a few barbed comments ringing in their ears, releasing them back out in the wild as bait.

Having split up to give the impression they were going their separate ways, the gang soon made it to the fairground. They stood nervously under its shadow by the main entrance, their mood having darkened since they'd left the clock tower. Everything felt different. Yesterday, under the pier, life had seemed fun and exciting. Now, one of them had been beaten to a pulp and their leader, when it mattered the most, was absent.

"He's late again," said Jez anxiously, his nervous energy all but spent.

"No he's not." Roper nodded his head towards Stanton and Heather appearing out of the crowd.

"Stanz!"

"Shut up dickhead, keep your voice down."

Sally chewed her gum furiously as she watched Heather approach. "Nice of you both to finally turn up." She spotted the bag. "Going anywhere nice, Stanz?"

Stanton didn't have time for pettiness. He'd been out of the loop since he'd rung Roper from the phone box and he needed to know what he didn't know. He moved his friend off to the side.

"Kenny?"

"All good. He'll be here later with some of his lads. Said he'd shut the pier a bit earlier and get here for closing just in case he's needed. Mentioned they had two people outside the pier all day keeping an eye."

"What about Armstrong?"

"Usual, still doesn't know his arse from his elbow. Wouldn't worry about him, told him I knew fuck all, although sounds like he'll be out looking for you tonight as well."

"Yeah well, I've always been popular. Anything from Mickey?"

"Nothing direct but he rang the house, left a message asking me to go to the office, said he had something for me."

Stanton spat on the floor at Mickey's obvious betrayal. They continued talking in conspiratorial whispers, their heads so close they were almost touching.

While the boys were distracted, Sally went to stand with Heather. She looked the younger girl directly in the eyes, speaking quietly but with menace. "See you didn't get the message yesterday. You chose to hang around, then?"

"Yes, that's right, I did."

Sally's eyes twitched as they narrowed in on Heather's face. "Don't say I didn't warn you."

Stanton and Roper rejoined the group.

"Let's get inside, it'll be safer." Stanton watched the others go in but Heather held back.

"I thought we were just meeting here, not actually going in?"

"We'll catch you up," Stanton shouted to Roper before turning back to Heather.

"It's the only place that's big enough for me to hide for a while, they won't think to come here, there are plenty of other places they'll be looking for me. Why, what's wrong?"

"I don't, I just, I just can't," she stammered, looking up at the sign over the entrance to the park.

Stanton wasn't sure what she was saying.

"Look, I can't mess around. It's dangerous for me out here, you've seen that today for yourself. Are you coming or not? I need to get inside. If you want to go home, that's fine. When I get back, I'll come and find you, I promise."

"If you come back."

"I'll be back. I think you'd miss me too much."

"Perhaps you'll miss me?"

"Unlikely."

Heather looked at the boy she had grown close to. She didn't want to go home ever, not just tonight. They'd been through so much and to lose it all now seemed pointless.

"I don't want to go home, James, but I'm scared."

"So am I, and if you tell anyone I said that I'll beat you up. But I'll look after you. I've told you enough times today."

"Promise you'll stay with me in there?"

He put his arm protectively around her shoulder.

"I promise. Besides, after the day we've had, we could do with some fun."

They walked together under the sign and into the fairground. It was already busy, the excitement already building. The whole town once again coming to life at the same time, the same place, every Saturday night in the summer, as it had for years.

It was the safest Stanton had felt all day.

THIRTY-SEVEN

THE FAIRGROUND WAS A FAMILIAR PLACE WITH FAMILIAR FACES and most of the two summer seasons Stanton had worked there were the best days of his life. Tonight the park was rammed, everyone there to squeeze as much fun, laughter and screams as they could out of the evening. It was exactly what he needed and he began to relax as they made their way through the heavy crowds.

They caught up with the others by the dodgems.

"You okay?" Stanton asked Heather quietly as they got closer.

"Just don't leave me, please. I'll stay with you until you get on that train, just don't leave me."

The bumper cars ground to a halt.

"Come on. We're on!"

Roper jumped in with Kat, while Jez ran aimlessly around trying to find an empty one. He noticed Sally was sitting in a car on her own and went to get in.

"You can piss off, Jez."

"Come on, move over."

"I said, piss off."

Sally could see Stanton stood at the perimeter talking to the ride operator and shouted over to him. "Oi, Stanz! Come on, I've got us one."

Jez tried again to take his place in the car, much to Sally's annoyance.

"Seriously, piss off, Jez, I won't tell you again. Stanz is getting in this one."

She looked over to see what was holding Stanton up, but he was still talking to someone.

She tried calling him again, only this time louder, then watched in disbelief as he and Heather got into an empty car together. He must have heard her calling, he wasn't that far away. Sally could see both of them laughing, no doubt laughing at her.

Jez was still standing by the car. "So, are you letting me in?"

Sally didn't have any excuse to say no, so he clambered into her car. It was the last space left, as all the cars were full. The excitement levels rose as people waited for the ride to start.

"Ready?" Stanton asked Heather.

"Ready!"

A voice came over the speakers.

"Stay in the car at all times. If you get stuck, please stay where you are, someone will come and help you. Okay, boys and girls hereeee we goooo!"

The operator in the control booth turned up the music, the electricity crackled in the metal grate roof, and slowly the cars all began to move. It wasn't long before there was a mixture of chaos and exhilaration. Cool and confident, Stanton was driving one-handed with his other arm draped over the back of the seats so that, from a distance, through jealous eyes, it looked as though his arm was around Heather.

"Look out!" Heather shouted, as they were hit hard from the side.

"Watch out!" she yelled again, as he turned the wheel with

Roper bearing down on them. Stanton only just managed to get their car out of the way in time.

"You're good!" shouted Heather above the music.

"All those cars I've nicked over the years."

Roper swore, his laugh disappearing as they swerved away.

"Got to be quicker than that!" Stanton shouted.

For a few minutes, all of Stanton and Heather's problems went away. There wasn't any spare time to think, no gaps or silences to let the past intrude. After a few more laps their allotted time was coming to an end, but Stanton had got them trapped in a pile-up, and he couldn't get them free.

Out of the corner of her eye, Heather saw Sally coming from the other side of the floor as fast as she could, heading directly for them. Her hands were gripped so tightly on the wheel they made her knuckles whiten, while Jez looked on, a bemused, unwilling passenger. Stanton and Heather were trapped, they could do nothing, watching Sally approaching at speed, urging her dodgem to go as fast as possible and slam directly into them.

Jez tried to intervene. "Sally! What are you doing? That's Stanz!"

Heather and Stanton, still blocked and unable to move, braced for impact. Given the speed Sally was travelling at, this was going to hurt. Getting closer, Heather could see her face contorted with rage and hatred, and she was only feet away from smashing into them when her dodgem powered down sluggishly and came to a stop just inches from their car.

The man's voice came over the speakers again.

"That's it, boys and girls. I hope you had fun. Last ride tonight will be 10.30 p.m., discount books are available in the kiosk. Please leave the floor as quickly as possible."

Stanton turned to Heather. "Come on, the waltzer next." He grabbed her hand and dragged her out of the dodgem.

They made their way through the heaving crowds towards the middle of the park where the waltzer stood. Roper took the opportunity to run and catch up with Stanton.

"It's busy," he said.

"Good."

"Couple more hours, and you'll be away."

Roper tried to say it as though it didn't mean anything to him. Unless Stanton asked him to go with him, he knew better than to suggest it.

"Yeah. When I get wherever I'm going, I'll call you, see what's happening. Keep an eye on things for me while I'm away?"

"Yeah, sure thing, Stanz."

To hide his disappointment, Roper fell back with the others.

They gathered at the bottom of the steps to the waltzer.

"You okay going on, Jez?" Stanton asked.

"Yeah, why?"

"Just that you normally scream like a girl on these things." He turned to Heather. "You coming on?"

"Only if I can sit next to you?"

Finally, with as little emotion as possible, he asked Sally. "What about you?"

She folded her arms and looked away hurt. It was the first time he'd spoken to her since they'd come to the fairground.

"Suit yourself."

Stanton turned and went up the steps with Heather by his side, Sally looking on enviously as Heather sat down and took what used to be her place. The attendant collected the money, pausing to whisper in Stanton's ear and pat his shoulder before moving on. He still had some friends around here and it might just matter tonight.

The ride soon started to move, slowly at first, steadily building momentum.

"Okay, boys and girls and mums and dads, are you ready to be

spun? Keep your arms inside the cart at all times, don't stand up until the ride has come to a complete stop and if you feel like you're going to puke, don't, we'll make you clean it up! Here we go!"

The music grew louder, the lights started to flash, and the ride gradually began to increase in speed. The shrieking, the screams and the shouts all began to build.

Heather held on, her hands aching as everything got faster and faster. Each time they made a revolution, she'd look up and see Sally watching them from the side, her arms still folded, her face unsmiling.

The waltzer spun around and around, Heather sliding from side to side and laughing inside the spinning carts. She'd forgotten what it was like to laugh like this. When the ride came back around again, Sally was still there in the crowd, just watching, but only watching Heather. She only had eyes for her. The waltzer went round once more, the cart spinning again and again, and there she was, refusing to move her stare away from Heather. Round and round and round, revolution after revolution and Sally was always the permanent feature in them all. Heather momentarily lost sight of her as the ride pulled her away and she was facing the other side, before whipping her back from where she came. Heather looked into the crowd. But this time there was only an empty space where Sally had once stood. She had only been out of sight for a few seconds but now searching for her among the smiling faces, it was clear Sally was no longer there.

Heather started to feel nauseous. All the spinning and movement had begun to make her feel unwell and she was relieved when the ride began to slow down and come to a stop.

"Anyone fancy another go?" asked Roper.

"Hell yeah!" shouted Jez.

"What do you think?" Stanton couldn't help but notice Heather's pale and bloodless face.

"Can we get off, please?"

"Sure."

They stepped out of the ride and Heather walked carefully down the stairs.

Stanton took the chance to lean into Roper's ear. "Let's split up for a bit. Might be easier, although I don't think they're here, anyway. You catch up with Kenny and his lads and we'll all meet at the entrance at closing."

"Stanz," Roper began.

"What?"

"You okay? You know what you're doing?"

"Yeah, it's all good," and he turned and ran down the steps to catch up with Heather before being swallowed up by the crowd.

Stanton turned to Heather as they pushed their way through. "You okay?"

"Yes, thank you. Sorry I got a bit dizzy on there."

"I need to stay until closing time, but if you want to go, just say."

"I know, it's just…" She let the sentence hang for a moment before changing the subject. "Where'd Sally go?"

Stanton shrugged. "Who cares?"

"I don't think she likes me."

"She doesn't like anyone. She's always been angry."

"That's not true, she adores you. Probably why she hates me."

Stanton noticed a shooting gallery. "Come on, over here, watch this."

He went up to a bored-looking man who was rearranging some prizes behind the counter. "Five quid, one shot to hit the bullseye, and I can have any prize."

The man laughed. "Five quid, one shot? Easiest money I'll make tonight."

"Any prize?"

"Yeah any prize, and I'll even throw my missus in as well."

Taking care to make sure no one was looking, Stanton opened the bag and took a note from the stolen money, which he put down on the counter. Picking up the rifle, Stanton noticed straightaway it had been attached to the counter by a short chain.

"Security," the man said. "Don't want you shooting any locals."

Stanton rolled his eyes. "Don't want anyone winning a prize, more like."

The weight of the gun had also been altered and the gun sight had been filed off altogether.

"Good luck, win me something," said Heather, leaning in.

"Any prize?" Stanton reminded the man.

The man chuckled. "Yeah, anything you want, Billy the Kid."

Stanton had shot fast-running rats from further away than this, although his air rifle was better than the thing he was holding. But the principle was just the same. If he could focus and cancel all the distractions going on around him, he was confident his nerves wouldn't let him down. Looking at the target, he estimated that the bullseye was about the size of a rat's eye. He adjusted his stance and squinted down the barrel. Stanton steadied himself, breathed in deeply and held it for a few seconds.

He pulled the trigger, the air rifle jolting back into his shoulder and he knew without standing up he had hit the target.

Red.

Bullseye.

Heather clapped excitedly. "Yes! You did it! Well done, James!"

Stanton laid the gun down and smiled at the stall holder. "Too easy. Let's have a look at that tray of jewellery you've got hidden behind the glass case. Bet you've got some nice stuff in there."

The man begrudgingly unlocked the glass cabinet and brought back a tray of jewellery and reluctantly placed it on the counter. Heather's eyes ran along the tray until they rested on something in the middle, hidden away as though it weren't meant to be seen.

"May I have a look at that, please?"

The man looked at where Heather was pointing and grimaced. "You've got good taste in jewellery at least," he said, glancing at Stanton before handing her a small silver locket.

Heather held it gently in her hands. "Yes, I'd like this one please?"

"Suit yourself," he grumbled, locking the tray back behind the glass.

"Here, I'll put it on for you." Heather felt Stanton's strong, smooth forearms gently brush her cheeks as he fastened the chain behind her, and his warm breath on the back of her neck.

Stanton pulled her over to a photo booth. "Come on," he said. "Can't have a locket without something to put in it."

They waited patiently for the pictures to develop. This was their second try, after laughing too much in the first one.

"Here they are."

Stanton picked up the photos. "Oh dear," he laughed.

"Let me see," Heather asked eagerly. "Oh my god, they're so funny! What am I doing in that one?"

"You keep them. You can put one in the locket, something else to remember me by."

"Thank you, I will."

"Hungry?"

"Very."

"Me too. I'll go and get some chips. Here, take the bag and wait over there."

Taking the bag, she went and sat on a wooden picnic table, her feet resting on the bench, watching as Stanton joined the queue at a food van. Being with him had somehow made life easier. He had given her a confidence she didn't think she could ever possess, a strength to do things she never thought she could do, and a desire to live in the moment and not worry about the consequences. She smiled at the absurdity of the day she'd had.

But the fairground still haunted her, as it did her family, that would never change and the sooner she got out of here the better.

The park was heaving and it felt like the whole town had somehow been packed in here tonight. Heather studied her new pendant. Tomorrow she would cut out one of the pictures they'd just taken and put it in there.

Stanton handed her the chips. "Here you go."

"Thank you, I'm starving—"

"—Where's the bag?"

"Sorry?"

"The bag," Stanton said urgently, "where's the bag?"

"It's—"

Heather looked down at the ground, she had put the bag there before sitting at the table.

But it wasn't there. The bag had gone.

THIRTY-EIGHT

Stanton could hardly speak. Having worked so hard to get the money, to get this far and then lose it now, at the very end, seemed incomprehensible, and to lose it in such a stupid way only made it worse.

"I asked you to keep fucking hold of the bag?"

He was incandescent with rage as he searched desperately around the tables for it.

"Where is it? Where the fuck is it? I need that money."

"I know, but honestly I—"

As Stanton urgently scanned the busy park, he soon came to the realisation it was hopeless. There were hundreds of people milling around. In less than two hours, he was leaving town and all he had to show for his efforts were the clothes on his back. It was hopeless, he had nothing, he was back to square one. He had stolen enough over the years to know that whoever took the bag could have run in ten different directions. It'd be long gone by now.

Heather looked frantically around the table, asking anyone close by if they'd seen it.

"It was here, I put it down just there, I haven't moved. I

swear, I hardly took my eyes off it, you weren't even gone that long. Oh James I'm sorry, I'm such an idiot."

Heather started to move away.

"Where are you going?"

"To look for the bag. We need to try."

"It's gone, don't bother."

Stanton sat down heavily on the bench. He was tired and fed up, his head throbbed with the chain reaction it had been suffering all day – problem, solution, action, disappointment. There was no choice in the matter now. He'd have to go back home and take the money from Margaret's drawer after all. It would mean travelling in the opposite direction to where he needed to end up, and in the dark, and back to one of the places he knew they might find him. It was practically suicidal.

Stanton leaned forward on his elbows just as Heather sat down next to him.

"I'm sorry," she said, leaning on his arm.

He knew there was no point being angry with Heather, she was out of her depth and had been all day. There wasn't a moment to waste from hereon in. Stanton got to his feet. He needed to get moving and he needed to do it alone.

"I think you should go home now," he said to Heather.

She rose slowly off the bench and was about to say something when Stanton saw she wasn't looking at him, she was looking at something over his shoulder.

Roper, clearly anxious and worried, was making his way toward them, pushing aside anyone who got in his way. He was already talking by the time he arrived.

"I've been looking for you for ages. Got a message off one of Kenny's lads. They've been to the pier, fucking loads of them apparently. Didn't take them long to work out you weren't there. They're on the way here now, you've only got a few minutes. We have about ten of us so we're going to try and stop them out the front."

Instinct kicked in. "I'll come and help."

"Don't be stupid. You stay here Stanz, don't move, don't leave until we come back for you. The park closes in half an hour, we'll be back."

Roper turned and disappeared back into a swarm of bodies.

"Quick, we haven't got time," Stanton said, taking Heather's hand.

"Where are we going?"

"We're hiding."

Stanton pushed his way through the crowds. His voice may have been calm, but his heart was pounding in his chest like thunder.

THIRTY-NINE

THEY LOOKED UP AT A LARGE FERRIS WHEEL THAT TOWERED OVER them and the queue of people waiting to go on which was snaking back into the distance.

"Are we are meant to be getting on there? Look at the queue, we'll never make it."

"Yes we will, come on," said Stanton, marching them down to the front, and together they ducked under the chain. The operator shut the doors on one of the capsules and turned to face them.

"All right, Stanz."

"All right. Can you get us on?"

"No problem mate, no problem. Let's wait for the next one, and we'll get you on then."

Behind them, murmurings of discontent rose from those stuck in the queue, but Stanton didn't care. He needed to get somewhere out of sight and right now this would have to do.

"Here we go, Stanz, ladies first."

The operator pulled open the gate and Heather got in quickly and sat down. Stanton whispered something to his friend before following her in. Straightaway the capsule started to rise slowly, the angry words from those still arguing in the queue below drifting away as they rose silently into the clear night sky.

Stanton sat nervously, willing the ride to go faster and higher, sprawling his legs across the capsule, almost corner to corner. They glided higher and higher, the noise and busyness from below slowly becoming less intrusive.

Heather looked over the side at the fairground as it moved further away from them.

"Like ants."

Stanton, who was momentarily resting his eyes, opened them and looked down.

"They're all fakers. The whole place is fake. Look at them down there. Sometimes I think the only real one is me. One day, I'll come back here and prove it. They'll see. I'll make them regret how they were to me. I'll show them, I'll show everyone. I'll show them all."

Down below, the lights of the town twinkled like fallen stars set against the blackness of the night. The Whale, having swallowed the sun a few hours before, had itself now been swallowed by the dark. Higher up, it was noticeably chillier and Heather wrapped her arms tighter around herself.

"Here," said Stanton, taking off his jacket and leaning forward to help Heather put it on.

"Thank you. Aren't you cold, though?" she asked guiltily.

"Nah, I'm good."

The wheel stopped turning as they reached the top, their capsule now the furthest from the ground as it swung gently in the void.

"We're not moving," said Heather, alarmed. "Have we broken down?"

"No. I asked them to stop it here for a bit."

Stanton needed to drag the time out as much as he could,

his mind obsessed with what might be happening down below. Up here, no one could see them, let alone reach them.

"You're lucky," said Heather.

"Could have fooled me," scoffed Stanton.

"But at least you're escaping. You're getting away from here. When you wake up tomorrow this will just be a memory to you, all of it, nothing but a memory. Even me."

"Easier said than done without any money."

Heather clasped her hands tightly on her lap. "I'm sorry, it's all my fault."

The wheel started turning again, sending them slowly back down to earth, back to whatever was waiting for them.

Stanton pushed himself further down in the seat. They were getting lower, and his safety was evaporating before his eyes.

"I'm not sure why, but I really enjoyed today," said Heather. "It's a shame it's over."

As Heather said those words, cowering lower in his seat, Stanton felt something he wasn't sure he had felt before. He felt lonely. He'd spent more years than he cared remember just looking after himself and being himself and never having to worry about anyone. But the past few days had changed that. He didn't want the ride to stop, he didn't want to get off and face whatever was waiting for him out there in the darkness.

They had reached the end of the ride and Heather sat patiently waiting for the man to open the door, but before he had time to do so, Stanton leaned forward and put his hand on the gate.

"Send us around again," Stanton said to his friend.

"No problem, Stanz."

"Give us as much time at the top as you can."

The operator gave the thumbs up and stepped away to let their capsule go past and Stanton and Heather were off again, rising up into the night sky. His instinct told him not to get off, there was danger out there somewhere waiting for him to appear. He liked the fact they didn't know where he was. The only problem with that was he didn't know where they were either.

"Why didn't you want to come onto the fairground tonight?" he asked once they were higher up.

"Sorry?"

"You said you didn't want to come here."

Being here with Stanton wasn't going to change Heather's past. He was going and she was staying. It seemed everyone left Heather eventually. She hadn't realised, but she was crying, the tears falling freely down her face.

The wheel stopped; they were back at the top.

"What's wrong?" he asked.

"James," Heather spoke softly, her head dropping to her chest, her shoulders slumping forward.

"What?" he said, moving his face so close to hers he could see the moon reflected in her watery eyes. "What is it, what's the matter?"

"James."

"What, tell me, what is it?"

"Something bad happened here," she began.

Stanton glanced over the side; the park was heaving with people. He wasn't sure if that was good or bad, his mind was half in the capsule and half down in the park. He turned back to Heather.

"What do you mean, something bad?"

She struggled to get the words out. They were trapped in her throat and at home behind the locked door.

"I…"

Stanton leaned forward. His face was inches from hers and as she looked deep into his eyes, she wanted nothing more than for it to be just the two of them on their own forever. Finally the words escaped, rushing up from her heart and out through her mouth.

"My brother, my little baby brother, he died."

Stanton brushed some tears from her cheeks. "It's okay," he said, although he was struggling to sound as though he cared. Stanton wasn't used to witnessing such raw emotion, he was better at fighting than he was at feeling.

"No, I'm sorry, James, I'm sorry. I shouldn't have come here today. I should have left everything as it was. I should have left you at the graveyard and left the memories out there where they belong."

She was throwing her arms aimlessly outside the capsule, which was still hanging stationary at the top of the ride.

"What do you mean, out there?" Stanton asked, confused.

"Out there!" she said, waving her arms.

The ride started up again, the capsule swinging under the new momentum. Stanton held on to the side.

"What do you mean, out there? You're not making any sense."

"Out there, James! Out there on the fairground, where he died, that's why I didn't want to come here tonight, because of that. But I wanted to help you, so I came anyway."

Heather pulled her face away from his hands and sobbed heavily into her own.

Stanton slowly sat back, his mind racing. It wasn't possible, too fantastical to be true. With urgency he leaned forward and pulled Heather's hands away from her face.

"Your brother died at the fairground?"

"Yes," she said, sobbing loudly. "Ow, you're hurting me."

He let go of her wrists. "When?"

"What?"

"When did this happen? To your brother?"

Heather looked puzzled. "Three years ago," she sniffed.

The blood drained from Stanton's already pallid face, his throat tightened so that he could hardly even get the words out.

"Your brother died three years ago? On the fairground?"

"Yes," she said in the smallest of voices.

He was starting to feel light-headed. It was impossible, improbable, practically unbelievable.

"How?" he asked urgently.

"How?" Heather wiped her nose with the back of her hand.

"Yes, how? How did he die? Your brother?" The anxiousness in his voice rising as quickly as they fell towards the ground. He grabbed her shoulders roughly.

"How? Tell me! How?"

"James, you're hurting me," she said, pulling back from him.

"Tell me? I need to know."

"There was, there was an accident. I wasn't there. I was with my mum. It was just Robert and Dad having a day out. They'd gone into one of the arcades."

He could see Heather's lips moving as she talked, but he couldn't make sense of what she was saying. He had buried the memory of that day, and here it was now being given back to him. Stanton leaned back as far as he could from Heather. Three years ago. A little boy. An accident. White trainers drenched with red blood.

It was Heather's turn to move towards him, conscious that something was wrong. She was speaking to him but the blood thundering in his ears made him deaf to her words. He played the accident over and over in his head. He had been told to fix the machine and instead he had spent the time chatting up some girls.

He got to his feet, the capsule rocking as it moved ever lower.

"James, sit down! What are you doing?"

It seemed to be taking forever to get back down to the ground, it felt as though the whole of time had stopped. He needed to get off right now. Looking over the side, he thought about jumping, but they were still too high. Staring dizzily out across the town, the horizon was rising as he himself was falling.

Then he saw them, the ones that had chased them on the pier that morning, and across town ever since. They were here, inside the fairground. Their sticky, spiked-up hair moving through the crowds like shark fins breaking the surface of the ocean. His safe space had been breached. They were still out there looking for him, hunting him down. They were not alone, he could see others, moving as a swarm, like a darting shoal. He thought he could see someone else with them. Sally? He couldn't be sure, they were too far away. Stanton quickly lost sight of them as the capsule dropped lower to the ground. He crouched down as low as he could. Had they seen him?

Heather reached out and touched his arm. "James, are you ok?"

He sat dazed, doubting himself about what he'd just seen let alone what he had just heard. But it was clear, tonight wasn't over.

Keep moving.

He needed to get out of the fairground.

"They're here."

It was all he needed to say for Heather to understand.

"Have a look over the top. Can you see them? There was a group of about five or six."

Heather peered over the edge of the ride that was only seconds away from coming to a stop.

"No I can't, I can't see them. Wait, oh my god…"

"What? What is it?"

Heather looked down at Stanton cramped on the floor. "I can see the bag."

FORTY

"WHAT? WHERE? ARE YOU SURE IT'S MY BAG?"

Picking himself up off the floor, Stanton peered over the side.

"Yes of course I'm sure, I've had to carry it enough times today. Quick, we're getting lower and we'll lose sight of it."

"Where?"

"There look, by the burger van, that man has it over his shoulder."

Stanton's eyes tracked to where Heather was pointing. He could see it now. It *was* the bag. At least it was still here at the fairground, but now they needed to get off this wheel and get to the man before he disappeared.

Nearly back on the ground, Stanton undid the latch before the operator could even get to it. "Right, as soon as this stops we need to get over to that bloke, we need to get that bag. Ready?"

They stepped out of the capsule and jumped off the ride, right into the streams of people moving in different directions at different speeds, most making their way toward the exits as the fairground began to close.

Stanton didn't have time for manners. He used his elbow and strength to barge heavily past anyone who got in his way.

"This way," he shouted to Heather, who was clinging on for her life.

Stanton spotted the man they were looking for. "There he is."

The ground was clearer now, there were less people to navigate and he pulled Heather towards the unsuspecting man.

"That's mine," Stanton said, making a grab for the bag.

"Sorry—"

Stanton didn't give the man a chance to saying anything further and snatched the bag off him, holding it protectively behind his back just in case he tried to make a lunge to retrieve it.

"That's my bag, where did you get it?"

Stanton was so furious it had been taken from it, he forgot to be relieved he had found it again.

"My son found it and brought it to me, he's gone with his mum to the toilet, he'll be back soon and you can ask him. We asked someone and they said to hand it in on the way out. I don't want any trouble. If that's your bag, take it." The man held his hands up and backed off.

"Did you open it?"

"No, no of course not, we were just going to hand it in, honestly."

Heather placed her hand on Stanton's arm. "James."

Her single word snapped Stanton out of his trance. He didn't have time to waste on strangers. He had the bag now, which might mean he had the money. If he had the money, his escape was back on.

Turning his back to the crowds passing by, he took a deep breath, unzipped the bag and looked inside.

The money was still there, the man hadn't lied.

He stuffed the money into his pockets. He couldn't risk anything like that happening again. The money was all that mattered.

"Come on, let's get going."

The main exit was likely to be the most dangerous, so they double backed on themselves and headed for one of the smaller gates off to the side. They ducked down behind a gallery of stalls selling food, giving them some respite from the heaving masses of people on the other side. They walked quickly but carefully, stepping over cables and squeezing past generators, until they got to the end and could see the gate. It was still busy here but not as busy as the main entrance.

They were out in the open once again and walking as calmly as they could the last few yards to what felt like Stanton's freedom. As soon as they were through the gate, he would head to the train station, making sure Heather was safe. Then he would get on the train and disappear. He had a new plan, he felt back in control. This could still work, there was still a chance.

"Stanton!"

The powerful bellow stopped them both in their tracks. They looked around to see who was calling him. Not for the first time today, Stanton's heart sank to his boots. It was Armstrong and this time he'd come prepared. There were policemen strung out across the entrance and the promenade.

"This way!" Stanton yanked Heather towards the main body of the park and back to where it was busiest. They heaved and shoved themselves deep into the thronging crowds, pushing as hard as they could against those shuffling their way out of the fairground. They had gone from avoiding the masses to now trying to lose themselves among those who were oblivious to the drama unfolding around them.

Stanton pushed aggressively, both of them stumbling and struggling to keep their feet as they swam against the tide, trying desperately to cut a way through and hopefully get to where he hoped Roper and the others would be. Behind them, the helmets of the pursuing police bobbed through the crowds. They were moving faster as people stepped out of their way.

"Keep going," he said to Heather as they squirmed through what felt like an immovable wall. "We just need to get to the other side."

Heather's arm ached from his grip as the crush of people moved in unison and shoved her harshly to one side.

"Is it much further?"

"We'll soon be clear. Come on, just don't let go of my hand."

Looking back, Stanton could see the police were also now struggling against the crowds. He gave one last concerted effort to push through, pulling Heather with all his strength as though he were hauling her out of quicksand.

Finally, they managed to get themselves clear.

But there was to be no respite. Through the gate to the side, the fight that had been happening in Stanton's absence poured into the park. Roper was at the heart of it, bloodied and battered, his arms working like a hurricane through a cloud of punks and thugs. Kenny was there with some of his lads, and Jez was in there trying his best, as he always did in a fight, the occasional glint of knives flickering in the moonlight.

Roper saw his friend and shouted at him through bloodied teeth. "Go, get out of here Stanz!"

Behind them, the police had broken through a crowd that was now trying desperately to move away from the violence. Stanton wanted to stay and fight, but he knew he couldn't. Pulling Heather in the opposite direction to the violence, he retreated back into the heart of the fairground, away from the ensuing carnage, away from the police and the chaos. The crowds had thinned and so their progress was quicker as they ran down the near deserted pathways and alleys. Stanton took them as far as he could to the rear of the fairground, checking frantically as they got there that they were truly on their own. Only when he was absolutely sure they were, did he stop, catch his breath, and gather his thoughts.

"I'm scared, James, really scared," said Heather, pressing up against his body.

"So am I," he replied honestly. He had long passed the point of bravado.

But there was no time to hang about and feel sorry for himself. He needed to get out of here and it wasn't safe to leave the fairground from the front, so they would have to try to escape over the back. There was no other choice.

"Come on, I know a shortcut," he said, looking at Heather, her face lit by yellow and red lights from a nearby ride. He hoped she couldn't see the fear in his eyes as he contemplated passing through the travellers' camp at night. He'd taken the shortcut a few times in the past, but never this late and never in the pitch black of night.

They set off slowly, neither looking behind as the music drifted away, an eerie silence having replaced the screams. The fairground workers busied themselves putting the park to sleep. If anyone was watching, they would have seen Stanton and Heather cross the line from light into darkness, his white t-shirt glowing in the fairground lights, until they could be seen no more; disappearing like ghosts swallowed by the night.

FORTY-ONE

THEY STAGGERED BLINDLY OVER THE UNEVEN CONCRETE THAT GAVE way to pot-holed tarmac, which eventually became a rubble-strewn wasteland. The lights and noise of the fairground now behind them, the only sounds were their own laboured breathing and stumbling feet as they tried hard to stay upright with the moon their only torch.

Stanton's mind was tumbling. In the space of twenty minutes, life had come at him so fast he wasn't able to control any of the consequences. He couldn't stop thinking back to the jetty. Would Heather have tried to kill herself if he hadn't been there? And was she only there because he had been an idiot three years before? It seemed like everything wrong and bad emanated from him. If he couldn't fix this, he might as well be dead himself.

"Is it much further?" asked Heather.

"No, a little bit more, let's keep going."

"What is this place? How do you know where you're going?"

"I told you, it's a shortcut I've used before."

The terrain gradually began to flatten out and became

easier to navigate, the rubble finally giving way to grass. Stanton stopped and looked across at what was in front of them.

The travellers' camp.

It was quiet, as most of the men were still packing up the rides and stalls down at the fairground. Stanton breathed deeply and Heather slipped her hand into his.

"Are we going to be okay?" she asked.

"We'll soon find out."

They walked side by side across the open space of the camp, past the remains of a burnt-out van. They could hear women's laughter coming from one of the caravans, smoke billowing from its vent as shadows moved across its windows. There was some music being played in another caravan, mixed in with loud angry shouts and threats. Heather moved closer to Stanton, until they were synchronised like marching soldiers. They looked straight ahead, not daring to look anywhere else, hoping that if they couldn't see anyone, no one could see them.

"Nearly there," Stanton whispered tensely, but just as they had almost reached the other side, they heard a noise and turned to see a large dog springing from the darkness. Heather screamed and Stanton put himself between her and the beast heading their way.

The dog was as black as the night that surrounded them, only its snarling white teeth shone in the moonlight.

The animal was now close enough to launch itself at them and Stanton braced, ready to at least try to land a punch on its jaw. Just as he began to draw his arm back, a steel chain tethered to the dog's neck caught fast and just stopped it from reaching them. Now the animal simply strained at the neck as it leered towards them, white foam dripping from its gasping mouth.

A man emerged slowly out of the darkness. "Samson! Down, boy!"

Immediately, the dog obeyed and stopped barking, panting to catch its breath as the taut chain cut into its thick neck.

"James," Heather said under her breath, squeezing his hand.

Even in the dark, the man drinking from the can looked like a giant. It was Big Tommy and Stanton hadn't seen him since he sold him the drugs two weeks ago.

"Samson! Here!"

The dog laboured back to its owner, the slack chain dragging noisily behind as it went.

"Now then, Jimmy," said the man, moving forward to pat the dog.

"All right, Big Tommy," Stanton croaked through a throat desiccated with thirst and fear.

Big Tommy took a long drink from his can. A caravan door opened and a woman stuck her head out to see what was going on.

"Bit late for you to be back here?" queried Big Tommy, his thick accent rendering what he was saying almost impenetrable to Heather.

Stanton wasn't sure if it was a question or a threat.

"We're just on our way home, Big Tommy."

"That so? This way, huh?" He took another long drink. The woman at the door of the caravan pulled her dressing gown tight.

Stanton swallowed hard. "Yeah, there was a bit of trouble on the fairground. I wasn't in the mood so I thought coming this way might be easier."

Big Tommy bent down and patted his dog roughly.

"So I hear. Seems you've not got many friends these days, Jimmy?"

This was taking too long. It was eating into what little time Stanton had left to get to the train station. He tried to make light of the situation so they could be on their way again.

"Seems that way. But you know me, there's always someone after me." He smiled nervously, not that anyone could see his face in the pitch black.

"What you got in that bag there, then?"

"Nothing much, just some bits. I'm going away for a few days." Stanton felt a bead of sweat running down his neck. "Are we good to be on our way, do you think, Big Tommy?"

The man finished what was in the can, crushed it with one hand and threw it behind him, before saying something to the woman at the door, who disappeared back inside. Big Tommy seemed to have all the time in the world.

"You got any more of that stuff you brought to me, Jimmy-boy? Made me some good money off that."

Stanton almost said out loud what he was thinking, that he was glad someone had because that stuff had brought him nothing but trouble.

"Sure thing, Big Tommy. As soon as I get back, I'll come over and we can have a chat about it?"

The woman appeared back at the door and handed Big Tommy another can.

"Sure. Maybe next time come back when it's light. You ought'en to be out back here in the dark, hey? It's a dangerous place out there sometimes, Jimmy."

Stanton slowly shuffled his feet in the direction they needed to go.

"Oh Jimmy, before you go, I hear you've come into some money?"

Stanton clenched his jaw. This town never could keep a secret. There was no point running, not back here, not in the dark.

The dog snarled, Big Tommy shouted at it to lay back down.

"A bit of spending money, that's all. For my holiday."

"Well, maybe so, but you know the rules, Jimmy."

Stanton wasn't sure that he did, he didn't think there were any rules back here. The woman from the caravan stepped out and walked quickly over the ground in her bare feet. When she got to Stanton, she held out her hand in expectation.

"Need to feed Samson Jimmy, otherwise he gets hungry. Or you can go back the way you came, no skin off my nose."

The implication was clear. Grudgingly, Stanton put his hand in his pocket and grabbed the rolled-up notes, realising his mistake of not splitting the money so he could at least have kept hold of some of it. He handed the money over to the woman, who scurried back to the caravan.

"Be on your way now, Jimmy," Big Tommy shouted, as he twitched his head to point the way for them to go, never once having left the shadows that hung around him.

They went on their way in dejected silence. In the space of a few short hours Stanton had got the money, lost it, taken it back and now lost it all over again; this time for good.

FORTY-TWO

THEY'D LOST TRACK OF TIME AND ALL SENSE OF NORMALITY, traipsing through the dark, feeling as though they'd been awake and alert for a week. They had no choice but to carry on though, as every time Stanton enacted a plan, he had had to change it. It felt like fate was always one step ahead of him.

They were soon out of sight of the camp, their hands brushing the long grass as they walked. Stanton was cursing himself for being back to square one with no more dice left to roll, when he abruptly held his arm out to stop Heather in her stride.

"What is it?"

"I'd forgotten how steep this bit was."

They both peered down a steep bank that ran away from them and into the darkness below.

"What's down there?"

"Home for you. Train for me."

"But what about the money?"

"I'll dodge the fare and worry about that tomorrow."

This was the sum total of his plan. He was at the last chance saloon, that was all that was left.

"It looks quite steep, James. How do we get down?"

"Like this."

Before Heather realised what was happening, Stanton launched himself down the hill, stumbling as he ran down the dry earth track that cut through the grass. Heather watched him career down the slope until all she could see was his white t-shirt in the murkiness below.

He shouted back up. "Come on, your turn!"

"I can't do that," Heather yelled down.

"You'll have to, unless you want to walk past that dog again. Come on. I'll catch you!"

The slope seemed to disappear into nothing.

"Come on, hurry up. It can't be scarier than that dog?"

"What if I fall?"

"What?"

"What if I fall down?"

"You won't! I'll catch you. Just aim for my voice."

"Promise you'll catch me?"

"No!"

She could hear him laughing in the darkness.

Heather moved her feet closer to the slope. It looked almost vertical and certainly not as easy as Stanton had made it look in his sturdy boots.

"Hurry up!" Stanton yelled. "Just stay on the path and away from the grass like I did. You'll be fine. Sometimes you just have to jump and trust what you can't see."

"Okay," she said, devoid of any confidence. "I'm coming down now."

Heather moved her feet to the very edge and felt herself starting to slip.

"Here I come!" she shouted, stepping down gingerly, first placing her right foot to gain some traction and then gently with her left, but before she could do anything, gravity took over. The angle of the slope started to work against her, and

Heather found herself hurtling downhill at speed, screaming loudly as she went.

Stanton heard her coming before he saw her arrive and when she did she was travelling much faster than he was expecting. He had no time to brace himself before Heather hit him full-on, her arms swirling wildly as she did so.

"Oh, fu—" he started to say, before the force of the collision kicked the wind from his lungs and sent them sprawling backward into the grass.

It took them a moment to regain their thoughts and bearings as they lay entwined. Heather was on top of Stanton, staring into his eyes, her hand resting on his chest. He smiled up at her.

"Well, at least you made it down."

They lay in the grass, neither of them wanting to move, their bodies and minds aching from everything they'd been through that day. Their heads were only a few inches apart, and Heather could feel his heart beating strongly through her hand, his arm still holding her waist from when he had caught her, their warm breath on each other's faces. She moved to get up, but Stanton tightened his grip, their eyes locking, both recognising themselves within the other.

Heather could feel her head becoming heavier as it started to fall forward and instinctively touched her lips to his. She moved her hand from his chest and put it on his cheek as their tongues finally met, his hand moving from her waist to the back of her neck as he kissed her harder.

Heather pulled herself away, fluttering her eyes over his face, not really believing what had just happened. They kissed again, not wanting to break the moment as they lay on a bed of dewy grass, under a cloudless moonlit sky.

"I need to go," Stanton mumbled. "I don't want to but I need to."

"Should I come with you?"

"The train station?"

"Yes, and then wherever you go from there."

Stanton got to his feet and dusted the grass from himself.

"Don't be silly, your life's here."

He held his hand out to Heather, like he'd done so many times since they'd met, and he pulled her close.

"Besides, it was going to be hard enough with just me and the money, no chance if it's both of us without *any* money."

From somewhere behind, a dog barked loudly, a timely reminder of the danger they were still in. Stanton started to walk away through the long grass.

"I can get you the money," said Heather quickly.

Stanton stopped and turned around. "Nice try. Come on, let's keep moving."

"No, James, honestly I can get you the money. I've just remembered something. I can get you all of it, maybe even more than you had before, and you can still catch the train."

Stanton held his arms out and turned three hundred and sixty degrees. "Very good, but I don't see any banks around here to rob."

"We're not going to rob a bank. We're going to rob my house."

FORTY-THREE

Heather closed the gap between them and held him by the waist. "It's true. When I was in my mum's bedroom this morning I looked for something in one of her drawers and saw a box right at the back that I've never seen before. It was full of money. A few hundred pounds, at least. Probably her escape fund so she can run away with her man."

To Stanton, this felt like another false dawn. The day had begun with hope and expectation, and was now ending in despair and resignation.

"My parents are at some boring family party, they don't normally get back until late. But we have to go now. It's about ten minutes from here and then twenty back to the station. Come on, it's got to be worth a shot."

They set off excitedly, re-energised once again by the thought of this new opportunity.

They were surrounded by acres of barren, unused scrubland that no one could find a use for. A back road snaked through it, like a racetrack, and sometimes late at night, that's what it became. But tonight no one was here, it was just the two of them, trampling a path as they walked through the waist-high grass.

Stanton quickened their pace as their feet finally touched tarmac and it became easier to walk. The road ahead only had one working light about two-thirds of the way down and they headed straight for it. Over time, stones had been used to break the other lights, and the council had given up replacing them. But the last remaining one had, for some reason, proved immovable, and it cast a weak yellow light about fifty yards away. Beyond that, a curve in the road would take them back to the heart of everything.

～

Stanton checked behind him. He thought he could hear a dog barking again.

Heather carried on talking animatedly about how she had found the money and how much she hated her mum right now. She was so engrossed in her monologue that she didn't notice Stanton falling behind. She turned around and was about to say something when she saw him stood motionless, staring at the road ahead.

"James? What's wrong?"

Stanton had always trusted his eyesight. It had never let him down before and he was convinced he had just seen something up ahead. He dared not move or blink for fear of missing whatever it was that had caught his eye. It was just past the solitary streetlight, in among the trees that lined the road. It was there that Stanton's eyes were now focused.

Heather walked the few steps back to see what was wrong.

Stanton saw it again. An almost imperceptible orange glow, small but bright enough to confirm his eyes had not deceived him. But he couldn't make out what it was. He watched again, as it slowly rose, hovered in mid-air and then grew brighter before falling slowly back down again. There was only one thing that could be. It was a cigarette and it meant someone was up ahead in the trees.

Stanton watched as the orange glow repeated its slow deliberate movement up, hovering while the embers burned brightly, before once again falling back down. Whoever it was, they were not there by accident. They were there waiting for something. Or someone.

He felt Heather clutch his arm tightly as she looked in the direction they'd just come.

"James!"

But Stanton didn't need to see what she was looking at, those black silhouettes fanning out across the road behind them. The moment he heard the dog barking, his instincts had told him to be alert. Then, when he thought he'd seen something up ahead, he already knew they were in trouble. You never walked this way unless you needed to, and very few people ever needed to. The instant he realised he was watching someone smoke a cigarette, it quickly all made sense to him. The fairground wasn't the trap. The fairground was the bait.

The real trap was this back road, the short cut, and Stanton had walked them directly into it. Those he had seen from the top of the Ferris wheel were never there to stop him from leaving the fairground. They were there to push him over the back of it. Away from the crowds, away from the gang, away from any witnesses.

He briefly resented Heather being there. She had weakened him, which in turn had endangered them both. But this wasn't her fault. It was his, and now they were in very serious trouble.

Stanton had been right; he had seen Sally at the fairground after all. Talking with them, betraying him to the enemy. He didn't want to believe she would do that; he'd hoped he'd been wrong but she knew this back road, he had taken her this way in the past. Sally had sold them out.

"Bitch," he said under his breath.

This time, they really were trapped. He could see in Heather's eyes that she was petrified.

"Don't worry, they're here for me, not you."

Turning his attention back to whoever it was up ahead, he watched again as the cigarette was raised and inhaled. This time, however, the person flicked the cigarette away, the embers scattering as it bounced across the tarmac. Whoever this person was began to emerge from the trees, walking deliberately and slowly toward them, their elongated shadow cast out across the road. Others also began to appear from the trees, spreading out like a net to catch a fish.

The individual had now reached the streetlamp, stepping under its glow, pausing for effect, looking in his direction and making sure Stanton could see exactly who it was.

It was Sonny.

FORTY-FOUR

"Well, you've been a busy little motherfucker."

With his grimy fingers, Sonny unbuttoned a breast pocket on his denim jacket and pulled out an already rolled-up cigarette. He left the words dripping in the air like laundry on a washing line. Sonny was smaller than Stanton and about ten years older and the nastiness oozed out of his every pore.

In the space of a few minutes, after hearing the last bark of the dog, they had been totally surrounded by ghost-like shadows, advancing from the trees or moving up from behind.

Sonny threw his head back and slowly blew the smoke from his nostrils. "Cat got your tongue?"

Stanton could feel his throat closing up, his dry tongue glued to the top of his mouth. "Look, Sonny, I think—"

Sonny pointed a finger directly at Stanton. "—Let's get this straight early on. I'm in charge here and I don't give a fuck what you think."

He left his finger hanging in the air for a moment before swivelling it like the gun of a tank, until it was pointing directly at Heather. "Who's your little friend?"

Heather had been scared a few times today, but never quite

as petrified as she was now. She quietly and fearfully whispered Stanton's name.

Sonny dropped his arm and started to laugh.

"Oh, it's James, is it? We're among royalty, boys. It's James now. Ooh la-de-da!"

"He always had ideas above his station, Sonny," said one of the gang members.

"Richie," said Stanton, recalling the last time he had seen him was only twelve hours ago, yelling from the top of the helter-skelter. "Not your normal Saturday night, you've normally got your face in a bag of glue by now."

Richie took a step forward, but Sonny stopped him.

"You'll have your fun, don't worry." He returned his focus to Heather. "Has he fucked you yet, love?"

Embarrassed by the accusation, Heather hid her face behind Stanton's arm.

Sonny smirked. "Well, he will. Don't worry. You'll get your turn. Proper little Romeo is our James." He bowed and doffed an imaginary cap. The others laughed and sniggered, enjoying Stanton getting his comeuppance.

"Look, leave her out of this, Sonny. If you've got a problem, we can sort it between us."

Sonny moved closer, flicking his half-smoked cigarette into the wasteland. "Don't you fucking tell me what to do. Do you understand me?" With each word, he jabbed Stanton's chest hard with a finger, staring into his eyes as he spoke, the strong potent smell of rolled tobacco filling Stanton's nose.

Sonny moved away and went and stood in front of Heather and smiled, his yellow teeth visible in the night.

"Funny looking thing, Jimmy. Not your usual type."

Stanton was feeling calmer than he thought he should be but he knew he needed to force the issue.

"Let's get this over with, Sonny, whatever this is."

"Oh, we will. Don't you worry about that, but let's start at the beginning, shall we?"

Stanton still had no idea; he had spent all day running from something he didn't understand.

"Well yeah, I wouldn't mind knowing where the beginning is, Sonny. You've been chasing me all day. I heard you weren't happy about something, and now here we are, and I still don't know."

"Don't get lippy with me, or I'll cut them both off that pretty face of yours."

Sonny pulled a knife from his back pocket, the steel glinting under the moon as he waved it between Stanton and Heather.

"You won't be kissing any bird again, let alone this thing."

Stanton clenched his fists.

"Aww, looks like lover boy has found his princess and wants to fight for her. Shame you don't pick your fights better, eh?"

From wanting to speed things up, Stanton needed to slow this down. The introduction of the knife and Sonny's sinister obsession with Heather had given this an ominous turn.

"Look Sonny, we've both been in enough trouble over the years, this is our world not hers. Let her go and we can sort this out, just me and you yeah?"

Sonny cocked his head patronisingly to the side. "Me and you? What do you think this has to do with me and you?"

"I just assumed—"

"—Well, don't fucking assume anything. No, no, no. This has nothing to do with me and you. But it has a lot to with you and my little brother."

Sonny lifted the knife up parallel with Stanton's face.

His brother?

"I think you've met him, Jimmy?"

Stanton was more confused than ever but tried to stay

nonchalant in the face of a situation that was as incomprehensible as it was farcical.

"If I've met him, it's news to me."

Sonny gave a fake laugh. "Trust me, you have. Care to guess where he is right now?"

Stanton shrugged, he didn't know and he didn't care either.

"How should I know where your brother is?"

He hadn't even know Sonny had a brother. In fact, he was starting to feel a little better. This was now clearly a misunderstanding and once it was cleared up, Stanton could start to get his life back.

"Okay, I'll tell you where he is. He's in the hospital."

"What's that got to do with me?"

"It's got everything to do with you because you fucking put him there." Sonny's tone was so cold, it felt like the temperature of the air had dropped.

"Me? Piss off, Sonny," Stanton said indignantly. "Honestly, I don't even know who your brother is…"

Abruptly, Stanton stopped himself from saying anything more. It dawned on him that he did know who his brother was because Stanton had just remembered a very important fact.

If you knew that Sonny had a little brother you also knew his younger brother was one of the punks that hung around town fighting, getting drunk and causing trouble. You might even find him one afternoon sleeping off his drunkenness in a backstreet bus stop as you walk past, frustrated at having just failed to steal some much-needed money. The final jigsaw piece fell neatly into place. It had been Sonny's brother that Stanton had beaten to a quivering pulp two days ago.

Sonny smiled as he read Stanton's white face in the dark.

"Yeah, now you're remembering. He's in hospital with a tube up his nose and they can't wake him up. You jumped him when he was on his own, kicked the shit out of him. Now the tables have turned and you're not such the big man when your shitty little gang aren't here. How is the fat one, by the way?"

Stanton's heart was racing, his mind hunting desperately for a way out.

"Who said it was me?"

"You what?" Sonny asked, puzzled.

"Who said it was me that beat him up?" Stanton felt confident with this line of defence. "Could've been anyone. Sonny, this is what happens. We fight. Always have and always will. It's just what we do. Ask Richie over there, or any of those ugly bastards. But it doesn't mean it was me. I'm not the only skinhead around here."

"Don't take me for a fucking mug," Sonny threatened. "We knocked on a few doors, asked around. Spoke to a lovely old lady who saw everything from across the road. There aren't too many pretty boy skinheads in this shithole."

The last remains of Stanton's confidence began to drain away.

"Turns out you're not as popular as you thought, Jimmy. A lot of people have been very helpful when it came to tracking you down. Seems there are some people around here with scores to settle, or business interests to preserve."

Stanton knew exactly who he was talking about. He thought of another angle.

"Alright, you got me. But my lot are bound to have another ruck with his lot again. Some you win, some you lose. Keeps us busy until the pubs open. I was fighting Richie on the pier a few days ago and he nearly cracked my head open."

Richie smiled at the memory but Sonny gave him a stare that wiped the smile clean off his face.

"You don't need to tell me how this works. My little brother is the biggest dickhead going. But that don't excuse what you did."

Stanton tried another approach, but he was running out of options.

"Look Sonny, just punch me in the face a few times, that's all I did to your brother. That way we're quits, no need to make this any worse."

It was hopeless, the look on Sonny's face was enough to tell him this was about to get a whole lot worse.

"Fuck this shit, I've heard enough. Lads."

With that simple word, everything changed. Richie and a couple of the others grabbed hold of Heather's arms and pulled her away from Stanton.

"James!" she cried.

It was life or death now for Stanton. He was fairly sure he could outrun this lot. He could drop a couple of the smaller guys and be up the bank on the right, through the back gardens of the houses and halfway to the train station before anyone knew what was happening.

Stanton noticed Jackson, the loser who had told him about the till full of money a few days before. He was part of the group now restraining Heather.

"You?" he mumbled in disbelief. Stanton had never felt so alone. Everyone had turned against him, even the lowest of the low. "Sonny, please. This has nothing to do with her."

"It does now, so shut it. We've had a little request come in, haven't we, lads? Something specific for the princess over here. The boys have done a lot of running around after you today, so I've lined up a little treat for them."

Heather struggled violently against the forceful grip that was holding her.

"Please James, stop them!"

Stanton felt powerless, the situation was getting out of control

"I've got money," he lied desperately.

Sonny hesitated. "How much money?"

"A few hundred quid. It's yours, all of it. I can get it tomorrow for you."

Theatrically scratching his stubble with the point of the knife, Sonny surveyed his surroundings.

"Nah, fuck it, but thanks anyway Jimmy. You're a dead man walking and have been for two days, plenty of places out here to hide a scrawny little shit like you. I'll get to you in a minute. In the meantime, you can watch."

Sonny moved towards Heather, grabbing her face with his rough, calloused hands.

"Who's going first?" he joked.

"Please!" Heather said, crying. "I want to go home, please. I won't tell anyone, I promise."

"I know you won't tell anyone," Sonny said, smiling in the darkness. "If you do, you'll end up in the same place as your boyfriend."

Stanton tried to move towards them but was pushed back.

"Sonny, that's enough. Leave her alone."

"James, please," Heather implored.

"Tell you what, I'll go first," Sonny said, moving his face next to Heather's so she could feel and almost taste his filthy beard. Sonny stuck his tongue out and slowly licked her cheek.

"Quite tasty. Bit salty, though. But she smells lovely."

Jackson was laughing and Stanton could see him moving his hands over Heather's body.

"Get your hands off her, you rat. Sonny, leave her alone."

Sonny ignored him, his thoughts now turning to what he was about to do. "You'll like this love, trust me. I know what I'm doing."

With his knife, Sonny hooked a button clean off Heather's blouse and moved in closer, rubbing his legs up against Heather's body as he roughly touched her small breasts.

From behind, Stanton spoke calmly. "I won't tell you again. I *said*, leave her alone."

Sonny was enjoying himself too much to bother replying and pushed his leg roughly between Heather's. Momentarily, Heather felt the grip on one of her wrists loosen. Taking her chance, she pulled her hand free and swung it as hard as she could at Sonny's face, her nails clawing at his skin like the talons of a bird of prey. They quickly restrained her again, but not before she'd drawn blood from Sonny.

"You fucking whore!" shouted Sonny, droplets of spit hanging from his beard as he reached to grip either side of Heather's mouth. "You want it rough? You can have it rough."

He brought the knife up to sit just below one of her eyes.

Down that deserted back road, the metallic click of a gun being cocked practically split the night in half.

"I said, leave her alone."

Sonny stopped what he was doing and slowly turned around. He found himself staring down the barrel of a gun, the handle gripped firmly by Stanton, his arm unfailingly still, his finger poised delicately on the trigger.

FORTY-FIVE

SONNY RAISED HIS HANDS IN MOCK SURRENDER.

"Woah, woah, woah Jimmy. A gun? Seriously, you got yourself a gun?"

"Looks like it's your turn to shut the fuck up, Sonny."

"Oh come on. We're only messing with you, aren't we lads?" Sonny looked and saw that some were already backing away. No one had mentioned guns when they'd agreed to get involved.

"This was never more than a friendly warning, Jimmy, that's all."

"Come here," Stanton ordered Heather.

She was still bound by the grip of those holding her, who looked at Sonny for what to do. He nodded his head, and they let her go. Jackson quickly saw his opportunity and ran away down the road as fast as he could.

"That's what happens when you pay rats to do your dirty work," scoffed Stanton, who, along with everyone else, watched as Jackson disappeared out of sight.

Heather went to him and he held her. His right arm, the one holding the gun, had not wavered an inch.

Richie knew a losing battle when he saw one. He melted back into the night, taking with him those he had brought along.

"Interesting," Sonny said to himself. He still had his own people but no one could deny the tables had just been turned.

"Pick up the bag," Stanton said to Heather, his strong and controlled voice giving her the courage she needed, and she put the bag over her shoulder. Stanton regripped the gun, the warm air was making it clammy in his hand.

"I'm sorry about your brother. I hope he gets better soon. Like I said, it's just what we do."

A gun was a gun and Sonny knew he was on the back foot. Stanton and Heather still needed to get past him and the others to get back to the main road.

"We're going now," said Stanton, pulling Heather gently as he slowly walked past Sonny, never once taking his eyes off his face, making sure there was enough space between them, knowing that any one of Sonny's men would do anything to take the gun off him.

"No worries, Jimmy. You do what you have to do."

Sonny turned his body around in perfect unison with theirs, his eyes set on Stanton's face, the uniformity of their movements making them look like two people dancing in the dark. Stanton walked Heather carefully backwards, the last thing they needed to do now was stumble. They were heading toward the bend in the road thirty yards away. Once there, they'd be safe.

But Mickey's old service revolver was beginning to feel heavy in Stanton's hand, the sweat began to loosen his grip. He was beginning to drop the gun lower, his muscles fraught from a day of tension and running.

"Look, Jimmy, why don't we sort this here and now? You've got the upper hand, that's clear. We can all see that. Let's shake on it, and we'll leave it there. You have my word."

Stanton let go of Heather's hand. "What do you mean?"

He re-gripped the gun, his wet palms making it difficult to keep hold of the handle while he used his other hand to wipe away the sweat that was running into his eyes.

"It means what I said. You're right. My brother's a bigger twat than you are. Always getting in scrapes. I told him he'd end up pissing off the wrong person and getting battered. I've better things to do than this. You probably did him a favour. He needs to grow up. I can't keep sorting his shit out. Come on, Jimmy, let's shake and move on."

Sonny held his hand out, slowly moving toward them both as he smiled. "No funny business, I promise."

"He's lying," Heather whispered.

Stanton looked into her eyes, which were red raw from crying.

Sonny and his gang crept forward.

Stanton looked quickly back at Sonny, his hand still outstretched as he inched closer.

"You have my word on this, Jimmy. It ends here, now, tonight. For you and her."

"Shoot him," Heather said coldly.

Stanton snapped his neck around to look at her. "What did you say?"

Heather stood on her toes and whispered, the red marks on either side of her face visible in the sallow light.

"They're all fakes, aren't they? They're all pretending. Isn't that what you said? We're the only real ones here."

She looked back at Sonny, who had stopped walking and was now only a few feet away.

"Last chance, Jimmy," he said.

Stanton turned back to Heather, his arm aching, his head pounding with pressure, his eyes beginning to sting with the salty sweat. "What did you say?" he asked her.

Sonny started to creep forward once more. "Last chance Jimmy, come on, I don't leave offers on the table for long."

Heather wasn't looking at Stanton, she was boring her eyes into Sonny's face.

"I said, shoot him."

Stanton switched his head back to Sonny and then quickly back to Heather. The gun felt like a brick, his head throbbed with words and choices, decisions and mistakes. Heather stood on tiptoes and gently kissed Stanton's cheek. It woke him from his inertia.

"Shoot him, James. Shoot him for me."

Turning back to Sonny and his gang, Stanton steadied the gun and gripped the handle tight. Closing an eye as though he were simply aiming at another seagull from his bedroom window, Stanton put his finger on the trigger and started to squeeze.

"Sonny," he said. "Go fuck yourself."

FORTY-SIX

The solitary lamppost threw its sickly light down on the road below.

As Stanton relaxed his grip, he felt the tension lift from his shoulders. Only now did he dare to blink. He could feel Heather's fingers digging into his waist as the adrenaline began to dissolve in his blood. Heather stood with her mouth gaping, looking at Stanton, his profile backlit and silhouetted, the streetlamp making it seem he was wearing a halo as a crown. No one had moved, it was as though their feet had been glued to the floor, like toy figurines strung out across the road, a cool breeze arriving and drying the sweat on all their faces.

"James?" she said.

"Don't worry, I know what I'm doing."

Stanton spoke directly to Sonny, the gun loose in his hand, his finger no longer on the trigger.

"We're leaving, it's over. I'm sorry about your brother but like I said, that's just the kind of shit we do. You said it yourself, it ends here now. Tonight."

Slowly, without take his eyes off Stanton's, Sonny began to lower his hands.

"Okay, Jimmy, if you say so."

There was nothing more to be gained by layering violence upon violence. Stanton had spent most of his life fighting or being fought, and he was tired of it all. He didn't want this any more than he wanted this town. If he could just wake up tomorrow somewhere else he'd be able to start his life again, but this time without the mistakes. When faced with a choice, for the first time ever he took a new, different path. Everyone expected him to shoot, but instead, Stanton simply lowered the gun down by his side and left it hanging, now limp in his hand between his leg and Heather's.

"We good, then?" Stanton asked.

Sonny picked some drying blood from the scratches on his cheek and gave the gun a furtive glance.

"Yeah, we're good. But Jimmy, I need you to know something."

"What's that?"

Sonny took his time to light another rolled cigarette.

"You're done. Here, in this town. There's no coming back for you. Ever."

Stanton wasn't sure if Sonny could see the corners of his mouth turn up slightly into an uneven smile. If that was the worst thing to come out of today then maybe his luck was changing after all.

"Okay Sonny, sure thing." He began to turn and walk away.

"No," Heather said, pulling Stanton back by his arm.

"What?"

She spoke quietly but urgently. "I asked you to shoot him."

"What? Don't be silly. Come on, let's go."

Sonny inched a little closer. "Everything alright there, Jimmy?"

Stanton tried to pull Heather away but she wouldn't move.

275

Instead, she stared straight back at Sonny. She could see him smiling at her, yellow teeth under a yellow light.

Before Stanton could react, Heather reached down and grabbed the gun from his unwary hand. She held it unsteadily and pointed it directly at Sonny.

"Oh this is brilliant," chuckled Sonny. "Got yourself a proper little bodyguard there, Jimmy…"

There was a burst of sound so loud it momentarily deafened those close by. Heather dropped the gun, her hands shaking uncontrollably.

Sonny screamed as he fell to the ground clutching his thigh, the blood already seeping out through his fingers.

"Fucking bitch shot me!"

Stanton came to his senses quicker than anyone. He reached down for the gun and pointed it straight at Sonny's gang members, who had once again started advancing on them. He fired a shot over their heads.

"Don't take another step."

"You're dead, both of you are fucking dead!" screamed Sonny.

Stanton waved the gun confidently, the only one who knew there were no more bullets left in the chamber. Like everyone else on that back road, he couldn't quite believe what had just happened and now he needed to bluff their way out. The night had just reached a new level of dangerous. If there was any lingering doubt that Stanton was leaving town and never coming back, that moment had passed.

"Any of you follow us and you'll end up like him." He used the gun to point at Sonny writhing on the floor in pain.

Stanton grabbed Heather's wrist and slowly walked them back towards the main road and safety, keeping the empty gun on them all the time, moving it from one to the other to ensure they all got the message.

"You'll be fine, Sonny, just looks like a flesh wound to me."

Stanton quickened their pace.

"I'll find you," Sonny shouted, his voice falling fainter as they neared the bend in the road. The further away they got, the longer the shadows of Sonny's gang crept out of the streetlight and merged into one to become a coagulated black puddle of hate on the road

"We're going to your house still?" he asked Heather. "I really need that money now."

Heather nodded.

Stanton was breathing heavily.

"You lead the way. Ready?"

Heather nodded again.

Stanton inched them round the bend in the road, never taking his eyes off those still gathered around Sonny prone on the floor. Finally, they moved round the bend and out of sight.

"Run!" Stanton shouted at Heather. "Fucking run!"

FORTY-SEVEN

THEY WERE STANDING JUST OUT OF SIGHT AT THE BOTTOM OF THE hill, looking up at Heather's house, having run here as fast as they could after leaving an injured Sonny on that deserted road.

"Your old man a millionaire or something?"

"Millionaire? Don't be silly, what makes you say that?"

"You've got a front garden."

"Most people have!" Heather laughed, before realising she had been to Stanton's little terraced house.

"There's a light on," Stanton observed.

"They always leave one on when they go out. The car's not there, they're out. I'll be five minutes, there should still be time to get to the station. You wait here."

Stanton watched as Heather ran quickly up the hill, pushing open the garden gate before disappearing out of sight.

Heather let herself in to what was a deathly quiet house.

The upstairs hall light and the living-room light had been

left on to give a sense of occupancy; even so, a loveless house will always feel cold and empty. As Heather passed the living-room door she paused and looked in, the metronome of the mantlepiece clock continued to tick away more seconds from an already frantic day.

Running up the stairs two at a time, Heather went straight to her parents' bedroom and put on the light. She had stood here barely half a day ago but it may as well have been in a different lifetime. Everything felt smaller, more insignificant. Heather felt the opposite, visible, relevant and more worthy, a stronger sense of being alive than she had ever experienced before.

The thought of Stanton, waiting down the road and reliant on her for the money, propelled Heather towards the dressing table where she had stood that morning. As she reached for the drawers, she caught a glimpse of herself in the mirror.

It was the first time she'd seen her face for hours and she almost didn't recognise herself. It looked red and felt hot, her hair was a mess. In the reflection, she could see something tangled in her hair. Reaching up, she pulled out a stalk of grass. It must have got caught among the strands when she had fallen down the slope and careered into James. She recalled the kiss that had followed. Heather noticed her mother's nail scissors on the table and they gave her an idea. Putting them quickly in her pocket, she began to look through the drawers.

Searching hurriedly, she began where she had first seen the box that morning. But her hand only found empty space. The box wasn't there. Frantically, Heather opened the other drawers and began to go through them all, in case her memory was failing her in her exhaustion.

Soon she had opened all six drawers, moved everything in each one but found nothing. The box had gone.

In desperation, Heather dropped to the floor and looked under the bed.

Where would she put it?

Getting back up, she spun on her feet to take in the whole room, her darting eyes searching for inspiration. They settled on the wardrobe. It was where her mum kept the old photo albums. They included photos from her parents' childhood as well as her own and Heather used to love it when they poured over them as a family, laughing at the clothes that were worn. But that all stopped a few years ago. Now the albums sat gathering dust, just fading images of faded memories. If her mum was going to hide anything, it would be in a place they no longer acknowledged – the past.

Opening the wardrobe doors, Heather stood on tip toes and reached for the top shelf. Unable to see, she used her hands to search blindly for what she was looking for. Moving aside a pile of musky albums, her fingers touched something smooth and lacquered. Instinctively, she knew it was the box. She had to stretch even further to get some purchase on it, her toes aching under her own weight. She finally managed to pinch a corner with her fingertips and manoeuvre it down.

Holding the box in her hands, she ran her fingers over the dark, shiny wood. Opening it, she was relieved to see the money was still inside. Her mum must have known that Heather had discovered it that morning. But it didn't matter now, nothing mattered except getting this money to Stanton. Reaching back up, she made sure to put the now empty box back exactly where she had found it.

Heather turned off the light, left the bedroom and headed back downstairs, but her feet had only just touched the downstairs carpet when she stopped. The front door was slowly opening and someone was coming in.

FORTY-EIGHT

HER MUM ENTERED THE HOUSE JUST AHEAD OF HER DAD AND THEY all stopped to look at each other, surprised that somehow each of them was the last person they expected to see in their own home.

"Heather, what on earth have you got on? Look at the state of you as well, what have you been up to? Have you only just got in? Where've you been?"

The volley of questions peppered Heather's mind so rapidly that she couldn't think quickly enough and stammered guiltily, "I thought...I haven't...I thought you'd be back later?"

"Well we're not and here we are. Close the door, Colin."

Heather's mum went into the lounge, carelessly catching the door frame with her shoulder as she went.

"Your mum wasn't feeling very well, Heather," said her dad, rolling his eyes and pretending to knock back a drink.

Heather needed to get the money to Stanton, she was worried he might have given up and left already.

"Heather," her mum called for her from the lounge.

She looked at her dad, his face resigned to the fact that more words were going to be said, whether anyone wanted to hear them or not. He flicked his head. "Better go in and see her."

Heather dropped her shoulders and went into the lounge to see her mum had already poured herself a glass of wine.

"Look at the state of you, Heather! Where have you been all day?" She flung her arm wide as though to indicate the answer was somewhere in the living room.

"Nowhere, I was with Libby and—"

"—Don't you dare lie to your mother."

"I'm not, Mum—"

Heather's dad sat down heavily in his armchair. "—Give it a rest, Jackie, for god's sake."

"Give it a rest? Give it a rest, you say, Colin? Well, yes, let's all give it a rest and let our daughter run around town with God knows who, doing God knows what, shall we? Who is this boy, Heather?" She took a gulp of wine and sat back down before standing straight back up again.

Heather was confused. "Boy?"

"Yes, boy, Heather; practically a man from what I heard and I've had to spend most of Uncle Terry's birthday party trying to pretend I know what's been happening in my own family. This'll be up and down the street by tomorrow. What will people think of us? We're not from the council estate, last I looked. I mean, the police, Heather, the police!"

"Mum, I don't know what you're talking about, honestly."

"Well I'll tell you Heather, shall I? One of Uncle Terry's friends said he saw you with some skinhead on the promenade earlier and you were both running from the police. That's what I'm talking about and probably so is half the street by now."

Heather didn't have the energy or the time to try to explain all that had happened today, or over the past few days for that matter. She was more bothered about what her mum had just said.

"Is that all you care about, what the neighbours think?"

"I don't know what's got into you lately Heather, you used to be such a nice, funny girl. But yes, I care about what people think. It's a good job someone does around here. Nothing wrong with having some pride, is there? If you had some, you wouldn't be hanging around with yobs all day long. I'll ask you again. Who is that boy you were seen with today?"

Her mum collapsed back down on the sofa in despair, swilling the wine in her glass before reaching for the bottle and pouring herself some more.

"They weren't yobs. You wouldn't understand anyway."

"Really? Well, they sound like yobs, and he apparently looked like a nasty piece of work. I suppose that thing you've got on is his?"

Heather touched the satin sleeves of Stanton's jacket, resigning herself to the fact that he was now probably long gone.

"Jackie—"

"—Oh shut up, Colin, you're no better. Where's that wonderful life you promised me at the alter?" She clicked her fingers. "Gone, that's where, just like that, along with all my dreams as well, and what do I get back? I'll tell you what. Nothing."

Her mum was back on her feet again, jabbing a finger at her husband before jabbing a finger at her daughter.

"Nothing, nothing, nothing! Heather, for the past few months, you've moped around here with a face as long as your arm. You don't do anything. No one can get a word out of you. It's almost as if you don't want to be here."

"Maybe I don't," said Heather dismissively.

"Oh, you don't want to be here? Where you get fed and clean clothes laid out for you every day, like it's some sort of hotel. You want to check out, is that what you're saying? Good, suits me just fine. Pack your bags when you want, both of you. Maybe I can start to get my life back. I'm sick of it, sick of it! Cooking, cleaning, running around after everyone."

"Seems like you have your life back to me. Can we stop pretending now? Can we stop the lies?" Heather said brazenly, the anger building inside of her.

"You must take me for an idiot. If I have such a wonderful life, perhaps someone can furnish me with directions to it and I'll book myself a taxi?" She laughed at her own joke.

Heather looked over at her dad and then back at her mum. It was now or never.

She started slowly; her words were calm but her thumping heart felt out of control.

"I know."

"Know? Know what?" her mum replied. "You don't know anything. You're just a silly schoolgirl showing off with your new friends. We've all been there, Heather. You'll learn the hard way. I certainly did."

Heather wasn't prepared to take any more. If the last few days had taught her anything, it was that she should be prepared to stand up for herself, to fight her corner, to be heard, to show them all that she was someone.

"I know what you've been up to—"

Her dad tried to interrupt. "—Heather—"

Heather's mum moved toward her daughter. "—Up to? Up to? I'll tell you what I'm up to, shall I?"

Heather screamed in her mother's face. "Go on then, be honest. *If you can!*"

Slowly, her mum drew a line across her forehead with her finger. "I'm up to here. Up to here with everything," she said, barely able to control the anger seeping out through every pore. She looked for the bottle of wine and saw that her husband had hold of it.

"I think that's enough now, Jackie."

"Is that right?"

"Yes, I do," he replied calmly.

"Well Colin, that's two of us that have had enough." She tilted her head as far back as she could and drained the glass.

"Why don't you tell him?" Heather demanded.

"Tell who, what?"

"Tell Dad."

"Tell Dad what? Stop talking in silly riddles."

Heather thought about Stanton. What would he do? He would curl those beautiful lips up into a sneer and just tell the truth. *Sometimes you just have to jump and trust what you can't see.*

"Tell Dad about your affair, Mum. Tell him about the man who keeps ringing here when he's at work. Tell him where you were last week, and the other night. Alison's leaving drinks, wasn't it?"

Heather started to laugh. "Do you know why that's so funny? Because you had leaving drinks for Alison about two months ago! That's a pretty long goodbye, wouldn't you say? Your problem is, you've told so many lies you've forgotten what the truth looks like. So go on, tell Dad, your husband, the truth."

Heather stepped back and watched with satisfaction as the life drained away from her mother's face as it paled under the accusation.

"Who's taking who for an idiot now? You've been having an affair behind our backs. Do you know what I'm going to do tomorrow? I'll knock on every door up and down the street, and all your precious neighbours will know as well. Then what'll you do? That oh-so-precious image you're so worried about will come crashing down! And look…"

Heather pulled the money out of the jacket pocket.

"Look Mum, it's your running away money. I found it this morning."

It sounded like a whip being cracked. It was short, quick and firm, a right-handed slap across the left side of Heather's face, the sudden, unexpected action bringing about a stunned silence that permeated the suburban living room. Heather could feel the pain heating up her face, her eyes began to water but she refused to let the tears fall out.

Her mum guiltily reached out to comfort her. "Oh Heather darling, I'm so sorry.

Heather, still in shock, looked at her dad. In the midst of the drama, he'd collapsed back into the armchair, the bottle of wine in his hand, his eyes staring vacantly at the floor. She looked back at her mum crying pathetically, the mascara running down her face in black streaks, before finally returning her gaze to her dad, sitting silent and motionless in his chair.

It was all so obvious. What was once hidden, was now staring them all in the eye.

"You knew," Heather said quietly to her dad, who didn't look up, as tired of the lying as anyone.

"Colin," Heather's mum said softly.

Heather felt sick. The secret she'd thought she'd been keeping to herself, making her ill with worry, was actually common knowledge. Yet again, she was the last to know.

"He was right," she said to her parents. "He was right all along. You *are* all frauds and liars. You're all pretending, all making it up as you go along. Grown-ups really are fuck-ups."

The clock on the mantlepiece ticked noisily, time moving inexorably on, leaving people and their lives in its wake. Heather couldn't understand why her parents were silent, why they were not reacting, why their eyes focused upon something over her shoulder. She turned around to see what they were transfixed by.

Standing in the doorway of the lounge, his face wracked with anxiety and fatigue, was Stanton.

FORTY-NINE

"Did you get it?" he asked Heather, ignoring whatever conversation had just been happening.

"Yes, here," she said.

Stanton grabbed the money. He'd contemplated heading for the train station. After watching Heather disappear into her house, he'd seen the light go on in an upstairs room and waited patiently for her return. A few minutes later, when he saw a car pull up and her parents walk up the path just as the upstairs light went off, Stanton had thrown his bag over his shoulder and prepared to leave.

But something stopped him, despite the pressure in his head telling him to flee. At that moment Stanton knew if he left he would be leaving something behind that he needed, and it wasn't the money. It was Heather. He took hold of Heather's hand. "Come with me."

"What?" Heather asked in astonishment.

"Come with me."

"I...I can't, I—"

"—You can," said Stanton. "You've been saying it all week,

that you wanted to get away, you even said it in the grass after we kissed. Well, this is your chance."

Heather turned to look at her parents, both stupefied by what was happening, barely able to muster the energy to challenge the stranger in their midst. Her dad was staring vacantly at the floor, her mum crying pathetically, the party mascara running down her face forging ravines of misery and regret.

The decision was easy. There was nothing here anymore, nothing worth staying for.

"Yes, yes I'll come with you." Heather rushed to kiss Stanton strongly on the lips, in doing so waking her mother from her malaise.

"What? What are you doing you silly girl, you're still at school."

"No I'm not, I'm sixteen now. I've left as of yesterday, Mum."

Her mum rose slowly out of her seat, the emotion and the wine conspiring to make it difficult.

"Colin," she said, trying to rouse her husband. "Who is this yob anyway? I shall call the police."

Stanton looked at the clock on the mantlepiece. "Come on, we need to go!"

"Just give me one minute," said Heather, pushing past Stanton and running back upstairs as he shouted after her.

"We'll get some clothes tomorrow, we haven't got time!"

But Heather wasn't going to her bedroom, she was going to her brother's.

Standing outside his door, she took aim and kicked it as hard as she could. The timber creaked but the door remained steadfastly shut. She steadied herself and kicked again, even harder, aiming at the lock. This time the door cracked loudly, and a gap appeared at the edge of the frame. Heather summoned as much strength as she could and kicked the door one more time, the wood splintering as the lock broke and the door gave way, swinging brokenly open to reveal darkness within.

No one was more shocked than Heather that she had managed to do any of that and she felt exhilarated as she ran back downstairs and into the lounge.

"I was never sure if you were stopping people from going in or keeping the ghost from getting out. Either way, it's out now. I've released the dead, Robert is free. Hopefully you can be as well. There's no need to pretend anymore."

Her parents hadn't moved, both of them paralysed, equal victims of their own bad decisions, parents who had simply become two people who didn't know what to do for the best.

"Let's go," Heather said impatiently as she headed to the front door.

Stanton was left alone to survey the corpse of a family whose body had his fingerprints all over it. His carelessness had cost them one child and now his selfishness was going to cost them the other. For a moment he too became paralysed, not with shock but with guilt.

"I'm sorry," he mumbled.

Heather's parents looked up at him, unaware of the miserable bond that held them closer together than they knew possible.

"I am, I'm sorry."

Stanton hung his head, then left the room, unable to see for one second longer the mess he had helped create.

FIFTY

I<small>F</small> <small>THEY</small> <small>THOUGHT</small> <small>THEY</small> <small>HAD</small> <small>RUN</small> <small>DOWN</small> <small>EVERY</small> <small>GODFORSAKEN</small> street ever built in this town, they were wrong. There were more, and they were racing down them to try to make it to the station in time. It all felt completely hopeless and desperate. Road after road, pavement after pavement. They were sick of them all.

Heather stopped, bent over and put the bag down. "Please, can we rest? I don't think I can run anymore. I've got a stitch."

Stanton ran back to her. "We're not going to make it if we stop!"

Heather raised herself slowly back up. "I'm okay, come on, let's go."

But all this effort was useless and Stanton knew it. They had started the day with all the time but none of the money. Now, they had the money but had run out of time. If Big Tommy hadn't taken the first lot, they would be there already. The station was still a mile away and they were down to just minutes, not the relative luxury of hours they once had.

Setting off again, Stanton walked quickly in front, his brain working overtime for a solution with every step he took. But his thinking was lethargic and drowsy with tiredness.

"Maybe you should go back," he said, stopping and facing up to the futility of the situation. Heather was in enough trouble, if she went back now there was still a chance for her.

"Go back? But why? You asked me to come with you. There's nothing for me to go back for."

"We can't get to the station in time, you're knackered. I'm not sure I can get there myself now. I definitely can't stay here tonight."

Up ahead, a car turned into the road, its headlights bouncing over the uneven surface. It was the first vehicle they had seen for a while and that was enough to make Stanton nervous. Accelerating noisily through the gears, the car made its way down the street toward them. The streetlights were too far apart for Stanton to see who was driving, but he could see it was a white Ford with a red stripe running up its side. Every sinew in his body was taut, poised ready for more confrontation as he searched his memory for anyone he knew with such a distinctive car. But, as it reached him, he saw it was just a young couple returning from a night out. He let out a long, welcome sigh of relief; he had nothing left inside to fight with. Then, without warning, the driver slammed on the brakes, the car's tyres screeching to an abrupt halt.

In panic, Stanton spun round. The car had stopped, the engine idling away, its exhaust fumes coughing into the night. Standing in the middle of the road and blocking the Ford's way was Heather, and she was pointing the gun at the windscreen.

FIFTY-ONE

"What are you doing?" said Stanton incredulously as he ran towards Heather, but in the short time it took him to get there he realised the brilliance of her idea. Just like at the helter-skelter, Heather's ingenuity might just get them out of an impossible situation.

"Genius," he whispered, taking the gun from her, his fingers feeling the warmth still emanating from its barrel. He knew the gun was empty but Heather didn't, and he wasn't going to tell her. Walking to the driver's door, he yanked it open aggressively.

"Get out, both of you."

The man did as he was told as did the woman in the passenger seat, where Heather was already waiting to take her place.

"Not a word to anyone," he threatened the young couple, who had moved to the side of the road and were gripping each other in fear.

Stanton got in the driver's seat; the engine was still running.

"Have you actually got a licence?"

Stanton familiarised himself with the car. It had been a few months since he had stolen one.

"Kind of."

"Kind of?"

"Kind of no."

"But you can drive, can't you?" Heather asked.

"Course I can."

Stanton pushed the gear stick and released the clutch. The car stalled.

Heather bit her lip and looked out of the window, noticing the couple whose car they had stolen were still there.

"Fucking thing," Stanton said, trying to hide his embarrassment. He turned the key again, revved the engine and engaged the clutch. The car began to move.

"Will we make it?"

He looked at the clock on the dashboard.

"It'll be close."

Stanton drove fast but carefully, hugging the labyrinth of backstreets which he would first cautiously peer down to check they were clear. Last thing he needed was a car chase with the police. He thought about just driving straight out of town. But they wouldn't get far. The couple whose car this was had probably already banged on someone's door and asked to use their phone.

They drove in silence; it was the first time either of them had not been on their feet since they had lain kissing in the long grass. Heather stared out at the last stragglers and revellers making their way home from clubs and parties. Winding the window down, she let in a rush of cool air. Closing her eyes, she allowed her thoughts to drift off, the streetlamps rhythmically flicking their light against her eyelids. Stanton interrupted the sleep that was starting to fall over her and Heather opened her eyes with a start at his voice.

"We're here."

"Already?"

"Yeah, the station's just over there. It looks clear, come on."

Stanton took the keys from the ignition, grabbed the bag from Heather and got out of the car, never once taking his eyes off the entrance to the station.

"But what's inside?"

"Dunno. Only one way to find out."

He took the gun out of the bag. He had thought about keeping it. Despite what Sonny had said, no matter where they went, this was unlikely to be over. But he was a changed man. Keeping the gun meant staying in a world of violence, a world he was desperate to leave. The longer he kept hold of it, the more time he had to use it. He went over to the kerb and, making sure no one was watching, dropped the gun down the drain along with the car keys.

There could be no going back.

Stanton grabbed Heather's hand and pulled her across the road, the fluorescent lights from the station drawing them in like moths to a flame. A taxi was dropping someone on the forecourt but other than that, there was no one around.

They went quickly into the station. The clock on the wall said 11.50 p.m. Somehow they had made it, but only by minutes.

"Piece of piss," said Stanton sarcastically, marching them towards the platform.

"What about a ticket?" asked Heather.

"A ticket? Seriously? In the space of about eight hours you've been involved in an armed robbery, shot someone in the leg and hijacked a car. I don't think dodging a fare is going to make things worse than that. Besides, this town isn't getting another penny out of me."

In the harsh, unforgiving light of the ticket hall, he looked at Heather's exhausted face.

"Last chance to change your mind."

She took the bag from Stanton and walked out onto the platform. There were a few people there but they didn't pay any attention to the unlikely looking pair that had just joined them.

Their train was in a siding, waiting to move. Once they were on it, they would be eighteen minutes away from the next town, eighteen minutes away from beginning the rest of their lives.

Above their heads, a large clock hung from the platform roof, its mechanisms clicking loudly in the quiet of the night, counting down the minutes to freedom.

Stanton smiled. "Five minutes to spare, loads of time. Come on, down this way."

They walked down to the far end of the platform, where the tiredness caught up with them both. Heather moved towards Stanton, giving him no option other than to hold her, with her back to the train, Stanton facing the way they'd come. The platform clock ticked down the seconds. Finally, it was just the two of them. No gangs, no police, no family and, in just a few minutes, no past.

Stanton dropped his chin onto Heather's head and closed his eyes but opened them almost immediately. In the distance he heard a motorbike. But it was travelling away from them and he relaxed again. He would be happier once they were on the train and it was moving.

"Where will we sleep tonight?"

Stanton didn't know. He hadn't thought that far ahead.

"I'll work that out when we get there." He gently kissed the top of her head as she pressed into his warm chest.

The clock ticked down, another minute gone, another minute closer to leaving.

In the siding, the train put on its lights.

Curiosity got the better of him. "Why'd you shoot Sonny?"

Pulling back, Heather reached up and ran a hand over his smooth face.

"Some of it was for you and some for me. I didn't want him to hurt you or cause you any more pain. But I panicked. I was tired, I wasn't thinking straight. Good job I closed my eyes."

"What do you mean, some of it was for you?"

Heather put her head back on his chest.

"When he touched me, it reminded me…of something bad." She hugged him even tighter.

"Please, not now. We can talk tomorrow."

"Here comes our train."

"I can't wait to get away from here, James."

"Me neither."

"I just want to be with you. To get over the river and sleep, and we can talk all day tomorrow and the day after and the day after that as well. Let's buy a map and open it and the first place we see is where we'll go. And when we get there, we'll start our lives all over again. No one holding us back, just us, just you and me. Both of us starting all over again."

His eyes felt heavy so Stanton closed them as he stroked the back of Heather's neck, thankful he wasn't on his own anymore. What she had said sounded good to him, perhaps too good, maybe he didn't deserve this second chance after all the mistakes he had made in life. He could hear the train approaching the platform, its methodical and hypnotic, metallic rhythm almost lulling him to sleep as it trundled alongside and came to a stop.

FIFTY-TWO

Further down the platform, people boarded while the guard waited patiently.

Stanton opened the door and helped Heather into the carriage, before following her inside and throwing the bag on an empty seat.

"Sit there. If anyone comes through that door, scream," he instructed, pointing down the train in the direction she was now facing.

Stanton stepped back down onto the platform and lit a cigarette. He was going to ensure he was the last person to step on the train. He watched as a few late stragglers rushed to clamber inside their carriages, making him smile at the thought of how easy their journey had been to get here compared to his own.

So this was it. He was finally about to leave this town, and Heather, who he hadn't even known a week ago, was somehow going with him. He had no regrets about either of these facts. He wasn't leaving anything behind that mattered. He would miss Roper more than Margaret, but he wouldn't miss anything else.

The guard checked his watch as a group of laughing young women echoed their way through the train station, their high heels click clacking over the tiles. Joking with them as they boarded the train, he slammed the heavy door behind the last glimpse of skirt.

Satisfied the platform was now empty, the guard took one final look at his watch and blew his whistle as he opened the very last door at the end of the train. As he lifted one foot inside the carriage, he noticed a skinhead youth standing at the far end by the very first door, his elongated shadow stretching halfway down the platform.

"Are you getting on?" he shouted.

Stanton took some quick final drags on the cigarette before dropping it and stamping on it with his boot, taking one last look around him before stepping, in harmony with the guard, back onto the train.

"Is everything okay?" asked Heather, looking up from what she was doing.

"Fine," he replied brusquely, pulling down the window and sticking his head out.

The train started to move slowly. No one was coming, there was to be no last-minute drama. The train was on its way, quickly picking up momentum and clearing the platform.

Stanton stayed at the window for a while longer, feeling the cool air rush over his face as though it were blowing away the last remnants of the town, watching as the station got smaller and smaller before it disappeared altogether behind a bend in the track. There was no going back now unless he planned to jump from a moving train. Stanton and Heather, receding like the tide in the bay. The only difference being, they wouldn't be back again tomorrow.

"Goodbye Morecambe," he uttered under his breath, the wind whipping the words from his mouth as quickly as he could say them, an indefinable pang hitting his stomach in the process. He turned to look at Heather, who was fiddling with her locket. Perhaps he would miss Margaret after all, daft and as toothless as she was, and maybe Stanton actually got something from looking after her.

The outskirts of the town sped by and he couldn't help but grin, thrusting his head back out of the window as he turned over the events of the past few days in his mind. His world had been turned upside down. Once the train started to rise and the town began to fall away below, the fairground stencilled black against the sky, he closed his eyes and breathed in as deeply as possible. He wanted to take with him a memento, the salty sea air he had inhaled every day for nineteen years but would never breathe in again.

Pulling his head back inside, Stanton pushed the window up. He didn't need to see any more, his face tingling as the cold wind was replaced by the tepid warmth of the carriage.

"Look," Heather said as he sat down next to her. She handed him the locket.

"I took my mum's nail scissors and used them to cut one of the pictures to get it to fit. What do you think?"

Stanton looked at the monochrome picture from only a couple of hours ago. The face he was looking at seemed young and fresh. He looked up at his reflection in the train window, the face looking back at him old and wizened.

Stanton closed the locket. "It's great. Here, let me," and he tenderly put it around Heather's neck.

"I'll never take this off, ever," she said, admiring it. She leaned in and Stanton put his arm protectively around her.

"Have I just ran away from home?" Her eyes closed as she spoke.

"I think so," replied Stanton, stretching his legs, putting his feet on the seat in front, his once pristine boots purchased with the money he stole showing the scars of a day that seemed as though it would never end. But somehow it had. Saturday was leaving and a brand-new day was about to make an appearance. Looking at his boots made him think about the money, which reminded him of Mickey. He thought about Kenny and the pier, the gang and Big Tommy and everyone else that had slipped through his life today.

Stanton was keeping his eye on the interconnecting door between their carriages when the train hit a low-hanging tree, banging hard against the window and making Heather jump.

"Don't worry, it's just a branch," he said, kissing her head.

"We're not coming back, are we?" she asked sleepily.

"Never."

"Promise."

"I promise."

"You won't leave me, will you?"

Stanton didn't answer. If he did, he knew he would be lying. He was going to have to tell her about the accident on the fairground. How his bone-idleness and desire for attention were responsible for the mess that Heather and her family were in. When he had looked at her mum and dad, broken, destroyed by all that had gone before, he too wanted to run down to the jetty and end it all. You can wipe the blood away from the trainers but you can't wipe the guilt from your soul.

"Would you leave me?" he asked in his moment of weakness.

Heather hugged him tighter. "Never."

"What if I told you something that made you hate me?"

Looking up at him, Heather touched his face. "There is nothing you could say that would make me hate you more than I hated my life before we met. *Nothing*."

Stanton lay his head back and looked up at the ceiling, the fluorescent lights making his eyes ache, the gentle snake-like rhythm of the train swaying his mind back and forth, memories pitching from side to side like water in a bath. He closed his eyes; he didn't want to but the lids were so heavy they felt like steel shutters being pulled down. His head fell listlessly against the seat as he felt Heather's breathing slow, becoming shallower as her body surrendered to tiredness, the locket still open around her neck.

The train would only stop once on the journey and that was when they arrived at the next town. It was impossible to miss, so a little sleep would go a long way, especially when, in only a few hours, they would both be starting their brand new lives.

Stanton was facing the same fight to stay awake, fluttering his eyes in a feeble attempt to retain consciousness, but it was a losing battle and he soon succumbed to the same swift sleep that Heather had already fallen into.

The only noise was the rickety, metallic lullaby of wheel against track which gently lolled their heads into an easy slumber, the very outskirts of the town whispering by. Their heads locked together like twins in the womb, fused by the events of the day, memories passing from one to the other as they dreamt fitfully, the nervousness still deep inside their thoughts. They had been through so much and yet their lives had not even started. Their pasts had drawn them together like magnetic pieces, merging their fates, their hopes and expectations settling like dust on the seat of a train that was delivering them to their future.

A train that was now, imperceptibly, beginning to slow down.

FIFTY-THREE

S<small>TANTON COULD SENSE THE DECELERATION BUT THE TIREDNESS</small> washed over him like a wave.

The train slowed some more, not that either of them noticed, lost as they were in their ethereal world. Heather twitched as she slept, her body reacting to the dreams in which she was still running.

Outside, the town was no more, lost amid the pitch-black night pockmarked by occasional lights from distant houses separated by fields and wide-open spaces.

The train was slowing to a crawl.

Neither Stanton nor Heather stirred, both suspended subconsciously, waiting for the slam of a train door that would wake them at the town across the river.

They dreamt hazily of each other and of the day just lived, the picture in Heather's locket on show for no one to see. It was just the two of them now, no family and no foe, just Heather and Stanton all alone in the world but with something within reach that neither thought possible a few days before.

Up ahead, an orange glow flickered on the track, burning

bright on an ebony canvas like the end of Sonny's cigarette on that back road behind the fairground.

The train lurched to a stop.

There was a fire on the line.

Stanton's eyes sprung open, adrenaline instantly replacing his fatigue as it poured through his body. Yet again he had been stupid. He cursed himself under his breath. The last week had been one bad decision after another, and now his idiocy had left them stranded on a train that was going nowhere. He gently took the scissors out of a sleeping Heather's hand and gripped them tightly.

There was no need for the train to stop; if it did, it was because someone wanted it to.

Stanton thought about the gun now and wished he had kept hold of it. A gun, even without bullets, was better than no gun at all.

Had he miscalculated?

Had he made another mistake, perhaps his final one?

The running might not be over.

The running might have only just begun.

ABOUT THE AUTHOR

M N Stewart is a highly respected finance professional who has written columns and leadership articles for both for trade and national press. *Goodbye Morecambe* is the first novel in a trilogy. He splits his time between London and Tunbridge Wells.

 x.com/londonmoneyFS

ACKNOWLEDGEMENTS

Sonny Marr, Gina Blaxill, Ali Clarke, Kate Pritchard, Claire Wingfield, Adam Hollingworth, Chris Budd, Victoria Straw, Alison Sudbury, Aaron Pritchard-Fern, Vicky & Millie Ashford, Charlie Bell.

Printed in Great Britain
by Amazon